Shameless

The Finn Factor, Book 6

R.G. Alexander

Shameless

Editing by D.S. Editing
Formatted by IRONHORSE Formatting

ISBN: 1537534548
ISBN-13: 978-1537534541

DEDICATION

Sometimes there are days…sometimes entire years that are more difficult than others. This year? Well if you're a Finn Club member you know this was mine. But there is always a silver lining. With every loss, I've realized how much I value the people still with me. With each bump in the road, I've learned and relearned and relearned again that I need to learn patience. Heartbreaks happen, but that's when your real friends—the ones that are still there when you come back after months of personal chaos, ready to greet you with open arms—are revealed. I have never been more grateful for the community of readers and writers I'm a part of. Never more humbled by their acceptance and compassion. There aren't enough dedications in the world to thank them, but I'll try.

For Cookie—love is the reason.

For Robin L. Rotham and every all night cp session, every mile traveled just to say hello—thank you for being my family and letting me share in yours.

For the Finn Club—You have gone all in for me and I'll always do the same.

For my readers… Thank you. And there's so much more to come.

Chapter One

Seamus Finn eyed his cousin with amusement. Chief of Police Solomon Finn was sitting on the floor in his dark blue uniform, a bewildered expression on his usually stoic face and his long, lanky legs twisted into a position that looked anything but natural.

And he was wearing a tiara.

Penny beamed as she pointed to her *very* uncomfortable tea party guest. “Uncle Younger’s pretty, isn’t he, Daddy?”

“I’m *not* pretty.”

Seamus covered his laughter with his fist and a well-timed cough.

“Don’t say that.” She reached up and adjusted his tiara, patting his cheek kindly before handing him an empty pink teacup. "You're a princess. Do you want some tea, Daddy? We're having a praxit party."

"*Practice* party," he corrected automatically, trying hard to keep his amusement in check.

"That's what I said."

Solomon sent him a warning glance. "Yes. Join us, Seamus. We need all the *praxit* we can get, since *someone* told her she has to mind her manners this weekend if she wants to play with her birthday presents tomorrow. I'm sure she has an extra tiara for you."

"Believe me, she does." He didn't tell him it was a king's crown and they'd picked it out together, because there were some things men shouldn't talk about with other men. Like how wrapped around their daughter's fingers they were. "Where's your brother, Penny? Didn't he want to play?"

Her mood changed swift enough to give him whiplash. She threw herself onto her small plastic chair, her lower lip protruding for all to see. "In his room. Being smart."

Being smart was something Jake had been doing under all their noses for a while now, but this year he'd raised the bar. In his first week of high school Seamus had been called in to discuss the possibility of his son skipping a grade. After going over the pros and cons at home that night, he'd let Jake make the final decision. And so his freshman had become a sophomore overnight.

Near the end of the year, his school counselor had sent him home with information on an advanced summer program that would give him college credits. It seemed way too early for Jake to start thinking about college, but he'd been so excited Seamus couldn't deny him the opportunity. He'd finished a few weeks ago, and was already getting ahead on his reading for the upcoming school year.

My son is a genius. I was ready for locked doors, strange mood swings and girlfriend problems. Not this.

A part of him wished Jake *were* upstairs sneaking kisses with a girl, or locking his little sister out of his room to play videogames with his friends instead of voluntarily reading thick textbooks by himself. He should be over the moon that his child was a book-loving prodigy—Seamus had always loved to read, though he'd never been as clever as his son—but Jake had been such a serious kid. Quiet and helpful and way too old for his age. He needed some fun in his life. At least one of them should be having some. Penny seemed to think so too.

"I hate school," she announced, still pouting. "School is worst than the zoo."

"Strong words," Seamus murmured sympathetically. "I know how much you hate the zoo."

She'd been there twice in her life and cried the entire time, begging Seamus to free the animals from their prison. His baby girl had a big heart and enough fire to grow up to be a future revolutionary. Or an incredibly passionate veterinarian.

"How about this? Why don't you march back upstairs and tell Jake if he doesn't come down for lunch I won't let him study for a whole week. That should do the trick. After that, Uncle Younger will take you both to get ice cream, then drop you off at Gram and Grandpa's house for your birthday weekend."

Since weekends were busy at Finn's—the pub he'd taken over after his father retired—his parents had suggested that they watch his brood so they could have two days of uninterrupted celebration. He could join them for the twins' birthday party tomorrow and not have to worry about the inevitable sugar crash that would follow before he went back to work.

Thank you, Mom and Dad.

"Ice cream?" Penny jumped up as if her chair was a spring, mood forgotten. "Can we get some for Wes and Little Sean too?"

His younger sons were already with his parents, shopping for and wrapping Penny's presents there, because if they were under this roof? She'd find them. "That sounds like a great idea."

"Okay. Make sure Uncle Younger drinks his tea, Daddy."

"You heard her," he said through tears of mirth after she left. "Drink your invisible tea, pretty princess."

"I could have you arrested."

Seamus turned toward the kitchen, still chuckling. "And I'd get a long, uninterrupted nap while my children wreak havoc on your peaceful metropolis. Your call."

Solomon took off the tiara and followed him, elbows on the counter as he watched Seamus finish making four turkey sandwiches and slice up a bowl of strawberries for his daughter. She'd started asking for them at every meal. He wasn't sure why, but it was healthier than her previous fixation with jellybeans, so he went with it.

"Thanks for taking the kids for me. I'm sure you have better things to do with your free time."

"Haven't had enough of it to find out." Solomon

lifted one shoulder in a shrug. "You know I usually work through lunch, but I have the information you were looking for."

The throb that instantly started at his temple told Seamus he wasn't going to like what he heard. "Did you get a name?"

"Bellamy Demir. I ran him through our computers but he's not on anyone's list. He's just some rich hotshot from New York with no priors. I'm thinking of asking Tanaka to get us more information. The hacker knows his—"

"No." Seamus interrupted, his voice rougher than he wanted it to be. "Don't mention this to Ken, okay? Please."

Solomon's eyes narrowed. "You know him." It wasn't a question.

"I do." It might shock him if he knew how well.

"And if you'd had any idea he was involved, you wouldn't have told me about your problem at all." Solomon scowled and rubbed the back of his neck. "Damn it, Seamus, what else are you keeping to yourself? I still can't believe you've been doing this for six years without anyone's help. You know I'm all for a man's right to keep a few secrets—I have a few of my own—but something like that? That isn't something you have to carry alone. No one should. With everything that came to light last year, it's a wonder no one found out."

"I know it." And if it weren't for the man he'd met five months ago, they never would have. Damn him anyway. Bellamy knew everything now. The secrets he'd kept due to expectations, and the one that was his lifelong obligation. His burden alone.

What was Demir doing? After months of silence, why now? Why this? "I appreciate your help, Solomon. I didn't mean to drag you into this, but I can handle it from here."

"You didn't drag me into anything. And you shouldn't keep this to yourself, Seamus. At least your parents."

Seamus sighed. "Not yet, okay? Things are finally back to normal. Dad's healthy, Finn's is doing great, Tanaka doesn't have men guarding our houses and no journalists are hiding in our bushes looking for the scoop on Senator Stephen. It's practically peaceful around here lately. I'll tell them, I promise. Just not right now."

"What about Demir?"

"I told you, I can deal with Bellamy. Now that I know it's him, I know exactly what to do." He forced a confidence he didn't feel, unwilling to let Solomon see how thrown he really was. "Let's switch gears. Tell me what your brothers are up to."

The change in topic did its job distracting Solomon. He was a lot like Seamus in that way, a big brother to his bones. Neither one of them knew how to turn it off.

"Get ready to have holes shot through your *practically peaceful* idea," Solomon grumbled. "Things on my side of the Finn fence are anything but."

"James?"

"Still avoiding me and everyone else. Nothing new there."

"Rory?"

Solomon sighed. "Better, but not back to his old self yet. Not since Owen's wedding."

Seamus knew Brady was doing great. Better than that, he'd told everyone about his and Tanaka's engagement. They hadn't set a date yet, but they were madly in love.

"Don't tell me Wyatt finally took off his shirt in the wrong place and got arrested," he joked weakly, hoping it was something that simple.

Solomon shook his head. "Noah's in trouble, Seamus. The kind of trouble only you could understand."

"That narrows it down."

"The morning show host popped up after eight months to tell him he was going to be a father."

"You're kidding." After Owen's wedding, Noah had disappeared with the one reporter Stephen had allowed to attend for two days, coming back with a wicked grin and an insincere apology for not turning on his phone. That was the last time any of them had heard of the woman until now. "Didn't he use protection?"

"Every time but one it seems, but once was all it took." He ran his palm over his short buzz cut. "She asked if Noah wanted the baby."

"Jesus." Seamus felt an ache of sympathy in his chest and pushed his own worries away to focus on Noah. "Has she talked to her family? If it's about finances or—"

"Her parents are in a retirement home in Florida and she doesn't want them to know." His cousin's expression was grim. "And I don't think it's about money as much as it's about her career. There's a talk show in Seattle offering her a spot and she's already found a place to live there. After she dropped her bombshell, she informed Noah she'd put the baby up for adoption if he said no. That was her original plan, but then she remembered the research she'd done on our family. She mentioned you and the kids specifically."

Great. Just like Mira. He'd always wanted to be the poster child for baby drop-offs. "What's Noah think about this?"

Solomon looked like he wanted to hit something. "Does it matter? He's twenty-eight and he and Wyatt live like they're still sharing bunk beds at home. Life is a frat house or a firehouse to them. Not exactly a lifestyle conducive to thinking *or* raising a child."

"Neither was mine," Seamus offered quietly. "You shuffle things around. You make room."

Solomon banged his fist lightly on the counter. "*You* shuffle things around, Seamus. He isn't you. He's never even taken care of a goldfish."

Because you took care of everything for him. "He might be a little younger than I was when Jake came into my life, but he's more together, whether you believe it or not. He's got a solid career, up to date payments on that townhome and a large, lovingly intrusive family that he's helped out more than once this past year. What did he tell you he wanted to do?"

His cousin's expression was despondent. "He wants to keep it. I don't know if it's because Elder beat the importance of Finn blood into all of us since birth or if he genuinely thinks he's ready for something this big. I told him to take some time before making his decision, but he's not listening to anything I say. No one is lately. You'd think I wasn't the oldest. That I didn't own a gun."

Seamus set a supportive hand on Solomon's shoulder. "No one listens to me anymore either. And now that they're all pairing up it's only getting worse. We'll be the last single stick-in-the-muds of the family. It's time we embraced it."

"Not cheering me up *at all.*"

If Solomon's laugh had a bitter tinge, they both ignored it. "Hey, I'm a bartender, not a life coach."

Penny bounced into the room tugging Jake in behind her. "We're hungry now. Jake needs brains."

"Brain *food,*" Jake said with a patient smile.

"We'll talk more later," Seamus assured Solomon, pasting on a cheerful smile and grabbing Penny, spinning her around as she giggled in delight before sitting her down at the small kitchen table. "This one has to eat her pre-birthday sandwich and drink her pre-birthday juice." He winked at Jake. "And tomorrow we have to do whatever Prince Wesley and Princess

Penelope want."

She loved that idea. "Can I make a list?"

When lunch was over and Seamus finally got them out the door with their bags and a harried-looking Solomon standing by his SUV, Jake came back to give him a one-armed hug. "See you tomorrow, Dad."

He knew that hug. "What's wrong, Jake?"

"Nothing." He shoved his hands in his pockets and looked down at his shoes.

"Spit it out."

"I think you should date," he blurted suddenly. "I'm old enough to take care of the kids, if that's what you're worried about."

Shit. "I know you are, son, but you'd be depriving your grandparents and aunts and uncles if you did that. They love spending time with you. Let's make a deal. You stop worrying about your old man's social calendar and just enjoy being a super genius, okay? I'll take care of everything else."

"Okay. But you're only single because you don't date, Dad. You always tell me to try before I give something up. You should try too." He disappeared after getting the last word.

He'd obviously heard part of his conversation with

Solomon. He wondered if he'd caught the news about Noah as well.

After they left, Seamus grabbed a bottle of water and went down to the basement where he'd made space amid his boxes and clutter for a personal gym. He spent an hour lifting weights, using his tread climber until he was soaked in sweat, and finished the circuit by punching the freestanding bag as if it owed him money.

You should try too.

He climbed the stairs two at a time and stripped before jumping in the shower. The sad, pathetic truth was that he *had* tried. No one knew what he was going through because of it or how much he'd changed. No one even suspected what had happened in Ireland. But Jake sensed *something* was different. He'd been making noises about Seamus dating for months now. How did he see what the rest of his family couldn't? What his own twin hadn't? How did his thirteen-year-old son know about the cracks in his heart?

It had been five months since he'd gone to Galway. Since he'd received the far too generous Christmas gift he still felt guilty about. Since he'd made a fool of himself and gone temporarily insane.

He'd tried to let it go. But every night when he closed

his eyes he was back there. Every time he had five minutes to himself…

Seamus gripped his hardening erection with a frustrated groan. Every time he was alone, *this* happened. When would the need go away? When would he finally get back to normal?

He leaned against the wall of the shower, stroking his shaft with the rough, desperate motions that he knew would bring him quick release—and zero satisfaction.

Why couldn't he forget Bellamy Demir?

Chapter Two

5 months ago…

Maybe he was overtired, but driving through the dark to the lit up hotel made the bleary-eyed Seamus wonder if he'd fallen down a rabbit hole and directly into an episode of *Downton Abbey*. It wasn't until his bags were taken with brisk efficiency and he was led to a lovely young woman at the concierge desk that it finally hit him. Kenneth Tanaka had made him reservations at a *Lifestyles of the Rich and Famous* style hotel. And yes, it used to be an actual Irish castle.

He was never going to be able to pay Ken back for this.

The driver that had picked up Owen and Jeremy at

the airport—before Seamus rented a car to go in the opposite direction—had assured them they were headed to the most romantic destination in Ireland to start their delayed honeymoon, but as far as Seamus was concerned, it couldn't be much better than this.

The woman took his information politely enough, but he could feel her curiosity in the glances she sent his way. Alone, wearing a faded Finn's Pub t-shirt and jeans, he knew he wasn't the usual guest for a place like this. He rubbed his stubble self-consciously and smiled. "This reservation was a Christmas present. My family thinks I work too much."

Understanding lit her gaze. "You're a lucky man then, Mr. Finn, and you're in for a treat. A few weeks here and you'll never be the same." She typed something into her computer and bit her lip, fingers pushing her short blonde hair behind one ear. "May I ask…when you say family…is there a Mrs. Finn?"

Seamus was almost too tired to catch the question. "Other than my mother and my brother's wife? No."

"I see. You have here that you'll accept calls to your room from your children, I suppose I just assumed…"

People always assumed. Wanting to hide in his room to get over his poor man's shock in peace, Seamus pulled out his phone and showed her the most recent picture of Jake, Penny, Wes and Sean. "This is my brood. It's the first time I've ever been away from them for longer than a weekend, so I wanted to make sure they could reach me if there was an emergency."

She gasped, gripping his wrist with surprising tenacity to keep the phone still. "Oh, now aren't they the most beautiful children I've ever seen! And those two are twins? My sisters are identical, and I can tell you, they were a handful growing up."

Seamus forced a smile. "They always are. Do you think I could get my room key? I don't mean to be rude, but it was a long flight and I had to rent a car."

She blushed. "Of course. I'll need a few more minutes, if you can wait over there."

Over there was a lobby with vaulted ceilings and seats covered in velvet cushions. Too nice for his old jeans, he thought with a self-conscious grimace. This was all like something out of someone else's dream, because Seamus lacked the imagination for anything this grand.

And then he saw *him*.

The late hour could explain the bare feet, burgundy silk pajama bottoms and unbuttoned white shirt. Since an employee probably wouldn't hang out in the lobby half naked, he must be a guest. Or the owner, since it was doubtful anyone else could walk around like *that* in a place like *this* without fear of reprisal.

Seamus had never seen a better looking man in his life. He was leaning against a thick granite pillar draped with some medieval coat of arms, eating a bowl of ice cream and staring unblinkingly at Seamus as if he'd been watching him for a while.

Had he? The man gave him a slow, sensual once over and an internal shiver of awareness raced up Seamus's spine. Instead of laughing it off or looking away, Seamus realized with a start of surprise that his body was responding in a way it hadn't in years. Not since Toby.

God, he hadn't thought about him in years. When he was a junior in high school, his best friend Toby had moved out of town, but not before admitting he was in love with Seamus. Not before he'd kissed him and touched him…and Seamus had let him. When it was over, he'd acted like an asshole—cut all ties and ignored Toby's postcards, trying to bury those memories deep enough that they'd never bother him again, though he'd never forgotten the feelings.

But he'd chosen a different path for his future. A path that would give him the family he'd always wanted and a life that would emulate his father's. A life to be proud of.

This man's attention made his reaction to Toby's awkward touches seem tame.

You're tired. That's all this is. Tired and hungry and out of your element.

But his body was buzzing with renewed energy and an urgency that stemmed from arousal. When the stranger licked the ice cream off his spoon, Seamus clenched his fists, feeling his dick harden and strain against his jeans in spite of his mental rejection.

He couldn't look away.

The man smiled in genuine amusement and interest, and his body straightened, shifting as if he meant to come closer.

Self-preservation made Seamus whirl back toward the front desk, warning sirens blaring in his head. "My key?"

The girl blushed again. "I'm so sorry, Mr. Finn. Patty has your key, and she'll take you where you need to go from here."

"Thank you. And please, call me Seamus." She could

call him anything she wanted as long as someone got him away from the stranger who made him more uncomfortable—more *aroused*—than he'd been in years.

"Mr. Demir. I didn't see you there, sir," the desk clerk said as Seamus followed a slender redhead with a luggage cart to the elevators. "Can I help you with something?"

The doors closed behind them before he could hear the man's reply.

Demir? Jesus, even his name sounds sexy.

Seamus sighed heavily as the elevator dipped gently and then started to climb. It had been so long since he'd experienced this kind of attraction that he'd almost convinced himself it was an aberration. The fact that he'd silently categorized himself as bisexual since Toby wasn't something he discussed with anyone. It was private and pointless, since no one of either gender had been in his life since he'd had the twins.

He wasn't ashamed or homophobic, that wasn't the issue at all. Two of his cousins were gay, and Jeremy Porter, Owen's husband and best friend since high school, had been bisexual for as long as they'd known him. And Seamus's twin brother Stephen was straight, but he'd fought for gay marriage in the state senate, so it wasn't like his family was backwards on the subject. But it still wasn't something they'd thought about or discussed on a daily basis—until Owen, their mother's pride and joy, fell for Jeremy and abruptly changed teams. That had shocked them all, but then sex and sexual orientation had started coming up all the damn time.

The thing was, back when Seamus was in high school, marriage and children had meant one man and one woman, and he'd accepted that he had to give up that part of himself to get what he wanted from life. It was worth it to him. But this last year had changed everything, and though he'd been happy as hell for his family's good fortune in the romance department, he sometimes couldn't help but wonder if he'd made a mistake all those years ago.

Now was too late for him to change direction. As a nearly forty-year-old father of four rambunctious children and the owner of a small but successful business, he'd barely had time to sleep let alone go out on a date in years. But he had a plan that, when and if he ever got around to it, anyone he dated had to be with someone he could see as a potential partner for the life he'd created. A strong role model for Penny. A supportive influence to help his sons become the men they should be. A friend he could laugh with and who would love his large family as if it were *her* own.

Nothing about what he was feeling right now fit in that perfect puzzle he'd been assembling in his head. Lust so forceful it made his body ache wasn't what he needed to make his life complete. It hadn't cross his mind because it simply wouldn't work.

Don't lie, he chastised himself as he got out on his floor and followed the girl down the hall. *It crossed your mind when your brother moved in with Jeremy, and again when your cousin found Tanaka.*

But just because he had a feeling didn't mean he had to act on it. He had to think about his kids. They were his priority—first, last and always—and nothing and no one was going to change that.

When the redhead led him to his room and opened the door to let him in, he was so distracted by his thoughts that he barely saw the huge suite with the walk-in shower and the bed that was bigger than his kitchen.

When she set his bags inside the door, Seamus tried to tip the woman—Patty, right?—but her eyes widened and she shook her head as she handed him the key. "That's all been taken care of in advance, Mr. Finn.

Word from on high is that you get anything you want. Your own key to the indoor swimming pool, and the VIP larder too, in case you have a late night craving. Any spa treatment we have is available for you with an appointment, and a schedule of outdoor activities like rowing and falconry is right there on your dresser. The sky is the limit."

Falconry? Damn it, Ken. "Thank you."

Patty nodded, backing out of the room. "I'll leave you to get some rest now, but if you need anything, just pick up the phone beside your bed and we'll get it sorted."

Finally alone with his thoughts, he prowled the room, restless and agitated. An image of the man—Demir—had been instantly burned into his mind's eye. After all this time, his body came out of hibernation for someone like that? Someone who looked like he was used to getting his way—not because of his money, though everything about him, including his presence here, said he had more than he'd ever need. It was the knowledge in his expression more than his damn silk pajamas.

The way he held himself with a confident, almost predatory stillness.

The hungry expression he hadn't even tried to hide.

And his body. Powerful was the word that came to mind when Seamus thought of his shoulders and broad chest. Powerful and masculine. His strong jaw was covered in dark scruff and his nose had obviously been broken at least once. His full sensual lips and long, thick lashes softened his hard angles.

But it was his eyes that had truly riveted Seamus. They were a piercing green so vibrant he could see them from across the room. Oddly, they made Seamus think of that picture of a bamboo forest the kids' dentist had hung on the waiting room wall, which he could never stop staring at. He'd thought then the picture had been manipulated, that a green like that couldn't exist in nature, but obviously he'd thought wrong. And those eyes were made more striking by his dark brown skin and the thick waves of silky, sable hair that framed his face.

Demir had seemed to know exactly how Seamus was reacting. He was no doubt used to it, and no doubt aware that when he walked around a hotel in his pajamas, he looked like a man on his way to or from his personal harem. He could be a poster child for excess. Or an underwear model. Or the hero on one of those romance books in the grocery store, where a sheik was holding a willowy blonde in his arms as if he owned her.

All equally irritating and disturbing mental images that Seamus didn't need to be thinking about right now. Or ever.

Jesus, the way he'd smiled at Seamus, as if he knew him, as if he wanted to use that tongue on his body instead of his spoon…

"Fuck." Seamus looked around at the expensive furniture and swore again, leaning against the wall and unzipping his jeans.

He sighed in relief when his heavy length dropped eagerly into his shaking hand. He'd tried to will the need away, but the temptation was too strong, and for once there was no one down the hall who needed a glass of water or another bedtime story. He didn't have to wait until midnight to sneak into his shower and find a little release.

And he needed some release.

He couldn't remember the last time he'd been this turned on thinking about a man. About anyone. Despite the occasional fantasy—and one visit to a gay porn website that had made him so paranoid about his teenage son finding it that he'd almost thrown away his computer—Seamus had no idea what being with a man would be like. Only that there was a part of him that had always wanted to find out.

Demir wouldn't be the type to let him use his inexperience as an excuse. He would be rough. Demanding. Impatient to see how far Seamus would let him go. How far he could make him go.

And God that thought turned him on more than it should have.

Seamus shuttled his hand over his erection and gritted his teeth, hating the man for making him feel this again. The confusion and desire. The lack of control.

In his fantasy, his anger didn't stop Demir from pushing him to his knees and making him swallow his cock. He'd wondered how it would taste since Toby had cornered him in his truck and said goodbye in a way that made Seamus come harder than he'd known was possible at the time. The way he'd been moaning as he'd swallowed every drop, Toby must have loved it.

He swore and muttered under his breath as dueling images fought for dominance in his mind. Toby's blond head bobbing frantically in his lap, lips wet and greedy on his cock, and the man from the lobby ordering Seamus to take more, to take all of him.

Demir won.

Seamus let his fantasy take over, the handsome forbidden stranger doing things to him, *with* him, that made Seamus cry out fall to his knees, his fist tight and brutal on his hard shaft.

He needed more.

He clumsily pushed down his jeans, licked his finger and slid it behind him, bending his body forward as he pressed his fingertip forcefully into his ass.

"Shit." It *hurt.* God, it hurt but he needed it. Needed to be filled the way the man in the porno had begged to be. It was like a wall inside him had fallen down and the flood of arousal was too great for anything less than everything. He couldn't get deep enough. He couldn't thrust his hips hard enough.

Fuck me. God, fuck me, please.

Demir's dark good looks and haunting eyes sparkled with the knowledge of what he'd done to Seamus with a single look. Laughed at him for his weakness while Seamus grunted and groaned in the quiet hotel room, his release coming in powerful spurts over his hand and onto the spotless floor beneath him.

When he could breathe again, need was replaced by embarrassment and determination.

"Jet lag," he muttered, wiping up the mess he'd made

on the floor before washing his hands and unpacking. Sure. Jet lag. That was all it was. A good night's sleep and some food, and his momentary weakness would be a memory.

He didn't believe a word of it but he'd fake it until he did. He'd hardly be at the hotel anyway so he'd likely never see Demir again. He'd come to visit Murphy's Brewery and his friend Gill, who he'd been emailing with for over a year.

This was a man's vacation, full of business discussions and brewing talk. He'd leave the gay romance to the professionals, since he didn't have a fucking clue what he was doing. Owen and Jeremy would make their mark on Ireland and Seamus would stay safe in Galway, learning how to improve his bar.

And if he had anymore fantasies about the stranger downstairs?

No one else would ever know.

Chapter Three

"Are you free this afternoon? I'm only asking because I think we should get married."

Gillian Murphy threw back her head and laughed, her dark curls dancing around her expressive face and making him smile. "You're great crack, Seamus. Four days ago you were fuming over me not being a man and now you're proposing marriage. How could I pledge my troth to such a mercurial man?"

She was one hell of a woman.

Gill Murphy, the man he'd been emailing back and forth for months about life, his kids and his plans for Finn's, was no man at all. *She* was the only daughter of Gable Murphy, the owner of Murphy's brewery and pub where he'd come to observe so he could start a microbrewery in his own bar.

Her breasts *were* a shock, not because of what she did for a living, but because she'd never given him a hint about her gender in any of their emails and he'd never thought to ask. He shouldn't have assumed, but luckily she hadn't held that against him.

It was surprising was how easy it was to be with her, in spite of her omission. After that first day, he felt like he'd known her his entire life. He liked her, more than he'd liked anyone that wasn't family in a really long time.

It was a relief to know he could still feel this way, especially after his experience with Demir at the hotel. That he could still find himself attracted to someone for who they were. That the feelings didn't overwhelm him and take away his control.

That they weren't all about sex.

With Gill it was exactly how he'd imagined attraction should be. An instant connection. A perfect fit.

And she knew *everything* there was to know about brewing beer. According to her father, she was the only one of his five children who took their business seriously. Which could explain why they were in some kind of financial trouble she didn't want to tell Seamus about. He'd only found out because her father liked to talk after he'd had a few drinks in the evening. He'd discovered that Gable's sons were "driving him into the poorhouse" because they enjoyed spending the profits more than doing the work involved in bringing it in.

They were all artists, he'd told Seamus with a scowl. A painter, a musician, an inventor and a poet who was more Seuss than Yeats as far as Gable could tell. None of them made a dime and they refused to give up their dreams just to help keep their family business afloat.

But Gill was too determined to let them go under, and too gregarious to let anything keep her down for long. She had a confidence that reminded him of his brother's wife, Tasha. Though, as far as Seamus knew, Gill wasn't as obsessed with kink or lasagna.

The more time he spent with her, the more obvious it became that if he had a soul mate in this world? She was it. He had no doubt she would fit right in with his family, and she made him laugh. Made him feel good about himself.

They were kindred spirits.

Exactly what you always wanted.

His biggest hurdle was getting her to look at him as something more than a friend who was great *crack.*

Which, he'd learned recently, actually meant fun. Wholesome, non-drug related fun.

They were walking on the rocky beach from the brewery to a small seafood restaurant nearby and, when she climbed over the divider, he gripped her waist and lifted her easily, as if he'd done it a thousand times before. "You think I'm joking. I've found a beautiful woman who takes care of her parents, can hold her own with her brothers and lives to talk beer. Frankly, I'm surprised you're not already taken."

"I've thought the same about you, Seamus." She winked. "Of course, then I remember a certain email where you told me your brother was voted your state's sexiest senator. It must be hard to compete with that."

"Funny." She was teasing, but she wasn't wrong. It was impossible to compete with Stephen and he'd long ago learned not to try. But she did say sexiest, and since they were twins he decided to take it as a compliment. "He's happily married with kids now. But I'm available." He squeezed her hand. "Also with kids. I know that sends a lot of women running in the other direction."

She turned toward him and placed their joined hands on his chest. "Shame on you, Seamus. If I didn't know you were joking—since like me you're not one for rash decisions—I'd tell you that any woman who can't appreciate a man who loves his children and family isn't much of a woman at all."

That wasn't the problem. Women *appreciated* him all day long. At the kid's afterschool activities, at the parent teacher meetings and at the pub. When they knew he was raising four children on his own, they couldn't *stop* appreciating him.

That didn't mean they wanted to date him. A large, ready-made family was a lot to take on, no matter how attractive they thought he was. And since one-night stands with tipsy pub patrons didn't sit well with him and gay bars were forever off the table? He'd taken a lot of late night showers over the years.

Being a father was the most important thing in his life, and he made no apologies for that. When he looked back on how they came to be with him, as unbelievable as those circumstances still seemed he wouldn't change a thing.

But he wouldn't mind having someone to share it with. Owen, Stephen and Jen had all found their partners. His parents were still madly in love. Seamus was the only single member of his immediate family left and this was the first time in years he hadn't been too busy to do anything about it.

What are the odds that you'd find two people to date after one week in another country?

One person. There was only one person he had the least interest in dating, and her name was Gillian.

He wasn't going to think about Demir today.

"You're not allowed to make that face on your vacation," Gill told him sternly, dragging him toward the large building—covered in an unexpected but cheerfully bright blue and green beach scene, complete with palm trees. "Bess will make everything better. She does things with chowder that will curl your toes, and her fish and chips are light as air. Better than anything anyone else has to offer."

After they'd been seated and Bess found out he was Gill's friend from "the emails", one platter after another kept appearing, and the curvaceous older woman looked so pleased when he cleaned each plate, he wasn't sure if she was ever planning to stop.

"Look at that," Gill laughed when another bowl of chowder was set down in front of them. "My brothers are lucky to get a biscuit between them with the tab they've left at her door, but she's definitely taken a shine to you. A good judge of character, Bess."

Seamus knew better. "She's seen pictures of my kids hasn't she?"

Gillian blushed. "Ages ago. They're beautiful, Seamus. I couldn't resist."

He figured. Along with all the appreciation he got instead of actual dates, women loved to feed him. Maybe they thought he needed all the help he could get to keep up with his young family. It honestly baffled him, but he wasn't complaining.

"Gillian." A husky male voice with the slightest trace of an accent spoke beside their table and Seamus froze with a spoon halfway to his mouth. "If I'd known bringing you with me would have resulted in this kind of king's feast, I would have done it days ago."

Gillian beamed over Seamus at the man who'd spoken and foreboding shimmered up his spine. "It's nothing to do with me, Bellamy. Seamus here has charmed Bess all on his own."

She stood and Seamus sighed, wiping his mouth with his napkin before doing the same out of habit. "Seamus Finn, meet Bellamy Demir, my dear friend and another tourist enjoying our fair isle."

He was better looking up close. Of course he was. He

was also wearing that half smile that could be interpreted as a knowing smirk, which reminded Seamus how much he'd started to dislike the interloper. He didn't offer to shake his hand, nodding sharply. "I've seen you at the bar." *Every day since I got here*.

"I'm sure," Bellamy said dryly, pulling *his* Gillian in for a warm hug. "I've been chatting this siren's ear off since I found her place. If she didn't have such brilliant business sense, I'd suggest she work in the tourism industry. She's already sent me on a few unforgettable Galway adventures."

Gill blushed. "Ever the flatterer, this one. But now I should have introduced you two sooner. You're both staying at the same hotel, I think, though Seamus isn't enjoying the amenities as much as he should. Do you know he's never been on vacation before, Bellamy? Can you *imagine*? Now he's here and the poor man has spent the last four days listening to me talk about my brewing process, barely poking his handsome head outside to smell the air. Lunch is the only time I can get him to relax without twisting his arm."

Seamus forced a smile for her. "You could get me to do anything, and you know it. Even eat poor Bess out of business in one sitting."

“Not a chance,” she denied lightly. “But I do think you two could find a lot to talk about. Bellamy might be the most well traveled man you’ve ever met. Sure and he can afford it, but still, I think you should take your vacation advice from a master. He knows how to make every moment count and he’s always on the hunt for a new adventure. The riskier the better.”

I bet he’s a master at all kinds of things.

Bellamy was studying him as if he were reading his traitorous thoughts and seeing his darkest fantasies. There was no way he could know how Seamus had spent the last few nights in his hotel suite. How many times he’d gotten himself off to that single scorching look in the lobby from a man he didn’t know.

Didn’t *want* to know.

“I’d be happy to help you in any way I can. If you like to hike there’s a beautiful spot I found this morning. Stunning view, very private.” He glanced back at Gillian. “Is this the same Seamus who owns his own little pub back in the states? The single dad who wants to start micro brewing?”

“The very same,” Gill confirmed with a wink at Seamus. “He bought the place from *his* Dad and he’s been making changes for more than a year now, working like a fiend to bring in a bigger, younger crowd."

"Smart," Bellamy offered in a voice that made Seamus grit his teeth. "Not all family businesses can make the generational transition necessary for growth without backing."

He didn't like the way the guy talked, Seamus suddenly decided. It wasn't the slight French tilt of his accent making everything he said sound pompous and obnoxiously sexy, it was his phrasing. It made it sound as if what Seamus was trying to do with his *little pub* was cute but unimportant. Complimenting him as though he were surprised he could string two sentences together, let alone make the *generational transition*.

He didn't like him at all.

Keep lying to yourself, Seamus. That always works.

"I should go before Bess brings another plate over," he said quietly to Gill, rudely ignoring Bellamy's words and gaze. "I need to get back to the hotel to wait for Owen anyway."

"Owen?" Bellamy's green eyes narrowed. "Gill said you were here alone."

Gill chuckled at the misunderstanding, not noticing how stiffly Seamus was standing or that his hands had curled into tight fists. "Owen and Seamus aren't *together*, Bellamy. Owen's husband wouldn't approve. Not to mention his mom. Seamus is—"

"Not interested in talking about his personal life with strangers," Seamus said with a scowl. When Gill's eyes widened in surprise, he wanted to smack himself. God, he was being a jackass. "I'm sorry. It's been a long day and I think I might need to rest before I join you at the bar."

"You're still coming though?" Now she wasn't sure. Shit, how could he convince her to date him when all he could think about was getting the hell away from her new friend?

"I wouldn't miss it. Your brother's been talking about his band for days. If even half of what he says is true we'll be in for a treat, I'm sure."

Gill smirked. "Nearly half of it is."

"Tonight?" Bellamy mused silkily. "I'd had other plans, but I'll change them for that kind of entertainment. I've been hearing about Gary's band myself."

Shit. Now he'd be spending the entire evening trying to entertain Owen and Jeremy while wooing Gillian Murphy and trying to keep all of them away from Bellamy Demir.

"Should be fun."

Right. Great fucking crack.

***

It felt wrong to be on this side of the bar. He was enjoying catching up with Owen and Jeremy and hearing about the tours they'd been on—and the few they'd been kicked off of for lewd behavior—but Seamus was still distracted. He had the strongest urge to pick up some empty glasses or grab a rag to wipe down a table or two.

Gill and her father were dealing with the crowd who'd come to see her youngest brother's band, and they were holding their own like champs, but neither of them had had a break all night. It couldn't hurt his cause to show Gillian that he was capable of something other than following her around.

It might also distract him from the asshole Gill kept talking to at the other end of the bar. Each time Demir smiled at her or reached out to touch her arm as he made a point, Seamus tensed.

He was trouble. He'd sensed it from the minute he'd laid eyes on the guy and the feeling got stronger each day. He was here nearly as much as Seamus was, and it wasn't like it was right next to the damn hotel. The location was why he'd rented a car in the first place. He'd seen him visit with Gillian's father and brothers too. And then at lunch today, he and Gillian were talking in a way that left him wondering what Bellamy's intentions were. Had he read him wrong? Was he flirting with the woman Seamus had set his sights on?

And what kind of adventures had Gill sent him on?

"I've noticed you eye-stalking your perky bartender friend all night. Does my usually oblivious brother have a crush?" Owen let out a low whistle as Gillian bent down to hear what Bellamy was saying. "If you do, it looks like you're not the only one. I'd beat him up for you but he's huge and my husband wouldn't sleep with me if I cracked my ribs playing wingman."

Of course Owen had noticed him. It would impossible not to. Bellamy didn't exactly fit in to the pale and predominantly ginger Irish crowd.

"Who *is* that?" Jeremy asked with quiet urgency when he caught sight of the man in question.

"Bellamy Demir," Seamus muttered. "Some rich asshole that's staying at my hotel and screwing with my vacation."

"Great name," Jeremy mused, grabbing his phone and slipping out the stylus attached to it, instantly starting to draw. "Thank God for Sketchbook."

"Are you really using that app to sketch another guy on our honeymoon—a guy easygoing Seamus hates, no less—right in front of me?" Owen sounded civil, but Seamus knew him well enough to hear the underlying jealousy. He was a little irritated at Jeremy himself. Demir was fast becoming his least favorite person, and the fact that Owen's husband found him attractive gave him another excuse to dislike him.

You hate him? Is that why your dick is hard? Why you're jealous of the way Jeremy is staring at him?

Jeremy didn't stop, but he did lean closer to Owen. "Come on, babe. He's not real. I mean he *is*, but look at him. No one looks like that in real life. He's all Arabian Nights meets MMA fighter. I do think he's perfect for the new character in Vini's next series though. He's definitely Dark Prince material. His eyes literally look like they're glowing from here."

So Seamus wasn't the only one who'd noticed that.

Owen's fierce expression gentled and he squinted at the image. "Damn. I don't like it, but I think you're right. He's just like you described him."

Seamus couldn't believe what he was hearing. "Wait, you're putting him in one of your graphic novels? As a *prince*? At least tell me he's a villain."

"Unfortunately, no," Owen grumbled, watching Jeremy's sketch take shape on the small screen. "Not officially. He starts out as a prick, if that helps, but it's all a funny misunderstanding."

Great, now he'd never be completely rid of the man. His son Wes loved Vini the misunderstood demon. "That doesn't help," Seamus growled.

Owen glanced up at that, eyes widening. "Whoa, what's he done to deserve *that* look? That only happens when there's an abusive drunk at the bar or a reporter trying to trip up Stephen and Tasha. Babe, Seamus has his *Hulk* face on."

Jeremy's attention bounced from him to the man he was drawing. "*He* doesn't look too intimidated by it. In fact, he's sending Seamus some amused side eye. What did he do, steal your hotel towels or something?"

He's not looking at me, Seamus wanted to correct Jeremy. He was too busy charming the pants off of Gillian to notice Seamus existed. What the fuck was he up to?

"We only met officially today," he explained, "but Gill's brothers talk about him. They say he's richer than Ken and Declan combined, but entitled in a way that would make them both cringe. His dad is some Turkish businessman and his mother was a French model."

The Murphy men liked to exaggerate almost as much as they liked slacking off, but Seamus was willing to bet at least half of that was true. They'd gotten the entitled part right.

"Turkish and French," Jeremy mumbled. "God, that explains his bone structure. Keep talking."

"He's invited them to visit him in New York, so he must live there, and Gill's father thinks he's got his eye on her. He told me I might have a fight on my hands."

It wasn't hard to imagine Gillian finding Demir attractive. He'd seen it right away, but no man wanted to admit his competition was ten times sexier than he could ever be.

If he *was* competition, and the chemistry Seamus was fighting was all one-sided.

Bellamy Demir got under his skin in a way no one else ever had. He dreamt about the man, did his best to avoid running into him… He'd never felt like punching someone without cause before, but Demir's confidence—everything about him—just bugged him to the point of violence.

And those mixed messages—giving Seamus

smoldering stares one minute and then putting his hands all over Gill the next—were enough to drive him to drink. Seamus wasn't sure he stood a chance with either of them. Not that he wanted a chance with Demir—that wasn't on the table. But with Gill looking at Demir like he'd hung the moon, Seamus might be out of luck with her as well.

Between the three of them, he didn't make the cut in the looks department and he knew it. He was ordinary at best. His short brown hair was cut for utility more than style. He had it done exactly the same way every month when he took his kids to the mall. The "Dad" cut, Jake had called it. Okay, so he was decently fit for a man pushing forty and had nice blue eyes like every other member of his family besides his cousin James, but that was about it.

The reason his twin was hailed as his state's sexiest senator had more to do with his attitude than his looks as far as Seamus was concerned. That, and the fact that most of the other senators he worked with were old or looked like they'd lost a fight with a hairbrush twenty years ago and never bothered with a rematch.

Seamus wasn't *that* bad, but he didn't have the aura of power or the charm of Stephen. Seamus wasn't anything to write home about. Or sketch impulsively in a pub in Ireland.

How did a guy like him compete with a *Dark Prince*?

How did he *resist* him?

"Earth to Seamus." Owen snapped his fingers in front of his face. "What do you mean a fight? Are you dating this girl? Please say yes. I'll send up the flares and we'll start celebrating."

"Not yet, but I'm working up to it." Seamus smiled at his brother, trying to take his mind off Bellamy and focus on the positive. "I actually skipped a few steps and asked her to marry me today. She thinks I'm joking, but I'm not so sure. I like her."

"Hold the phone." Owen put his finger in his ear and wriggled it around. "Did you say you asked her to *marry* you?"

"You don't approve?"

"*I* do. She seems fantastic." Jeremy set down his phone-turned-sketch pad on the bar. Seamus had gotten his attention. "But four days is a little quick to start planning a wedding. Is the vacation sex turning your head? Have you two already…?"

"No, we haven't. How could we?" Seamus waved that question away. "We're surrounded by Murphys most of the time, and they all live under the same roof so it's not like we've had a lot of opportunities for privacy. Even if we did, she's not the kind of woman that jumps into bed with men she hardly knows."

"But she'd marry one? And by the way, *every* woman is that kind of woman if she wants you badly enough." Owen was staring at him like he'd grown another head. "You really haven't had sex with her? At all? No make out session in a closet? No under the table action or orgasms on either side? How are you walking without a limp right now? Are your balls permanently blue or what?"

"Owen." He really didn't want to talk about this.

"Don't use your *Dad voice*, it doesn't work on me. And I'm sorry, but the nineteen-fifties called and even *those* prudish sons of bitches say you should be sharing her bed instead of a milkshake at the drive-in. How can you know you want to marry her when you don't even know if there's chemistry?"

Jeremy dug his elbow hard into Owen's side. "Excuse your brother, Seamus, he's oversexed and used to instant gratification in all things. But there's nothing wrong with being a gentleman." He looked at Owen and spoke loud and slow. "*Gentleman.* That means you open her car door and ask about her day before you unzip and demand a blow job."

"I think you should stick to your phone art, babe. You don't know women as well as I do." He pointed at Seamus. "I appreciate the fact that you even jokingly proposed to someone who isn't in some kind of trouble." He narrowed his eyes. "She's not right? This wasn't a rescue proposal or anything? She doesn't need a green card to escape the country?"

Seamus glared at him in answer.

"You heard the same thing I did, right, Jeremy? He *likes* her. That is the wrong L-word for marriage. I *like* sleeping in on my days off. I *like* pizza."

Jeremy raised an eyebrow and covered his smile by rubbing his beard. "You more than like pizza, Owen. Let's be honest. If it was legal to marry one of those meat pies, I'd have had competition."

Owen wouldn't be distracted. "He hasn't even *tried* to sleep with her. And he's hanging around with us while that the sultan of sex appeal over there flirts with his girl. No one else is seeing a problem with that?"

"He's also sitting right here," Seamus warned darkly.

"Then you tell me, Seamus." Owen's expression was genuinely mystified. "If you're serious about this woman, why don't I believe it? You're a Finn, man. Where's the fire?"

His brother winced and Seamus knew he was regretting the way that had come out, if not the sentiment. "I'm not like you, Owen. You've always jumped into everything with both feet and no fear. That's what made you unstoppable on the football field and irresistible with the ladies, and it's how you started a successful company as soon as that diploma was in your hand. But some of us need time to think things through. And in *your own experience*," he added pointedly, "sometimes sexual attraction shows up *after* an emotional connection."

He took a quick drink to calm his ire and then continued, "Gill and I built a friendship online that I don't want to lose by moving too fast. And I'm not punching the pompous playboy over there because this is her place of business and I respect her family."

"But what about—"

"Sex?" Seamus held up his hand. "Of course I want sex, Owen. But I'm a grown up and can, on occasion, think with something other than my dick. And what I think is that maybe what *I'm* looking for is better for me. Something solid and lasting, that isn't always unpredictable and doesn't consume all the oxygen in the room. I like Gillian. A lot. I can see her in my life. *With my children.* I know that doesn't sound fiery enough for you, but that doesn't mean it can't be good."

Owen opened his mouth to keep arguing, but Jeremy stopped him with a hand on his arm. "Whatever it is you need to be happy, Seamus, that's what we want you to have." He glanced back down the bar and shook his head. "If you like her, I'm betting she's too smart to fall for that perfect camouflage anyway. That's probably why he keeps looking over here. He knows you're a threat."

Bellamy was more of a threat to the future Seamus had envisioned for himself than anything else. He *couldn't* give in to this sudden, unreasonable attraction for a gay fling right when the perfect woman was within his reach. He might never find someone like Gillian again. He might never have the time or inclination to try.

He might end up alone.

Owen swore and grabbed Jeremy's hand, pulling him abruptly off of his bar stool. "I need to borrow my husband for a minute, Seamus. I'm sure you understand. We'll be back after I remind him who he belongs to."

"Owen—damn it." Here? He was probably taking

Jeremy to the bathroom for a quickie. Seamus should be used to it by now. No one around them could deny that what they had was fiery and passionate. But, whether Owen wanted to admit it or not, the years of friendship and trust that had come before it made that intensity possible. Made it last. Most people went a lifetime without feeling something like that.

Seamus actually felt like a fraud after his anti-fire speech. He gave advice to the lovelorn in his family all the time, but when it came to his own love life? *Of course* he wanted sex and fire. *Of course* he wanted what everyone else had. But he had no idea how to get it, let alone what to do with it when he did.

You felt it with Bellamy.

That was too much. If a few hot glances had put him in this state, all that could come from anything more was scorched earth and regret.

Sometimes it seemed as if his life were on backwards and inside out. He had four children, but he'd never been in love. Not really. Sadly, his friendship with Toby was the closest he'd come; only he hadn't realized it at the time. He wasn't good at reading signals with women and his experience with sex had been… Well, it hadn't been earth shattering, but it hadn't been so awful he didn't want to try it again. Admittedly that was based off a very small sampling.

Maybe he wasn't the kind of guy who could handle the Finn fire. It didn't mean he had to be alone, did it?

The loud beeping coming from his pocket had him standing, his mood instantly lifting. Gill caught his eye as if she'd heard the sound over the din, and he held up his phone up and shrugged sheepishly, making her grin.

"You're an angel, Seamus Finn," she called in a loud, clear voice. "Say hello to them from me."

Maybe tomorrow he could ask her to join him and introduce her to his family.

He walked outside, the music and loud voices fading as he moved toward the back where the brewery was shut down for the night. He used the app Ken Tanaka had put on his phone so he could talk to the kids.

His son's face appeared less than a minute later and Seamus felt a wave of love and homesickness roll through him. "Hey Jake."

"Hey Dad." He glanced behind Seamus and squinted. "Good, you're outside. I'm attempting to disprove a hypothesis. Is it raining there? I can't tell."

"A hypo-what now?" He joked, glancing up at the clear, star-filled sky. "Actually it hasn't rained all day.

Has Gram got you watching the weather channel again? Tell her it's not really a show."

"We're at Aunt Jen's. Grandpa has a stomach bug and Gram doesn't want us to catch it."

Good call, Mom.

Five-year-old Wes got in front of Jake, blowing his white-blond bangs out of his eyes in frustration. He needed a haircut. "You should come back right away, Dad. Uncle Rory says it's always raining because of the curse."

Hell. Rory was there? "The what, son?"

But it was Wes's twin Penny who peered over her brother's shoulder and answered. "The curse, Daddy," she yelled into the phone as if they were playing with a tin can on a string in the backyard. "The curse because of *the fairies*!"

Seamus thought he heard someone cackling in the background. Fucking Rory. "Could you put Uncle Rory on the phone, sweetheart?"

His youngest cousin's voice came through loud and clear. "Rory isn't available at the moment. Not because he's afraid you'll ban him from the bar for life or anything, but because he's being chased by a baaaaansheeee!"

Penny screamed and giggled and Seamus saw Little Sean running past the camera after her, all smiles, before Jake angled the phone back to himself. "Where's Aunt Jen, Jake? Uncle Declan? Please tell me there is an actual adult in that house right now."

Jake was watching something off camera, smiling. "Rory's an adult, Dad. Technically. I'm looking out."

"Of course you are. I'm not seeing any blood and you still have all your limbs, so I suppose that's something."

"He's an EMT. If we were bleeding, he could probably fix it." He lowered his voice. "I dragged a mattress into my room and we've all been sleeping in there. Aunt Jen is fine with it."

"Good man." He cleared his throat, knowing Jake had no doubt done it for Wes, who wasn't a big fan of sleeping by himself unless he was in his own bedroom, and Jen's house was the size of a shopping center. "I'll talk to you tomorrow okay?"

"Sure."

"I love you, Jake."

"Me too. Night."

The phone went dark and Seamus slipped it into his pocket, wishing he were there to tuck his kids in instead of arguing with his brother and competing with some wealthy demi-god for Gill's attention.

"Did she say fairies?"

The voice behind him nearly gave him a coronary.

"Shit." Seamus turned to find Bellamy Demir leaning against the wall, his hands stuffed in the pockets of his slacks and that irritating smirk on his face. "I didn't see you there."

"Sorry." He didn't sound sorry.

"My daughter," he explained simply, surreptitiously glancing around for an escape route.

"She sounds adorable. And a lot like my mother. She sent a text warning me about standing in fairy rings before I got here."

Seamus lowered his eyebrows suspiciously. He texted his model mother? That didn't sound like the man he'd decided Demir had to be. "Huh."

Nice, Seamus. He'll think you can't form a damn sentence.

Bellamy didn't seem to notice. "Was it Owen or his husband I caught staring at me a few minutes ago? They both look a little rough around the edges, and they've had a lot to drink, but I was sure he was looking. Is he interested in adding a fourth for the evening?"

That was more like it.

"*A fourth?* That's my brother and his new husband you're talking about," Seamus said stiffly, a clear warning in his voice. "They're on their honeymoon, and trust me, two is their magic number."

Seamus thought he saw relief flash in Bellamy's eyes. "Owen is your brother? I'd guessed they were trying to lure you into a threesome, since you didn't want to talk about them at lunch."

Seamus's mouth nearly fell open. What about him said he'd be down for a threesome?

"I suppose them being newlyweds explains the behavior." Bellamy's laugh was wicked. "They're in line for the bathroom right now, wrapped around each other like no one is watching. Not that I mind, but I *have* heard Gill's father warn a few couples apart this evening. This is a family establishment you know."

Bellamy had added the last bit with Gable Murphy's clear brogue, but Seamus wasn't laughing with him. He considered himself a peaceful, good-natured man, but no one talked about his family. Particularly not this ass who was distracting Gill and Jeremy with his magnetic appeal. Distracting Seamus and making him lose sleep.

He stepped into Bellamy's space and grabbed a fistful of soft cotton without thinking. "If they bother you so much, Mr. Demir, maybe you should leave."

"Call me Bellamy, Seamus." He looked down at the fist still gripping his shirt with an intrigued smile. "That's a surprisingly short fuse you have. Gillian never mentioned that. But then, I don't imagine she gets you as aggravated as I seem to."

Seamus let him go hastily. He didn't enjoy losing his temper, but this guy seemed to like stirring the pot. "No, she doesn't."

Thank God.

Bellamy seemed pleased. "Well, don't hold back on my account. I bet you could do some damage if someone got you worked up enough."

"No one's ever tried."

"And you'd rather they didn't, I can see that. Don't worry, you hide it well. That big-but-harmless routine has everyone fooled."

Seamus scowled. "Are you *trying* to pick a fight?"

It sounded like it. Everything the man was saying felt like a challenge.

"Usually. But that's not why I came outside. I was curious about your evening appointments." He glanced at the pocket where Seamus had stashed his phone. "They're lucky to have such an attentive father. How many children do you have?"

"Don't take this the wrong way, but I've heard about you too, and I'd rather not discuss my kids with a pampered bully. Especially not one that's after Gillian."

Bellamy grinned. "Is there a right way to take that? I'm flattered you've been asking about me, so I'll give you pampered," he acknowledged. "And too forward on occasion, though I'm working on that. But I'm not after Gillian, Seamus. I think you know why."

"I don't, actually."

"I'm gay."

Every muscle in Seamus's body tightened with awareness. Oh God. Something in him had known the second he saw Bellamy. How had he known? "You're gay?"

Bellamy laughed again. "All my life. Did Gable tell you I wanted Gillian? He thinks everyone with a dick is after his daughter. I heard you were interested in her too."

"The difference is, I am." Seamus crossed his arms over his chest, relieved but still on the defensive.

Bellamy tilted his head, his hair falling over his forehead, and his eyes practically glowing in the evening shadows. "Really? I could have sworn you were just good friends."

First Owen and now this jackass. What was he supposed to do, toss her on the bar and publically stake a claim?

He could see Bellamy doing something like that. Dragging Seamus to the center of the room and kissing him with those soft lips until he was begging for more, audience or not. Taking his cock out and—

"I've only been here a few days," he said, desperate to distract himself. "These things take time."

"Not if you're doing it right." Bellamy pushed himself off the wall and moved closer. "In my experience, you either feel it or you don't. And when you see something you want? You do whatever you have to do to make it yours." He licked his lower lip and watched Seamus with hooded eyes. "Not that it's any of my business, pampered bully that I am, but it's not really fair to lead her on when your feelings are…elsewhere."

Seamus shook his head in denial. "My feelings aren't elsewhere, and your experience isn't mine." Their experiences were light years apart. Different solar systems. "Look, I don't really know you, and you definitely don't know me. Let's save us both some trouble and keep it that way."

He started walking away again, ready to get some distance from the disturbing man. The only good thing that had come out of it was the fact that he knew Bellamy Demir wasn't interested in Gill. He was gay. Not a rival, but still a dick.

You want him and he's gay, you idiot. Take what you want for once in your life.

No. He refused to think about that. It wasn't an option. It would never be an option.

"I do know one thing about you," Bellamy called after him.

"What?" He looked over his shoulder impatiently.

"I knew the second I saw you that I wanted to fuck you."

CHAPTER FOUR

The universe had it in for him.

"You know Ken Tanaka?" Owen stared slack-jawed at Bellamy Demir, all his earlier jealousy forgotten. "Man, talk about a small world."

How was this happening? After the things Bellamy had said outside, Seamus had decided he never wanted to speak to him again, but somehow he'd wound up sitting right beside him at a table with Owen, Jeremy, and Gillian.

He glanced down at his beer. He was going to need a lot more if he wanted to forget what Bellamy's graphically sexual words.

I knew the second I saw you that I wanted to fuck you.

Who said that to someone they hardly knew? He was probably just trying to shock Seamus. If so, he'd done his job. He couldn't stop thinking about it. It was almost surreal to know that if he wanted to, he could actually hook up with a man tonight. This man.

Not that he would, because hookups weren't his thing, no matter what the gender, right? But if they *were*….

Bellamy grinned at Owen. "Hell, yes I know him. Long hair, tattoos, and dangerous with computers or ropes depending on his mood, right?"

Seamus stiffened. Had they dated or something? "What do you know about ropes?"

"Probably more than you, Mr. Mom." Owen was teasing but he shook his head subtly, reminding Seamus that when it came to kink, he shouldn't talk about things he didn't understand.

He had a point. Seamus didn't know anything about BDSM other than what Owen and Tasha threw out in casual conversation, and that was more information than he needed. Even if he were inclined, having a houseful of kids would make indulging in that kind of thing impossible.

Bellamy barely hid his smile. "You said he's with

someone exclusively? Are you telling me he's finally found the man who can keep him in line?" He winked at Gillian, whose cheeks had gone deep red at the topic, though she tried to hide it. She looked especially lovely tonight, Seamus thought almost defiantly. And he *did* want her, damn it.

Of course he did.

"Their cousin Brady," Jeremy answered in a louder voice than necessary. Bellamy was right, he and Owen had both had more than a few shots of whiskey to wash down their beer. Seamus was glad they weren't driving anywhere. "His brothers call him Gigantor and he used to be a Marine so…"

Bellamy nodded, as if that explained everything. "A giant Marine would do it, I imagine."

"Tanaka's the reason we're here," Owen shared as he wrapped his arm around Jeremy's shoulder and started playing with his husband's shirt collar. "Seamus too. We got a honeymoon for Christmas, and my big brother got to meet Gill." He raised his glass with his free hand. "To Gill."

Seamus would drink to that. "To Gill," he said with absolute sincerity. "You'll never know how glad I am that you ended up being Gillian."

She laughed at that and reached up to kiss his cheek. "I'm glad you're glad. But I'm still not marrying you, Seamus Finn. At least, not today." She glanced over at Bellamy and her smile flickered for the space of a heartbeat. "I really need to get back to work, but I'll see you boys later."

When she left Jeremy and Owen were chuckling and whispering in each other's ears. "What's so funny?"

Owen was wearing a goofy grin. "Nothing. We're glad too. Glad she's not a damsel in distress. Glad she's not pregnant and on the run. Glad she didn't trick you into—"

"That's enough," Seamus interrupted grimly, too aware of their audience. "I know you're enjoying yourself, but even if you don't think *I* do, *she* deserves more respect than that."

Owen ducked his head sheepishly. "You're right. I'm sorry, Seamus. I think I'm drunk."

"I know it. Let's get some coffee in you ASAP." Jeremy said to Owen, pulling him to his feet. "No more whiskey tonight. Maybe ever. You might not be Irish enough to handle it."

"I'll show you how Irish I am." Owen's voice faded as he stumbled away.

Seamus was embarrassed, and once again alone with a man he didn't want to have anything to do with. A man he had no idea what to make of. "I think I should join them. They get distracted when they're alone together, as you made sure to point out. They could end up being arrested before the night's over."

"I see." Bellamy leaned back in his chair, frowning pensively. "Just so we're clear, you're solidly in the closet then? The hints were all there but I'm used to ignoring things I don't want to know. You're so relaxed around your brother and his husband, but they don't know you're bi, do they?"

"What I am is my business." He wasn't in any closet. There were aspects of himself he chose not to focus on. It wasn't the same thing at all.

"We've been circling each other for days, and I know you've been watching me almost as much as I've watched you. Now you're jumpy and tense and you can't even look at me. Was I too pushy? Are you afraid I'll jump you right here in the middle of this bar?"

The thought had crossed his mind, but it hadn't scared him. The fact that it hadn't was the problem.

Seamus forced himself to glare into intensely green eyes. "I'm not in the closet and I'm not avoiding you because you're gay. Maybe I don't really like you. Maybe we don't have anything in common."

"What's not to like? And we both enjoy spending our evenings at Murphy's, we both know Tanaka… We've both wondered what would happen if you let me kiss you tonight."

"No one's wondering that but you," Seamus muttered, knowing it was a lie.

"Too pushy again? I apologize. I know I come on strong. I've never believed in wasting time, but with you I might need to take a different approach. Talk to me, Seamus Finn. Tell me about yourself."

When he hesitated, Bellamy's lips tilted. "That's fine, I'll start. Kenneth sent you here on a vacation to a brewery. This brewery. And you've been emailing with Gillian since last year, is that right?"

"Yeah?"

"You don't seem like the kind of guy who would accept such a generous gift. You like to work with your hands and earn things on your own. Am I right?"

Seamus nodded, in spite of himself. "I think it was more an intervention than a Christmas present. The whole family knew about it before I did."

"A workaholic. Why am I not surprised? Still, a trip

to Ireland is no small thing. Did he owe you? What exactly did you do for him?"

"If anything, *I* owe *him*." Seamus opened and closed his fist on the table. A nervous habit. "He's even looking after the bar right now. He's a good friend."

"Yes, he's always generous with his friends. Very involved."

Trying to unclench his jaw, Seamus took a drink before giving in to his curiosity. "So you *did* date?"

Bellamy found that funny. "Tanaka? Never. But we're good enough friends that I thought I knew his MO. I have a hard time imagining him playing house with one man, even if your cousin is as big as they say."

Then you don't know him as well as you think. "He's not playing at anything. They're in love." Seamus felt his lips curving upward. "My kids call him Uncle Necky."

That made Bellamy laugh. "I love it. And good for Tanaka. If anyone deserves it, he does. Speaking of love and family, is she still in the picture?"

"Who?"

"The mother of the children you don't want to talk to me about."

"No."

"No? That's all you're giving me?"

"Yes."

Bellamy sighed, but his expression was almost playful. "Heads up, gorgeous. Pampered bullies used to getting their way don't like monosyllabic answers to leading questions. If you're not going to talk, I'll have to be forward again and explain exactly what I've imagined doing to your body before, during and after I get inside you. I've been thinking about it a lot."

"You can't stop pushing, can you?" Seamus fought a shiver at the images Bellamy's words brought to mind. He wanted to know.

He *didn't* want to know.

"They're out of the picture," he said swiftly, desperately trying to change the subject.

"*They*? So more than one woman and they're *both* out of the picture? Now you have to tell me more. Do you snore? Leave the toilet seat up? What is it?"

He didn't have to tell him anything. He *never* had this conversation because no one understood. Not really. His family loved and accepted all the kids, but none of them could resist the good-natured ribbing at his expense. They called him Father Goose or Mr. Mom. Any time he left to run an errand, they'd tell him to be sure he didn't come back with another baby. People who weren't related to him usually thought he was a fucking doormat or a fool.

Or worse.

Who cares what he thinks about you? Tell him. You'll never see him after this trip, and maybe he'll lose interest and run screaming in the opposite direction. Or do you want to hear about what he wants to do to you?

Yes.

"Fine," he said again, reaching for his beer. "You asked for it. I have four kids and they had three mothers."

"Had? What happened?" Bellamy asked, his husky voice low and soothing. "Marriage not a good fit for you?"

He should let him think that, but Seamus found himself shaking his head. He wasn't anything like his uncle.

"I've never been married. I was only with one of them." He swore then, because it sounded strange to say and it was none of this man's business. "This isn't a bar conversation you have with a stranger."

"I know." Bellamy covered his hand and Seamus bit back a moan at the heat that instantly flowed into his body from that small contact. “But I’m a pushy stranger who’s friends with your friend Tanaka, a man you know has great taste in people, so tell me anyway.”

He didn’t know why he obeyed the soft command, but once he started talking, he couldn’t stop. “I used to eat at this diner near my apartment every night. I’d walked there and back so many times I started recognizing faces. Making friends. There was a guy who ran the hot dog stand and listened to audio books, another who sold t-shirts and cheap cell phones and…there was a woman near the alley who always seemed to have a fresh set of bruises. I was worried about what she was selling, but she looked so sad and no one ever approached her. I imagined it was because of the quiet six-year-old boy who sat at her feet and never took his eyes off her, as if he were protecting her or afraid she would disappear.” His throat tightened. “He got to me, that kid. I started bringing them hot dogs and food from the diner, but she never took any for herself and she wouldn’t say anything to me other than ‘Thank you’. She didn’t seem like she belonged there, but I didn’t want to push. She was very skittish.”

Seamus could see it all as if it had happened yesterday. “One night it got so cold, and it was snowing so hard, that I tried to get her to go to a shelter, but she was terrified of that idea. I didn't know why. I finally convinced her to stay one night at my place instead. All I could think about was the little guy shivering beside her in three layers of clothing. I offered her a warm meal, clean clothes and a shower. I even told her the name of my cousin, so she could call the police station and ask for him if she didn't feel safe."

"What happened?"

"She was so surprised when I fed her and made up the couch for myself without asking for anything in return that she almost cried. But then I fell asleep. I don't think it was for long, but by the time I woke up she was gone, and Jake was sitting quietly on the bed, looking so lost I swore he knew she wasn't coming back."

"She ran away?"

"The police didn't find her body for two days. I think she did mean to come back for her son. They said her boyfriend caught her sneaking in to get their things and some money and… Well, since she didn't have any living relatives, I started taking steps to adopt Jake myself."

Bellamy swore and shook his head. "That's fucking

tragic. Poor woman. And you. I can't imagine it was easy. One night of kindness and suddenly you're a bachelor adopting a child."

Seamus nodded. "It should have been impossible. But I used every family contact and pulled every string I had. All I knew was that I had to take care of him. He'd already lost too much."

Bellamy hadn't stopped touching him, slowly running his fingers over the back of Seamus's hand, somehow soothing and arousing at the same time. "You said you had four children?"

He wanted to know more? Why wasn't he changing the subject and looking uncomfortable? Why wasn't he looking at Seamus with pity? "Jake and I were on our own for a few months when I met a woman who was temping in his pediatrician's office. She was funny and attentive with Jake, and having her flirt with me was a nice change after all we'd been going through. So when she asked me out, I said yes."

He paused, knowing there were some things he still couldn't say out loud to anyone. "When Presley found out she was pregnant with twins, she didn't handle it well. She wanted out, and I got sole custody of Penny and Wes as soon as they were born. They've never met her."

It was for the best. For everyone.

"Did you love her?"

He couldn't lie. "No. Not the way she needed me to."

"And your youngest?"

Seamus looked down at his hands. This was usually the point in his story where his family starting making jokes about his talent for chasing away women who kept leaving babies on his doorstep.

"Before my father retired, a woman showed up at Finn's one night, tired, broke and extremely pregnant. I wasn't there, but Dad said he felt compelled to let her stay in the place we have behind the bar, rent free, until she got on her feet."

See? He wanted to say. *The apple didn't fall that far. Dad's a sucker too.*

"He started asking me to look in on her and make sure she was okay." Seamus shrugged. "So I did. I let Jake come with me to bring her groceries and they played cards and, despite the fact that she'd left an abusive situation, she seemed surprisingly together. My mother took her to see her doctor and even threw her a small baby shower. I think everyone was hoping I would..." He shook his head. "But there was never anything but friendship between us. Mira had big dreams of traveling and being an actress and I was already firmly planted with a family."

But for a month or two it had been like being married—without the sex, attraction or common interests. It hadn't sucked and she'd been nothing like Presley. God that sounded pathetic, but he probably wouldn't have turned it down.

"Let me guess," Bellamy said softly.

Seamus nodded. "When the baby was born she named him Sean, after my dad and me. She knew all about how I'd ended up with Jake and the twins. My family had talked me up a little too much, I think, trying to impress her, but instead it had given her ideas. She started saying her child would be better off with us. With me. That if I really knew what she'd come from, I'd take him anyway."

"You don't strike me as an easy mark."

Something that felt like gratitude washed over him. "You might be the only one who doesn't think so. I'm not, but I'm not an asshole either. I told her it wasn't going to happen. I was already over my head with the three I had. I tried to help her find another way. I offered her money, work, the chance to go back to school. But I couldn't lock her in that apartment and force her to take care of her baby when she'd already made up her mind. It took years to find her and get her to sign his adoption papers. But that's what I did, with help from Tanaka, because of what Jake said the morning after she left."

Bellamy tilted his head. "What did he say?"

"He wasn't happy she was leaving, but he told me that he knew Little Sean was supposed to be a part of our family. That his grandparents and Mira had taken care of him before he was born so Jake could have a new baby brother to love." Seamus smiled a little at the memory. "I couldn't argue with that. But I did tell him this was the last time and it meant we could never get him a puppy. I had to draw the line somewhere."

Bellamy's expression was a strange mixture of incredulity, admiration and something Seamus couldn't name. "I knew you were too good to be true, but I had no idea you were an actual angel. It never occurred to you to call social services or look into foster care, did it?"

Seamus tugged his hand away and ran it through his hair, not sure if he'd just been complimented or not. "Of course it did. I was a thirty-two-year old man living above a garage that first time. My twin brother had already made a name for himself as a lawyer and entered public office." His lips twisted ruefully. "I, on the other hand, still had no clue what I wanted to do with my life. I worked as a handy man, doing odd jobs to pay for my rent, my membership at the old boxing gym on the corner and my evening trips to the diner, and nothing else. I was drifting. Once I looked at Jake and realized he needed me to know what I was doing? Things started clicking into place."

Jesus, that's enough now, he doesn't need a novel. "I'm sorry. I have no idea why I'm telling you this. I'll—"

The warm hand was back on his arm now, squeezing, and it stopped him cold.

"I'm glad you told me. You're a fascinating man, Seamus. Gorgeous and kind. And boxing, huh? I thought so." Bellamy's eyes were a sparkling distraction. "There's something careful about the way you hold yourself. Especially when I make you mad. Do you still get in the ring?"

Seamus looked down and saw a fresh beer. Where had that come from? He'd been so lost in the memories and the conversation, he honestly had no idea.

Boxing. Right. "I hadn't for a while, but Brady and

Ken have been getting me back into it. I don't have a lot of time, but I made a gym in my basement so I don't get that old man gut and become the total dad cliché."

"Whatever you're doing, it's working for you." Bellamy licked his lower lip and studied him. "There's a bar on the other side of town with a backroom perfect for brawling—one of the adventures Gillian sent me on, and I've gone there once or twice after coming here. In fact, there are fights going on right now. Come with me. I think you'd enjoy yourself and we could celebrate the fact that you don't dislike me anywhere near as much as you thought you did."

"That's not really my style." Seamus tried to frown in disapproval, but he was already thinking about it. "And who said I don't dislike you?"

"You did. With every word. Weren't you paying attention?" Bellamy smiled wickedly behind his mug. "Did I mention it's usually full of fighting Finns? I wonder if they're any relation."

Aw hell. There was no way he could know Seamus was supposed to be looking for his cousins. He hadn't even tried yet; he'd been too busy discussing brewing techniques and following Gillian around like a puppy. Too busy avoiding his attraction to Bellamy. "You don't say."

"Don't say what?" Owen asked, sliding back into his seat with a cup of coffee in his hands. "What did we miss?"

Bellamy told him about the Irish "fight club" and Owen got a look on his face that made Seamus cringe. Hell. Not *that* look. Since birth, the brat had gotten whatever he wanted when he used *that* look. "We have to do it, Seamus. We can't leave tomorrow without experiencing something like that."

Seamus turned to scan the room for Gillian, but she was leaning over the bar in deep discussion with a smitten old regular. She'd never miss them. "Sure. Why not?"

Sure? Why not? Three reasons, idiot. And they're all named Bellamy. You know, the guy you think is an asshole? The guy you can't stop thinking about? The guy who seems more interested in your ability to throw a punch than your collection of children?

Actually, that part was kind of…nice? Was he a bad father if he admitted that?

"Good man." Bellamy got up and put a strong hand on his shoulder, squeezing and sending another jolt of desire through his system. "You can't spend your entire vacation watching Gill make and serve beer. It can't be *that* different from how you do it at home, can it? This is exactly what you need to get that adrenaline pumping."

His adrenaline had started pumping the second Bellamy touched him.

Owen talked about their travels for most of the cab ride, which was good because Seamus was too busy wondering if Bellamy was pressing his knee against him on purpose, and hoping his brother was too drunk to notice the erection that was getting impossible to hide.

They finally got to the narrow, darkly lit bar and Bellamy nodded at the bartender as if he knew him, and then led them all directly into the back room. It was packed with men in various states of undress. The smell of smoke, blood and sweat permeated the air.

"Holy shit," Owen said, stunned at the chaos around them. "Is this a fight club or an orgy? Is the price for a ticket a piece of clothing? Because I'm in."

Seamus chuckled, feeling nostalgic and surprisingly comfortable. "They're shirtless, not naked, Owen. And don't take yours off or someone will think you're asking for a fight."

"That's my cue." Bellamy sent Seamus a sizzling look that made his ears hot. He pulled a flask out of his pocket and took a short swig. “Hold my things?”

He pulled his shirt over his head, handing that over along with the liquor, and then raised his hand as he met the gaze of someone across the room and nodded.

“I’m next,” he said without glancing over again.

“*You’re* fighting?” Seamus hadn’t expected him to participate. Didn’t rich people place bets and watch safely from the sidelines as poor men, roosters or whatever strange thing they felt like putting a wager on entertained them?

You need to stop falling asleep to British television.

“I have to do something to impress the sexy, saintly father of all orphans, don’t I?” Before Seamus could respond, he lowered his voice and added, “Don’t bet against me or I’ll take it out on your ass later.”

He didn’t have a clue how to respond to that, unless it was to say *Yes, please*. And that didn’t feel appropriate.

“He’s taking off his shirt? What is happening right now?” Owen wondered loudly behind him, making Seamus tense until Jeremy spoke and he realized they hadn’t heard Bellamy.

“Bloody fisticuffs? Shirtless man-on-man wrestling? Imagine we’re at our club, Owen, only there are rounds instead of safe words and no one cuddles after.”

"Oh, there are safe words," Bellamy drawled, waggling his eyebrows at the newlyweds. "*Mercy* is one. *Shit, you broke my nose*. That's my favorite."

Seamus couldn't hold in his laughter, but he kept his eyes on the other men in the room so he wouldn't have to admit he was enjoying Bellamy's company.

This felt like something right out of an old movie. Young and old were equally represented here. A man with a face covered in freckles held ice wrapped in a bar towel to his black eye, laughing at a burly black man who, judging by his expressive hand gestures, was clearly telling a knock-out story of his own. Most of the men were currently focused on two fighters dancing around each other in the center. They were either on the last round or they were taking a nap on each other's shoulders.

"Do you see any Finns here tonight, Demir?" he shouted over the din of jeers and encouragement directed at the two exhausted fighters.

"Bellamy. And other than you, it doesn't look like it. I did give one of them one hell of a fat lip the other night. They might still be recovering from the humiliation."

"You punched my cousin?"

"So protective." He sent Seamus a speaking look. "You haven't even met them yet. Trust me, that little rascal deserved it. And I'm up. Wish me luck, gorgeous."

Gorgeous? Why the fuck did Bellamy keep calling him that?

And why do you like it?

As soon as Bellamy walked away, Jeremy poked Seamus in the back. "Hey, I need to get Owen some fresh air. Our All-American is turning a shade of Irish green that isn't pretty. We won't go far, okay?"

Seamus gave Owen a once-over. He did look like shit. "Do you need—"

"No, no, we're good," Jeremy assured him. "Watch the fight, please. You need to know what you're up against for Gill's affections. Here's hoping his perfect jaw is made of glass, because that body is ridiculous."

"Wha—?" Owen moaned.

"Nothing, babe. Come on."

A bell rang and the shirtless Bellamy winked a greeting at his opponent, raising his fists. Seamus was dimly aware of the shouts and all the people shoving wads of money into the air, but the man he'd come with held all of his attention.

As he watched the fighters begin to take shots at each other, Seamus came to a realization. At the fancy spa-like hotel *and* the wholesome bar Gillian and her family owned and operated, Bellamy stood out like a sore, handsome thumb. Someone that didn't belong. Didn't fit.

But this...*this* seemed to be his natural element. There were no dress codes or rules and no crowds to impress. It was dirty and dark, heavy with raw aggression and primal impulses. They were just men proving themselves in the most elemental way.

That's what Bellamy was—a force of nature. He was thoroughly masculine and clearly dominant as he played with his opponent, moving with a light grace that belied his size. Without his shirt, there was no question he was all muscle. Not the regular muscles people got at the gym by doing shoulders on Wednesdays and abs and back on Fridays. Not the body beautiful expensive personal trainers always delivered. Bellamy had a *pulling a sled full of boulders in the snow* kind of body. Jeremy was right—it was ridiculous. This wasn't a guy you'd bump into at the grocery store. Not in this century.

This wasn't a guy you turned down if he wanted to fuck you.

Bellamy licked his lips and said something clearly off-color that made his opponent roar and lunge, his anger and impatience earning him a hard jab to the ribs when he missed.

God, he's too cocky for his own good. And too sexy for mine.

Seamus wasn't sure how long the dance, taunt and jab routine lasted, but it was enough time for both men to develop a sheen of sweat on their skin. Long enough for Seamus to take another swig or three from the flask, because it was hot and he didn't want to look away long enough to get water.

Or risk moving the shirt away from the tent his jeans were making.

Something inside him was responding to Bellamy's energy. His body was practically vibrating with the need to take a turn. He wanted to fight. He wanted to push his way into that circle, strip off his hot shirt and take a turn.

With Bellamy. After days of denying his desire and forcing himself to hate the man responsible for igniting it, he wanted to look into those beautiful green eyes and prove he could give as good as he got. Maybe some physical activity would get rid of this edgy sensation buzzing underneath his skin. A good workout had always done the trick before. He was sure Demir could give him that and more.

I knew I wanted to fuck you.

Before Seamus realized what he was doing, his shirt was off and joining Bellamy's in his arms. He moved closer to the fight, taking another deep swig from the flask. At that moment Bellamy met his gaze over the crowd and froze, his eyes widening slightly as he took in the challenging smile stretching Seamus's lips.

A fist caught Bellamy in the temple and rang him like a bell.

"Shit," Seamus muttered as Bellamy stumbled. He pushed a few men out of the way until he was right at the edge of the makeshift ring, but before he'd taken more than two steps, Bellamy was shaking it off, bouncing on his toes and laughing. *Laughing.*

"Lunatic," Seamus said out loud. That had been a hard hit.

A narrow trickle of blood ran down the side of Bellamy's face, but he came back stronger, no longer pulling his punches and making short work of his sparring partner. Seamus couldn't help but admire how quickly Bellamy had bounced back. Neither could the crowd around him, if the approving shouts were anything to go by.

Moments later the other man was waving him off and smiling with a mouth full of bloody teeth. Bellamy shook his hand and pulled him in to pat him on the back.

As bets were paid out, Seamus was pushed by unknown hands into the circle, and Bellamy reached for their shirts and his flask as he stepped back into the crowd without a word.

A shirtless stranger with tattoos on his forearms and two missing front teeth grinned at Seamus, lifting his fists.

Suddenly it didn't matter that it wasn't Bellamy. It didn't matter which one of them the men were betting on. Hard-won skill took over and his focus pulled in tight around him. The sounds of the crowd dulled to a wordless white noise as Seamus circled his dancing partner with a calm he didn't feel.

Toothless was a hard brawler, his first two combinations forceful and bone jarring. Seamus blocked him, protecting his ribs before paying him back in kind.

You want Gillian.

Where's the fire?

Bellamy. Bellamy is the damn fire.

He parried another jab that slid past his chin. Then

another, and another, until something in him snapped. As though he were disembodied, he saw his fists fly out with two quick pops to his opponent's cheek and a surging uppercut to the man's jaw. His blood was pumping so loudly in his ears he didn't hear the shouts of surprise that turned abruptly to stunned silence as Bellamy and someone he didn't know held him back.

"Fight's over already," Bellamy said, smacking Seamus on both cheeks. "He's done, Seamus."

He looked down in horror at his opponent. Still smiling, with a face covered in blood and a bruise already blooming on his cheekbone, Toothless let his friends help him up and he held out his hand for a friendly, forgiving shake.

Seamus hadn't wanted to hit him that hard. He hadn't meant to...

Fuck. He shook off the arms holding him, his hand barely grazing the other man's before he pushed through the crowd and out of the room without looking back.

The bartender called out to him as he strode through the front of the bar. "Your friends went back to the hotel. The big guy with the beard was holding up the blond, who, if you don't mind me saying, was a few more sheets than three to the wind. Said they'd see you at breakfast tomorrow."

Seamus, still reeling, felt the words like another punch in his side. He'd been acting like a brainless street thug while his brother was so shitfaced he'd had to be carried out? "Damn."

The older man laughed and waved away his concern, but he was eyeing Seamus warily. "He'll be fine in the morning. My wife always says Americans spend five days in Ireland, but only remember two. Lightweights, every one."

"Thanks." Seamus walked out the front door without another word, determined to find a taxi and get back to the hotel.

What had he been thinking? He didn't fight when he wasn't in control, but tonight he'd gone berserk on some stranger who'd done nothing to deserve it. He didn't do that. He never did that.

You threatened to break a reporter's arm once, his guilty conscience reminded him. *And you would have hurt that blogger if your sister hadn't punched him first.*

Toothless hadn't threatened his family. He wasn't hurting anyone. He'd only wanted to go out to the bar with his friends and have a friendly sparring match.

Proud of yourself, Finn? Feel like a man now?

"Hey, gorgeous," Bellamy called. "You want your shirt back?"

Shit, he needed to get his head on straight. "I forgot you were holding it."

He put it on and started walking away, but Bellamy—still shirtless—followed close behind him. "If you can wait, I'll call my driver. He's right around the corner and he can take you back to our hotel."

Our hotel. Seamus shook his head. "You don't have to do that."

Being alone with him was *not* the best idea. Not now.

"Are you okay?" Bellamy asked after he made the call.

No. I hit that man. I want to kiss you. I'm not okay at all. "Worried about my brother."

"Are you sure? You look a little pale. Does your lip hurt?"

Seamus reached up to touch it, surprised to feel the blood and the slight split. "I'm fine. But Owen can usually hold his liquor. I should know. He might really be sick."

There was a hand on his back, rubbing small soothing circles over his too-tight muscles. He didn't step away from it. He wasn't sure why.

"I'm sure he can, on a normal night," Bellamy assured him. "But if a man drinks Irish whiskey, beer, *and* whatever Gillian's brothers were giving to him earlier…"

His stomach knotted up. "What were they giving him?" And why the hell would he take it? *Jesus, Owen. You know better.*

Yeah? So do you.

"All I know is it was glass-cleaner blue, it looked homemade, and he was drinking it from a jar with the redheaded brother. George, I think. The one who keeps insisting he's a poet? I imagine he's in the same shape as Owen right now."

"Idiots," Seamus muttered, turning his head to thank Bellamy for distracting him. The words died in his throat when he saw the unmistakable desire in his eyes.

Unnerved, he stepped away from the hot touch on his back. "Thanks for inviting us tonight. It was fun to watch, but I should have left it at that."

"You aren't the kind of man who'd be satisfied just watching," Bellamy drawled.

"The *fighting*," Seamus clarified, throwing a dark look over his shoulder. "You're good at it." *You never lost control, but I don't have any around you.*

"I'm good at a lot of things."

Jesus, did this guy never give up? "I'm interested in Gill."

"I know you are." Bellamy was following him back toward the shadows of the building. "She has a lot to teach you about running a brewpub."

"As a *woman*," Seamus said, more loudly than he'd planned. "I'm interested in dating Gillian Murphy."

"I don't blame you, but you're *sexually* interested in me, Seamus." Bellamy raised his brows expectantly. "Are you going to deny it?"

He couldn't, but he wasn't going to admit it either. "I *want* to be with Gillian."

"I hope you're giving her some say in that. She's a fairly independent woman, in case you haven't noticed. Have you? Noticed?"

"Noticed what?"

"Let's put it another way. Have you thought about her naked?"

Seamus instantly tried to conjure up the image so he wouldn't have to lie. It wasn't unusual that he hadn't, was it? He wasn't a teenager, for God's sake, staring at every pair of breasts that went by, but he'd noticed her body. She was small with narrow hips, and breasts that would fit in his hands. Hair that was a shade or two darker than Bellamy's, though you couldn't compare the two because Bellamy's hair was more like three shades in one. It was clear he'd spent a lot of time in the sun.

Fuck, stop thinking about him. "Yes, I've thought about her naked."

"And when you think about Ms. Murphy naked," Bellamy said, smiling as if he knew how full of shit Seamus was, "about spreading her legs and making her come, does it get you so hard you have to touch yourself? Do you rush back to your hotel room every night and jerk off imagining her beneath you?"

Seamus clenched his fists so hard they hurt. He did, but not for Gillian, and somehow Bellamy knew that. The bastard. "I'll let that go because you might have a concussion and you're giving me a ride home."

"That's nice of you. You are, you know," Bellamy added. "*Nice.* It must be exhausting. A part of you thinks so too—I saw it when you knocked that man off his feet with your combination. He didn't even see it coming. I don't think you did either."

"No." *But I should have.*

Bellamy's voice gentled. "Are you beating yourself up about it? Wondering what your kids would think if they could see you now?"

How the *hell* did Bellamy read him so easily? It was pissing him off all over again. "Look, Bella—"

"Were you thinking about Gillian when you were watching me fight?"

"I was thinking about fighting, you asshole! I don't fight with Gillian. She never drives me this crazy."

Bellamy beamed at that, then flinched and swore, raising his hand to wipe away a streak of blood from his cheek.

Seamus instantly forgot his own anger and anxiety and moved closer. "Are *you* okay? Maybe you should sit down and let me—"

His back hit the brick wall and he grunted as Bellamy pressed his hot, damp torso against him. His face was so close Seamus could see flecks of gold in the brilliant green gaze. "I'm a man too, Seamus. I also have two parents that, while nowhere near as attentive as you seem to be, love me in their way and would give me anything I asked for. I'm not an orphan, I'm not broken, and I don't want to be another person you feel the need to take care of. That isn't what you need."

Seamus swallowed and licked his lips, a part of him loving the contact, needing it, and another part wishing he weren't so weak around this man. "How do you know what I need?"

Bellamy's smile transformed, suddenly more feral than sensual. "You're so bottled up you're ready to explode. So hard that if I touched you the way I wanted to? You just might. I don't know all the reasons you have for denying what's been happening between us since that first night in the lobby, but I can't anymore. I want you, Seamus. I think you know how much. And no matter how much *you* wish it weren't true, or what elaborate explanation for it you have in that head of yours, you want me too. All you have to do is admit it."

Before he knew what he was doing, Seamus reached up and grabbed Bellamy's throat, sidestepping as he swung the big man around and pressed him against the wall. He stared into those bright green eyes, feeling their hearts pounding against each other's chests. He thought he might feel more than that, but he didn't want to acknowledge it. Couldn't. "It doesn't matter what I want or what I admit. This shouldn't happen."

He kept waiting for Bellamy to break free, to try and kiss him. To slide a hand between them and grope the erection he couldn't explain away. That was something he could stop. He could use it as an excuse to push

Bellamy away from him and claim that it was all one-sided. That he wasn't affected. Aroused just by breathing Bellamy's air.

Instead Bellamy let out a rumble from deep in his chest and pressed his throat into Seamus' hand like a dare. A challenge. Their torsos were pressed to each other, their breaths mingling and their gazes locked in some battle of wills Seamus didn't entirely understand. He just knew he couldn't be the first to look away.

When headlights splashed over them like cold water, Bellamy's sigh rippled through his body. "Damn. You have some pretty blue eyes, Seamus. Has anyone ever told you that?"

Seamus dropped his hand from Bellamy's throat and stepped back, embarrassed at losing control again.

Bellamy merely smiled and casually strode toward the car, motioning for Seamus to join him. "After you."

They drove back to the hotel in silence, and when they arrived Seamus said an abrupt goodbye and made a beeline for his suite. He got inside, turned the lock and slid down the door, gripping yet another Bellamy-induced erection in his hand and staring blindly at a picture of a small white sailboat on a choppy, storm-tossed sea.

Yeah. That about summed it up.

CHAPTER FIVE

Seamus wrapped his arm around Gillian as they walked out of the brewery, tugging her up against his side. "I've got so many ideas now. I wasn't sure how I was going to create what I wanted in my limited space but—" He shook his head. "You're brilliant, Gill, I hope you know that."

"I do," she answered breezily. "Don't go telling my brothers, though. They're fragile creatures with egos like ruffled feathers." She winked and clarified, "In constant need of stroking."

When he laughed, she smiled and hugged him closer. "It's good to hear you laugh, Seamus. You've seemed a bit down the last day or two. Do you want to talk about it?"

"I have?" He hoped he looked surprised. He was down and more than a little dismayed at how often he'd had to take himself in hand thinking about things he didn't need to be thinking about. Where was his self-discipline? Everything he wanted—a mate, a mother for his children—was finally within reach and he couldn't stop sabotaging himself with fantasies of sweaty sex with Bellamy.

But of course he couldn't tell Gill all that.

"I miss my kids," he finally said. At least that wasn't a lie. "How sad is that? In seven years, I haven't had a single break from being a full-time father. Now here I am in another country, learning the mysteries of beer from a beautiful woman and…" He shrugged. "I miss them."

"So you still think I'm beautiful? I was wondering since you haven't asked me to marry you today." She was teasing him. And staring at him expectantly as if waiting for him to make an admission.

"I'm trying not to come on too strong." *And dealing with the fact that after years of drought, I have two people I want…with different parts of my anatomy*. "My Gillian proposal schedule has me asking again tomorrow, in case you needed time to prepare."

She hugged him again, then stepped out of his arms to hold his hand. "I wish I'd prepared better for your visit now that I know. There's a three-day music festival not far from here, but it's sold out. Bellamy got to catch the rowing regatta but most of the gatherings I love happen after you leave. If you'd brought the kids you could have stayed longer."

Seamus sent her a look of disbelief, though a part of his heart was melting at her mention of his kids. "Are you kidding? I'm having a great time."

Gill mimicked his expression. "The bartender is having a good time after crossing the ocean to go to another bar? Galway is a beautiful place, Seamus. Even if you just take a tour by yourself, you should go out and enjoy it. You don't know when or if you'll ever see it again."

He kissed her hand with a playful smack of his lips. "I *am* enjoying it. This is why I came here."

"The only reason?"

Seamus thought of his father. "I do need to track down a few Finn cousins before I leave. Dad made a *before I die* request."

Gill chuckled. "That's serious. It still sounds more like a job than a vacation, but you're a good, obedient son, so off with you."

"What, now? I thought we'd have lunch with Bess again."

She was already pushing him toward his rental car. "I have some financials to go over with my father. We're going to eat while we work, so you should go back to your castle, King Seamus. And maybe get a massage at the hotel spa before you search for your cousins—methinks you could do with a bit of pampering."

"I've never had a massage," Seamus admitted, more than a little tempted. He'd seen the ad for the spa in the hotel amenities book and dismissed it, but now he had time on his hands and a little pampering sounded pretty damn good.

"Never? Now that's a crime," she said, shaking her head. "No wonder you're so tense. Ask for Connor—his hands are magic."

Seamus hesitated. He was already horny as fuck because of one man—letting another slide his hands all over him might push him over the edge. "Connor? Is he another brother?"

Was she blushing? "Only an old friend who gives me a discount for my sparkling personality."

"A massage from a guy doesn't sound very...

relaxing. Don't you have any female friends who offer discounts?"

"What would your brother think of a question like that, Mr. Finn?" Gill teased, reaching past him to open his car door for him.

"I think he'd understand," he said uncomfortably. "I'm new at this. Shouldn't I start with a woman and, you know, work my way up to the pros?"

"It's a *massage*, Seamus, not a boxing match," she said with an eye-roll. "And women are every bit as ruthless at finding your knots and working you into a puddle of goo. Trust me, he's the best."

"All right, fine, I'll make an appointment with Connor, if he's available." Seamus grinned. "Look at how good you are at giving me orders already. We should get married."

She laughed and spun around, her curls a wild tangle around her head. "See? You're already in a better mood. And he'll be available. I'll make sure of it. Unless you're too relaxed to stand upright afterward, I'll see you back here tonight."

As he drove away he couldn't help but wonder at his repeated proposals and her continuously amused reactions. She still didn't take him that seriously…and it didn't bother him as much as it should. Why had he done it in the first place? Why did he keep doing it?

Because you keep waking up hard after dreaming about Bellamy?

No. He wouldn't do that to her. Jesus, he hoped he wouldn't. Gillian was too amazing to dick around with. She deserved a man's entire attention—the kind of attention he was starting to realize he might not be able give her. It might have been possible before Bellamy woke up that part of him that had been hiding on a forgotten shelf for half his life, but now? He wasn't sure. And that would never be fair to her.

As for Bellamy, dreaming about sex with that demanding, cocky… Well, it definitely didn't mean it was going to happen. All it meant was that he was horny as hell and no one had ever talked to him the way Bellamy had before. Everything he said was so overtly sexual. Sensually aggressive. It was disconcerting how strongly Seamus responded to it.

The view of the lush, green Irish countryside distracted him from his thoughts, the way it always did. Driving up the road to the luxury hotel/castle was always surreal.

Every time he pulled in it felt like he was sneaking

into someplace he didn't belong. He was an ordinary guy. Velvet sofas and brocade? Tassels on everything? Not his style. Still, it was a once-in-a-lifetime experience, and one he'd been spending too much time in the brewery to take advantage of. If Gillian hadn't brought it up, he might have ignored the spa for the entire visit, but maybe a massage was a good idea. He definitely needed to relieve some stress.

He called the front desk to ask about scheduling Connor and smiled when the woman told him Ms. Murphy had already called and gotten him scheduled as Connor's next appointment. When he wandered down to the spa, a young woman at the desk, lost in whatever was playing on her iPod, jumped in surprise when she saw him.

Blushing, she pulled out her earbuds and pointed toward the hallway past the desk. "Go into the changing room and put on the bathrobe, sir. You can leave your clothes in one of the lockers."

"My clothes?"

"Your clothes," she confirmed.

"All of them?"

Now she was looking at him as if he were slow. "Your pants and shoes and things? Put them in a locker.

Then go down the hall to room B. That's Connor's room. Just turn the knob and go right in."

"Ah, got it." Seamus bit his cheek to keep from laughing as he followed her instructions. He kept his underwear on and held on to the belt of his robe, uncomfortably aware of his lack of pants as he went to room B and knocked once before turning the knob.

Mother. Fucker.

There weren't that many guests at the hotel, but this was too much. Bellamy Demir was sitting on the massage table, his long legs hanging off the side as a younger man rubbed his shoulder. And he was naked, from his flexing feet to the dark hair on his thick, powerful thighs. His skin was glinting with massage oil and the thin white sheet on his lap barely covered his—

Sweet, Jesus. The sight was already making Seamus's dick hard beneath his robe.

"Seamus?" Bellamy gave him a look of surprise. "I didn't expect to see you until tonight. Are you Connor's next victim?"

Seamus scowled. "Did you know I was coming here?"

"He didn't, but I did," the young man said. "You must be Gill's friend. I'm Connor."

"Seamus Finn," he acknowledged with a grudging nod.

Connor was a tall, athletic redhead with a full beard. He had one hell of a smile and, annoyingly, looked like someone Gillian should marry and have ten kids with instead of Seamus. "Gill called not an hour ago and said if I didn't see you this afternoon, she'd close my tab. Can you believe that woman? You'd be doing me a favor if you stuck around."

"She's very spirited," Bellamy remarked as he sat there, letting Connor lift and lower his arm. "Has she always been like that?"

Seamus was trying not to notice his nudity, but it wasn't easy. He wanted to look. He wanted to touch. He wanted to take what Bellamy had so willingly offered.

Wanted it so much he could taste it.

Was it hot in here?

"Since she was in braids." Connor sighed, smiling fondly. "I told you earlier I have stories that would curl your hair."

"Really?" Seamus hadn't planned on saying anything. Or looking at anything but his feet.

Bellamy's laugh was a little forced. "Now you've piqued his interest, Connor. He'll want every Gillian story you've got. Poor man has a crush."

"Join the club. We're done now, Mr. Demir. I want you to ice your shoulder in a few hours and try to stay out of the fights for at least a few days. It takes some time to recover from a torn rotator cuff, even after surgery and therapy." Connor handed Bellamy his robe and he held it in front of his waist as he stood up.

Why aren't you putting it on, you exhibitionist?

Bellamy's expression said he hadn't wanted to talk about his injury. "Don't worry about me, kid. My shoulder feels better already. Seamus is the one in desperate need of relaxation. He's very bottled up."

And whose fault is that?

"Gill said the same thing." Connor changed the sheet swiftly and efficiently, washing his hands before patting the table. "Take off your robe and lie down so we can get started."

"See you later, Finn."

Seamus wasn't ready for Bellamy to leave. The compulsion was so strong he started talking before he could rationalize it away. "I've been meaning to talk to you about my cousins, Bellamy." He glanced awkwardly at the floor and flexed his hands. "If you have time?"

Bellamy stilled and tilted his head, watching through

his lashes as Seamus set his robe on a nearby chair and climbed onto the table in nothing but his underwear. "I can make time. What did you want to know?"

Following the instructions, Seamus lay down on his stomach, his hands folded underneath his head, as Connor dropped a sheet over his lower half. He was glad he wasn't on his back. The last thing the guy wanted to see before he started massaging him was his erection.

"Did you happen to catch a first name? I promised my father I'd find—" Seamus lost his train of thought as warm oil was rubbed onto his back and shoulders. "*Oh my God.* What the heck was that?"

"That's a massage," Connor laughed. "And I'm thinking that was just the beginning. You might be sore tomorrow because your back is a mess, Seamus. May I call you Seamus? Gill's been talking about your emails since they started, so I feel like I know you and that big Finn clan of yours."

Seamus's eyes were practically rolling back in his head. How was it possible he'd gone his whole life without experiencing this? "Mmhmm. Huh? Seamus. Sure."

"Good. She told me this was your first vacation and now I believe it. Have you been spending every day stuck in the brewery?"

"It's great there." He could actually feel the tension in his shoulders melting away and taking his worries with it. *Some* of his worries…and not all of his tension. As long as Bellamy was around, that wasn't going anywhere. "It's like the Disneyland of beer."

Bellamy's husky chuckle made Seamus open one of his eyes. He was sitting in a chair against the wall, his robe bunched up in his lap while he watched Connor massage him. "Aren't you going to put that on?"

"I'm hot-blooded," Bellamy said with a shrug. "And this fabric soaks in the oil. But I can put it on if it makes you more comfortable."

Please.

"No, that's fine."

Bellamy's lips curved. Cocky bastard.

"Have you been to Disneyland?" Connor asked as he kneaded Seamus like bread dough.

"With the kids, yeah. So technically I've been on vacation, just not an adult vacation." He snorted. "It was great. Penny got sick on the teacups, Wes had to pee every five minutes and I lost Jake in the haunted house. But they had a good time."

Bellamy's quick grimace told Seamus all he needed

to know. Of course *he* didn't like kids. He probably didn't like sunshine, either, the miserable, sexy SOB.

"Have you had a chance to go to one of the nightclubs in town?" Connor asked. "Any restaurants? There's a sailing tour that most of the tourists love."

It was clear he agreed with Gill and every member of Seamus's family about his needing to relax, but Seamus was too distracted to respond. Connor had found the central location where all his stress met, and the feeling as he broke it up was painfully good. "*Right there.* Oh, God, that's good, Connor. Gill was right about you. I… Yeah, *right there.*"

"You asked me about your cousins?" Bellamy's sharp voice broke through his ecstatic haze. "Do you want me to help you find them or not?"

"Sure." Seamus opened his eyes again, feeling drugged and lightheaded. Bellamy was too handsome. Not pretty like Rory and Noah, or generally good-looking like Owen, but punch-in-the-gut glorious. Especially his eyes. They looked like contacts. No one's eyes were really that shade of green.

Seamus focused on the small cut near Bellamy's temple, where he'd taken that punch during the brawl. "Does it hurt?"

"Not at all."

"How did you tear a rotator cuff?" He hadn't noticed him favoring his shoulder during his fight the other night.

Bellamy's silent glare made his cock twitch. Luckily Connor answered for him. "Mr. Demir already had an injury from last year's bull run in Spain when he went to Turkey to participate in a large wrestling event a few months ago."

"Bulls?"

Bellamy was still glaring. "I hadn't done it before. Now I know why."

Connor chuckled. "After he told me about the wrestling the other day, I watched some of the videos and saw him in action. He was good, from what I could tell, but I have to say I have *never* seen people wrestle like that around here."

Wrestling and running with damn bulls? God, no wonder his body was built like that. "Like what?"

"Connor, I don't think Seamus needs to see that in the middle of his massage."

"Don't go getting modest now." Seamus glanced up when Connor's hands left him to slide his phone out of his pocket. "Weren't you the one telling me all about it?

The oldest continuing sport in the world. A true test of endurance."

He handed Seamus his phone and pressed play. "This is only a minute long, but you'll get an idea. Watch while I get to work on your back."

Seamus forgot how to breathe. *Slickly oiled muscles. Leather pants. Two bodies locked in a struggle for supremacy that looked more like an erotic embrace. Strained expressions and masculine grunts. Bellamy forcing his hand down the back of his opponent's pants for a handhold.* "Holy shit."

It looked like fucking porn, and for an instant, Seamus *was* that guy, locked in that fierce, sweaty embrace with Bellamy's hard, hot hand gripping his ass. The sensation was shocking, and when the video was over, he set the phone down as if it were made of dynamite, his pulse pounding in his ears, his cheeks blazing. He was *not* going to search for that video tonight when he was alone in his room.

"Now that show-and-tell is over," Bellamy said, his face a mask of restraint, "did you want me to help, Seamus? Or am I just keeping you company?"

Imagining what other kinds of "help" Bellamy could be offering, Seamus licked his lips, his now fully erect cock pressing painfully against the table. Connor was rubbing his lower back, close enough to his ass that Seamus was teetering on that brink between hoping they'd go lower and hoping they wouldn't. Damn that video! Now all he could think about was getting someone's hard hands on his ass.

He shifted his hips and made a sound of pure pleasure so sexual he had to make an excuse for it. "I had no idea this would feel so good."

Bellamy stood up abruptly, his chair banging against the wall. He reached into his robe pocket and handed Connor a wad of cash.

Who carried that much cash in a bathrobe?

"Seamus and I need to have a private conversation, Connor. Can we have the room?"

"But his hour's barely started."

"I think that should cover it. Go relax before your next appointment."

Connor gripped the crumpling bills in his hand, hesitating. "You won't tell Gill, then?"

"Your secret is safe with us. Go now. Please."

Connor left the room and Seamus pushed up onto his elbows, blinking at Bellamy, suddenly wary. "Why the hell did you do that? That was my first massage and I was enjoying myself."

"You were enjoying yourself too much." Bellamy walked around him to stand where Connor had been and tossed his robe onto the chair. "But far be it for me to take a first away from you. I can massage you while we talk."

"Y-you?" Large, hot hands shoved Seamus back down and started working out the kinks in his lower back with a skill that rivaled Connor's.

Fuck me, that's good.

He couldn't let him know how good. Or that every time Bellamy touched him, the desire inside got sharper, stronger and more demanding. That he couldn't think about anything else but…more. He wanted more.

"Maybe we should get Connor back in here," he said, painfully aware of the arousal thickening his voice.

Bellamy's chuckle was dark. "I know you warned me away from you the other night, but you don't want to traumatize the boy, do you, gorgeous?"

"What do you mean?"

His response was close to a growl. "If you could have seen the way you were moaning and humping the table, you wouldn't have to ask. Imagine friendly, easy-going and very straight Connor's reaction if you'd climaxed from a simple massage."

"Shit," Seamus swore, trying to drag himself out of his relaxed stupor. "I didn't mean to—"

"I, on the other hand, won't mind seeing you let go at all." Bellamy tugged the sheet down and slid his oiled hands beneath the cotton fabric of Seamus's underwear to massage the curves of his ass. "May I?" he asked innocently.

Seamus stiffened, then moaned. "Maybe…you should stop, Bellamy."

Bellamy's hands froze in place. "Do you want me to?"

Now was the time to say *Yes, I definitely want you to stop,* to get up off this table and walk out. Why couldn't he do that?

"No," he whispered.

"Good. You need this as much as I need to touch you," Bellamy murmured, "and I think you want me to be the one who gives it to you. Not Connor. Not Gillian. Not anyone else."

Seamus lifted up on his elbows again and glared over his shoulder. "Are you really that arrogant, or is this just an act?"

Bellamy's fingers dug into his ass and squeezed, the

sensation unmistakably erotic. "You asked me to stay and watch another man touch you the way I wanted to. And I saw your face when you watched that video. It's not arrogance if I'm right. You want me, and your reaction put me in a state I don't like, but it's one that I'm getting used to around you."

Seamus couldn't help himself. He glanced down and away, swallowing hard. He'd never seen another man's erection before—well, not this close and never *that* erect. It was electrifying. Hard and long and...

Mouthwatering.

Bellamy is naked and aroused with his hands on my ass.

"We shouldn't do this here," he said breathlessly.

Anywhere. You were supposed to say we shouldn't do this anywhere.

"Do what? Talk about me doing you a favor? I'm going to find your cousins, if that's what you're worried about. In return, you're letting me practice my massage skills on your amazing but frightfully tense body. It's a simple, innocent barter."

Innocent, my ass. "Why are you willing to do this when I haven't agreed to sleep with you?"

"You must be turning me into a masochist." His

underwear was nudged down to his thighs and Bellamy began a deep, sensual massage of his buttocks. "God, that's a sweet ass, gorgeous. Does this feel good? Should I stop now?"

"Don't stop." It scared him how much he liked having Bellamy's hands on him. *It's been a while since someone touched you like this, sexually or otherwise. That's all this is.*

An image of Bellamy pinning him down the way he had that wrestler in the video flashed behind his eyes and Seamus swallowed a strangled groan.

"What do you want, Seamus?" When Seamus couldn't reply, Bellamy continued in a soothing tone, "There's no pressure here, just an offer of pleasure. Would you like a deeper massage? A more intimate touch? Because I'd love to give you that."

"You're a tool of the devil," Seamus grumbled without opening his eyes.

"Is that a yes?"

"Dammit, just do it. Nothing else, though." *Because at least then I can pretend this is just a massage.*

"Only my hands, you mean? Yes, Seamus, I can do that."

When those magic hands left his ass a minute later,

he almost complained. But then Bellamy moved closer, leaning over his body to massage his shoulder blades.

Seamus flinched when he felt the wet tip of an erection press into his ribs, his mouth suddenly watering again. "Oh, Jesus."

"I didn't do that on purpose. You've seen how hard you make me," Bellamy muttered. "Touching you is better than touching myself in my room, thinking of having you just like this. I could do this for hours."

Maybe it was his imagination, but Seamus thought he could actually smell Bellamy's arousal, could almost taste it, and the feel of those hard hands on his flesh... Christ, he hadn't known it would feel like this, so hot and stark and vivid in his mind, in his senses. No one's hands had ever felt this good.

"I couldn't take this for hours," he admitted quietly.

"You can take a lot more than you think." Those hands slid down to his ass again, one oiled finger slipping between his cheeks and massaging him *there*. Pressing but not pushing inside, just circling with a skill that stole his breath. The sensation was so intense his hips lifted off the table in reaction. "Oh God."

"You don't even realize how responsive you are," Bellamy murmured. "How much this body is telling me.

I bet I could make you come like this."

His hips were already tilting back toward Bellamy's hands, rocking, reaching for something he'd barely allowed himself to dream about. "Bell, what are you…"

"Bell? I like that. Maybe someday you'll call me that when I'm sucking your cock.

"This is such a bad idea," he groaned. So why did it feel so damn good? He'd had no idea his ass was so sensitive until he met Bellamy.

Gentle laughter rained around him. "You must like bad ideas, Seamus. I bet if I wrapped my fist around your cock, I'd feel how ready to pop you are. Are you close? Tell me."

"Yes." He wanted to beg for it. It was a fight against his most basic urges and, damn it, he wanted to *lose*. "Fuck me, yes, I'm so close."

"I will, gorgeous," Bellamy whispered into his ear, pressing that finger between his cheeks and stroking his ass. His other hand curved around the back of Seamus's neck possessively, snagging in his hair and making him groan. "I can't wait to see you stretched around my cock. You've thought about it, haven't you? No matter how dirty and wrong you think it is, you still wonder, don't you? You still want."

Seamus struggled against him, wanting to lift up, to take more, but Bellamy's strong hand kept him flat against the table.

"You want me," Bellamy continued. "You're going to come all over this table for me, aren't you? You're about to unload on Connor's nice clean sheets, wishing I'd stop teasing and stick it inside you already. My finger. My cock. *Anything*."

"*0h God*. Do it now," Seamus cried, moaning louder when Bellamy instantly obeyed, sliding thick, oiled fingers deep inside his ass. "*Jesus*. Bell—Christ, that's—"

"That's right, gorgeous. Fuck my fingers. Take what you need and come for me."

Seamus slammed his hips back, coming with a loud shout. Coming so long and hard he soaked the thin sheet beneath him.

Fuckfuckfuck. This wasn't supposed to happen, he thought as soon as he came back to awareness.

He struggled for breath, his heart pounding against the massage table. The silence was heavy with lust and tension, and though he'd just come, he could feel his body readying itself for another round. He could also feel the evidence on his back and hip that Bellamy had found his own release. He couldn't look at him. Not now. Maybe never again.

"Seamus?" Bellamy whispered urgently. "I wasn't planning on taking it that far, but don't make me apologize. Come to my rooms and I can show you exactly what you do to me. Exactly how good it could be between us. Don't say no."

Seamus felt a pang of fear so strong he almost jumped from the table.

He should have, and to hell with the stain on the sheet, because what he actually did was worse—he said the first thing that popped into his head. "I'm thinking of sleeping with Gillian."

Oh fuck, why did he say *that*? He had no plans for seduction, tonight or any time soon, and as far as he knew, neither did Gill.

Bellamy's hands disappeared suddenly. "I see. Well, good. You should get that out of the way. The longer you wait, the more you're prolonging the inevitable."

"Get sex with Gillian *out of the way*?" Seamus jerked to a sitting position, dragging the sheet over his lap as he struggled to yank his underwear up behind him. "What the—"

"You won't do it, Seamus. In fact, I dare you to try, just so you can finally realize that you're not sexually attracted to her at all. I know it, she knows it—I think everyone knows it but you." Bellamy circled the table and picked up his robe. "Better to find out now."

"Of course I'm attracted to her. You know I've already asked her to marry me."

Bellamy froze with his robe half on and stared at Seamus for a few seconds before his eyes narrowed. "I thought that was a joke. Has she accepted?"

Heat flared in Seamus's cheeks. Why the hell couldn't he keep his mouth shut? "She's thinking about it. Now get the hell out of here so I can get dressed."

"All right, I'll go," Bellamy said as he circled the table for his robe. "But you know this isn't finished, Seamus. And as soon as you stop denying it, I'll be right here. I can be just as stubborn as you, and you just showed me that you're worth the wait."

After he left, Seamus slumped over with a groan. He couldn't be alone with Bellamy again. That was painfully obvious.

And he would talk with Gillian tonight if the opportunity presented itself. Ask her for a kiss at the very least. Not because Bellamy had practically dared him to, but because he needed to know. He *did* know, dammit—he found Gillian very attractive—but he also knew that he hadn't yet had the kind of physical reaction to her that he'd had to Bellamy from the very first instant their eyes met. He needed to see if he could make it happen.

Then? He was willing to try just about anything to shake off these long-buried and unwelcome feelings that he couldn't seem to control anymore.

My finger. My cock. Anything.

He had to get Bellamy Demir out of his head.

Chapter Six

"I didn't know you could dance like that, Seamus." Gillian's cheeks were flushed and she was breathless. She hadn't held anything back on the dance floor.

He was glad she'd agreed to spend some time with him while she wasn't working, even if it was still at Murphy's so she could keep an eye on things.

"Neither did I," he answered honestly. "I can't remember the last time I did it in front of people. Maybe senior prom?"

"You truly are deprived." She shook her head reproachfully as they walked toward the bar. "No massaging, no dancing, no holidays. You should enjoy life more, my friend. You only have the one."

He caught a glimpse of Bellamy brooding on his

usual stool. He'd been watching them all night, a knowing expression on his face, and Seamus had an overwhelming urge to escape him. To prove him wrong. "Get some air with me?"

Gill glanced at her father before nodding and taking his hand, letting him pull her out the front door. He walked her over to the far end of the building where the music and noise faded and spun her around as if they were still dancing.

"Seamus," she laughed. "Stop, you're making me dizzy."

He looked down at her and thought of all the plans he'd been making a few days ago. Everything was different now and he didn't like it. He'd been sure this was what he wanted. *She* was what he wanted. It would be so easy.

"Gillian Murphy, would you mind if I kissed you?"

She bit her lip, studying him the same way he'd been studying her. "Seamus Finn," she started, just as formally. "I would be insulted if you didn't at least try."

He cupped her cheeks with his hand and pressed his lips gently to hers as she leaned into him with a gentle sigh. Her lips were sweet and soft, opening easily to invite him in. Their tongues explored each other's mouths with light, almost teasing curiosity. Gill lifted her hands to his shoulders and he tugged her closer, gripping her carefully around her waist.

There's nothing wrong with this, he told himself. It felt good. Comforting. Familiar, like everything else about her. He could be content kissing her for the rest of his life.

A memory of Bellamy's hands on his skin made him pull away abruptly.

Gill licked her lips and studied him with a tender smile. "That was very nice."

"It was." *And I'm an idiot.*

"You're a good man."

"That doesn't sound promising," he said ruefully.

Her expression was incredibly kind. "It is. There aren't many of those around, you know. Believe me." She bit her lip. "But I think we both know I'm not really the one you want to be kissing."

Seamus frowned, but she shook her head before he could deny it. "Even if I hadn't seen the sparks flying between the two of you all week, or realized that Bellamy only showed up at the bar when you were around… Connor told me about your spa session."

"Son of a bitch."

She cupped his hot cheek. “Don’t blame him. He never could keep a secret from me. And there’s no shame in it. You, of all people, should know that. Certainly I’m not the one to judge you. My oldest brother sleeps on both sides of the bed, and our pub was the place to be in Galway to celebrate when we passed marriage equality.”

Her kindness was salt in his wounded pride. “How can you be so understanding? I’ve proposed to you. I *kissed* you.”

Seamus let her tug his head down and press his forehead against hers.

“We’re friends, aren’t we?” she said. “And I think we both wondered if we could be more because, well, wouldn’t that be perfect? I’d be an idiot not to at least think about it. You’re gorgeous, smart and kind, and you’d do anything for the people you love. And you know your beer. Exactly what I’ve always wanted. But sometimes what we think we want isn’t what we really need, is it?”

Seamus sighed. “Thank you for stroking my ruffled ego.”

She laughed softly and kissed his cheek. “They don’t know? Your family?”

"No. I've never… My friend in high school tried but—" He took a shaky breath and shook his head against hers. "I wanted children. I wanted what my parents had. Throwing that away on something I wasn't even sure about…"

Her expression was full of compassion. "The world finally caught up, Seamus. You can have it all with anyone now. Man or woman."

Seamus grimaced. "I can't have what I want with someone like Bellamy, Gill. He's nothing like us. He's not that guy."

"He could surprise you." At his derisive snort, her lips quirked. "But if he doesn't, don't you think the man who's never had a vacation or danced since his high school prom deserves one wild, hot fling with a sexy man who clearly wants him?"

He'd denied his feelings for so long, it wasn't easy to accept what she was saying. But the fact that she was saying it meant more than he could ever express. "You don't hate me?"

"I could never hate you, Seamus Finn. Honestly, I've been wanting to thank you. I thought I couldn't give my all to my job and have a family of my own, but you've shown me I can because you do it every day. And it's nice to have a peer appreciate what I've made here. Believe me, you'll not be getting rid of me easily."

She wrapped her arms around him and he buried his face in her neck, enjoying the moment of complete acceptance she was offering. Whether or not he took her advice, he'd never forget this.

Gillian tensed in his arms and pulled away with a supportive smile. "I think I'll go make sure my father doesn't need my help. We'll talk more later." She glanced over his shoulder. "Hello there, Bellamy."

If he was hoping for some time to come to terms with what just happened, he wasn't getting it. When he turned, an angry Bellamy Demir was striding toward him.

And just like that his heart was racing. The way it should have when he kissed Gillian. The way it never did for anyone else.

Bellamy waited for Gillian to disappear before he spoke, his voice hard and cutting. "Looks like it went well, then. Was it worth the wait, Seamus? Did you set a date?"

Every muscle in his body tightened until he felt like he was vibrating. "None of your business, Bellamy."

He tried to walk around him but Bellamy got in his

way. "I lost the dare, didn't I? I deserve to know how it went."

Seamus felt his own anger rising to meet Bellamy's and crowded him like he was looking for a fight. He bumped him with his chest and shoulders in a repeat of what the man had done to him a few days ago, advancing until his back was against the wall. "What exactly do you want from me, Demir? Why are you there every time I turn around?"

"I've been asking myself the same question. Is it too much to ask for you to admit there's something between us?" Anger made his slight accent more pronounced. "Something you don't have with Gillian or anyone else?"

Was Bellamy jealous? "I don't *want* there to be anything between us! Don't you get that? I have a plan for my future and you don't figure into it, and if you're honest, I don't figure into yours either. Oh, you think you want me, or maybe I'm some kind of challenge to stave off your obvious boredom—like those fights, I don't know. You run with fucking bulls, so hanging around a bar every night waiting for me to *come out of the closet* must seem pretty damn dull to you." He shook his head, telling himself to let him go. To step back and walk away. "I don't even know why you're here. I don't know anything about you, and strangers don't get a say in who I can and can't kiss."

Bellamy was staring at his lips. "I was here for a meeting with the hotel's owner. I stayed for you. And after what we did on that massage table, I'm not as much of a stranger as you'd like to believe."

He'd stayed for *him*? "I haven't had sex in a few *years*, Bellamy. And when I say a few? I'm practically a damn cicada."

Bellamy lifted an eyebrow. "I know it hasn't been seventeen years since you've had sex, Seamus."

He growled in frustration, at Bellamy, at the erection threatening to bust through his zipper. "It feels like it. What I'm saying is, I'm not ruled by my sexual urges and I'm not in the market for a one-off. Am I physically attracted to you? Obviously yes, but you and I don't make *any* sense at all. I had a blowjob in high school. That's the sum total of my experience with guys and the only experience I was ever planning to have. That's what you've wasted a week on. Let's just chalk it up to a physical reaction to outside stimuli. Hell, Connor or any one of Gill's brothers could have done what you did and gotten the same reaction."

It was like poking an angry bear. Bellamy's eyes narrowed and he got right back in Seamus's face. "Is that what you believe? That you got off because it had been a while since you'd had any *outside stimuli*? Fine. Let's do a little chemistry experiment."

That was the last thing he heard Bellamy say before their positions were reversed and he was pressed between the wall and a hard male body. Then his mouth was claimed with an animalistic growl.

Oh God.

Seamus pushed half-heartedly at Bellamy's arms until he felt strong hands grip his wrists. *Yes. That's what I need.*

He bit Bellamy's lower lip hard, but that only made Bellamy buck and grind his unmistakable erection against him. *Harder.*

His tongue warred with Bellamy's inside his mouth and his body was still vibrating, but with a new kind of tension. His blood was pounding, so much of it going straight to his dick he felt like he might pass out.

He shouldn't want this. It didn't make sense.

Yes. Please. More.

Bellamy let go of his wrists and flattened his palms against the wall on either side of Seamus as he continued his carnal exploration. *Too much.* Seamus had nowhere to hide, nothing left but raw reaction and need. He'd never been treated like this before. This wasn't a getting-to-know-you kiss. This was a *fucking starving, have to have you* kiss. It was brutal and devastating and he never wanted it to stop.

He needed to touch him. Bellamy let one of his wrists go with a tug and Seamus went for the man's zipper with trembling fingers. When Bellamy lifted his head to stare at him, Seamus almost whimpered at the loss of contact.

"Don't worry, we're not done. I just want you to know whose tongue you're sucking into your mouth. Who you're moaning for. Not Connor. Not Gillian. I want you to understand how you're responding to me, Seamus," Bellamy rasped. "*To me.*"

Seamus followed his gaze and groaned as he watched his own hand pulling Bellamy's erection from his unzipped jeans. He was stroking Bellamy's thick cock as if it were his own. The sight was as hot as it was surprising.

"Don't you fucking stop now," Bellamy ordered roughly.

As if he could. Bellamy's cock was big. So big, and hot and smooth and heavy in his hands, and he didn't want to let it go.

Stop now, Seamus. If you don't want this, stop right now.

"I keep seeing you on that massage table," Bellamy breathed. "You came so fast I was almost disappointed. I wanted you to beg for more so I could fuck your ass with my fingers and feel you tightening around me. I wanted you to turn your head so I could push my cock into your mouth." He pushed his hips forward with a low groan. "Tighter. Grip it tighter, damn it."

Then his mouth was consuming Seamus again. Rough and aggressive, his teeth scraping and his tongue demanding everything Seamus had to give. He used both hands and tightened his fingers instinctively around the thick hard flesh, fists that Bellamy took full advantage of.

"Yes. *Fuck—*" Bellamy's words became garbled and he started to mutter in a language Seamus didn't understand. But he knew what it meant. Every man alive knew what it meant. He was close.

He's fucking me, Seamus thought in amazement. *He pinned me against the wall and now he's using my hands to get himself off.*

It was the realization of too many long-repressed

fantasies, and his own erection was trying to bust through his zipper in reaction. It needed. It ached. It wanted a fist of its own. A mouth to wrap around it.

Why wasn't Bellamy touching him?

"God, that's good," Bellamy rasped in guttural English. "I'm going to come like this, Finn. You're so hot, I can't wait anymore. Lift up your shirt, gorgeous. I need to…"

He didn't wait for Seamus to obey, but instead dragged up his shirt and covered the hands on his cock with his own, letting out a broken moan as he came. And came. *Fuck*. And came some more.

They watched together as spurts of his hot release splash over bare skin. Seamus felt it drip down his chest and flat stomach. The proof of what they'd done covered him. Marked him.

Seamus couldn't stop looking at it.

He didn't have time to come back to his senses, because Bellamy was finally touching him, watching his own fingers with avid eyes as they spread the results of his release all over Seamus's chest and stomach.

"I never appreciated this until now," Bellamy murmured absently. "I've had men beg for me to come on them, but it felt too possessive and messy. I never wanted to leave any part of me behind."

Seamus tensed at the mention of other men, but Bellamy eased his fears. "With you it's different. I want to cover every inch of you in my come. I want to fill your mouth, your ass and paint your body until you're sticky with it. I want to own you."

Holy fuck. "Bellamy that's not—"

"Nice?" Bellamy offered with a raw twist of his lips. "No it isn't. There's nothing nice about the way I feel. But I'm honest. Are you ready to be?"

When he didn't answer, Bellamy stepped away from him and stuffed his still partially aroused length back in his pants. "My car is here. Have you been drinking?"

Seamus shook his head, tugging his shirt down and grimacing as the fabric clung wetly to his skin.

"Then get in your rental and follow me back to the hotel. There's no way you can go back inside. Not like that."

He wasn't wrong. Had Bellamy done this on purpose so Seamus wouldn't spend the rest of the evening with Gillian? Was it jealousy or mindless passion?

"Stop thinking," Bellamy ordered arrogantly. "Your dick's hard as a rock, your lips are swollen and you're covered in me. Drive back to the hotel, get changed and

I'll meet you in your room with my file on your Galway relatives."

Seamus knew his face was red from embarrassment and arousal. "You have a file? I just asked for one name."

He smiled and licked his lips, his eyes dropping to the denim tent Seamus' dick was pitching. "I'm thorough and detail oriented. You'll enjoy that about me later."

When he didn't move, Bellamy took a threatening step toward him, a growl rumbling in his chest. "Seamus Finn, if you don't get in your car right now, I'll drag you kicking and screaming into mine. Then I'll suck your cock in front of my driver. I'll let him hear you moaning like a whore and I won't stop until I make you come in front of him. Maybe not even then. Do you want to do that to the man while he's trying to drive?"

Seamus turned and walked to his car without another word, his heart pounding. His drive back to the hotel was filled with so many racing thoughts that none of them made any sense. Panic was warring with desire for dominance in his brain. This was insane! Bellamy wouldn't fit into his life, so why let him do all these things to him?

Technically all Bellamy did was kiss you. You touched him. You did everything else.

Everything else. Jerked him off. Let him come all over his chest. *Wanted it.*

He'd crossed the line, and Bellamy hadn't even needed to ask.

I'll suck your cock in front of my driver.

"Fuck." Seamus undid his pants and pulled himself out. Right there on an empty Galway road, with Bellamy's taillights guiding him back to their hotel.

He could imagine it. Eyes watching curiously from the rearview mirror as Bellamy knelt on the floor between his thighs and sucked him off.

"Jesus, that is so wrong." He'd never had exhibitionist fantasies before. What was the man doing to him?

He licked his palm and stroked his erection, rough and fast. He was going to explode if he didn't find some relief.

Then he licked his lips and tasted Bellamy. Felt the burns on his chin from his beard and wanted more. This wasn't normal, even for him. It was like something alien had taken him over. Something inside him that wasn't Seamus, wasn't the man who wanted a simple, traditional relationship.

Something that just wanted to be fucked so hard he couldn't move.

"So fucking hard," he muttered, letting the car slow to a crawl as he lost himself in the rhythm.

Make me take it so fucking hard. Oil me up, pin me down and make me— "Fuck yes! *Bellamy*."

His trembling fingers clenched and unclenched on the steering wheel as he let the climax roll through his body. God, that was intense. What the hell was happening to him? He didn't do this. He wasn't sure he knew anyone who did. What kind of irresponsible pervert couldn't wait until his car was parked? Couldn't wait until he was alone in his room?

He cleaned himself with his already ruined t-shirt and zipped his pants up again. And then his phone beeped. "Mother fucking—"

Seamus glanced in his rearview mirror and ran a hand through his hair, breathing deeply before looking for the app to call his kids.

There was a new text message on his phone, but Seamus didn't recognize the number.

I know what you're doing back there and I love how shameless you are, but that cock is mine. I don't like it coming without me.

How could he possibly know?

"It's not yours," he said without any real heat to the tinted back window of the car in front of him. "I don't even like you."

But that wasn't really true anymore. If it ever had been.

He opened the app before he could think about it.

"Hey, Dad."

"Jake. Wait, what's happening behind you?"

His oldest son smiled, ignoring the chaos at his back and his father's guilty expression. "Little Sean found Uncle Declan's shaving cream. He gets a bunch at once because it has to be shipped from another country."

"That makes perfect sense. Tell me everything."

Thank God for reality. He needed a good dose of it right now.

***

Seamus swam in the full-size indoor pool until he'd gotten out most of his restless energy. He'd texted Bellamy, telling him he needed a few hours to think before they looked over the files on his family.

"So think," he muttered to himself.

If he did that, he'd have to concede that he'd been acting like a chickenshit for the better part of a week. Using Gill, his own inexperience, and even his kids as an excuse not to face what was happening to him head on. Like the adult he'd assured his brother that he was.

He wanted Bellamy Demir.

Denying it was only making things worse, making everything feel dysfunctional and unhealthy. It wasn't unhealthy to want sex. He hadn't had it in six years, and the last time he'd lost his head the way he did every time Bellamy touched him?

Never.

After advising his family to make brave choices, and even giving his mother shit for denying her true feelings, what kind of hypocrite would he be to do the same?

Just sex. It didn't have to be more than that. Hot, life-altering sex that would tide him over as long as it took to find someone he wanted who'd fit into his life with the kids.

Bellamy was the perfect choice. The only choice, because Seamus couldn't find it in him to resist anymore. It felt inevitable. Necessary.

I knew from the second I saw you I wanted to fuck you.

"So did I."

"Talking to yourself? I was looking for you."

Seamus swallowed some water and sputtered as Bellamy entered the luxurious poolroom, pushing a large silver trolley weighed down with food. His nerves were doing belly flops in his stomach. "You found me."

"It wasn't hard." Bellamy shrugged. "A little bird told me you come here every night."

"I don't have one of these at home so…" Seamus stopped talking to swallow when Bellamy opened his robe and let it fall to the floor. "I'm taking advantage while I have the chance."

"Good philosophy." Bellamy pulled a file out from underneath a bowl filled with chocolate-covered strawberries and waved it toward Seamus. "I have what you want."

"You do?" Jesus, did his voice crack?

He set it down and watched Seamus tread water, completely comfortable with his own nudity. "I found Finns everywhere, but only a handful in Galway that are directly related to your father. Two young thugs, a wildcat and a senior citizen. Their contact information is in this file."

Seamus kept his eyes on Bellamy's, refusing to let

his gaze wander lower. Not yet. "I never asked, how did you put that together so fast?" And why had he done it at all?

"I have people." Bellamy started walking toward the pool. "I pay them an obscene amount of money and they give me whatever I ask for."

Seamus wanted to say something clever. He wanted to walk out of the pool, grab Bellamy and take what he needed. He wanted…

He finally took a good look.

This wasn't fair. It just fucking wasn't. No one looked this good completely naked. There was always something. An inch you could pinch. An oddly shaped mole. Something.

Except on Bellamy. He was like a Spartan. Maybe he did that *300* workout because *goddamn*. Every ridge and curve of his body was perfect and lightly dusted with dark hair. His big, strong thighs framed an erection Seamus couldn't stop staring at. Long and thick and flushed with arousal.

It was as perfect as the rest of him.

Dammit, his mouth was watering again. "Jesus, Bell, are you coming in here or not?"

"I'm planning on doing a lot more than that,"

Bellamy said as he lowered himself into the pool. "The last few hours all I could think about was you jerking off in your car like a teenager with my cum still covering your chest."

Seamus moaned and dunked his head into the water, desperate to cool himself off. When Bellamy reached him, Seamus didn't resist the hands that slid his swim trunks down his thighs until he was just as naked. He had no desire to try.

"If you thought I could leave you alone after that, you're delusional." Bellamy paused. "Unless you aren't ready to admit what you want."

"*This* is crazy," Seamus whispered harshly as Bellamy touched him and tugged him against his naked body.

"Let's be crazy."

"Yes. Oh God." He shuddered. "I've never—I don't know if I can—"

"You're a natural. Trust me, you'll figure it out," Bellamy spoke against his throat, walking them toward the sloping wall of the shallows. Seamus felt his back scrape against it, and the rough treatment actually turned him on.

Bellamy guided him up until he was leaning on his

elbows out of the water, then covered him with his body and took his mouth to mute the surprised cry that escaped him.

Oh shit. Bellamy's cock was grinding against his erection, sliding back and forth as his tongue plunged deep into his mouth. Seamus couldn't resist cupping the bare ass above him to pull him closer, but the move had him underwater in seconds.

"Fuck," Bellamy laughed raggedly. "This isn't going to work."

Seamus's instant disappointment was embarrassing, but instead of moving away, Bellamy dragged him out of the water as if he were weightless and flung him onto the wide, cushioned lounger beside the pool.

Damn.

"Where were we?"

Lost, Seamus answered silently. Lost in a kiss that wasn't gentle or safe or romantic. A man's kiss that was hungry and vulgar and almost violent. And it was so fucking hot he couldn't get enough.

Bellamy growled when Seamus squeezed his ass this time, pumping his hips in reaction. "I want inside you *now*."

Yes. Seamus held back the word, biting down on his

lip. "Until you, I've never had anyone—"

"Believe me, I know," he snarled. "That tight little virgin ass still needs to be taken care of. Then I'll be the first. The only one to fuck it."

Or maybe I'll fuck you, Seamus thought, but before he could reply, Bellamy's hands moved between them and gripped them both, stroking their wet, hard shafts together. "Bell, shit, that's…"

"Sexy? Perfect? Say it. Give me something, Seamus. I need you to tell me you like this."

Seamus swallowed and nodded jerkily. "You know I do."

"Give me more."

He didn't know what to say that would get Bellamy to keep doing what he was doing. "I love it, Bell. *Please*."

"Begging works," Bellamy groaned. "I need to get inside. Hang on."

He leaned over and adjusted the lounge until it was completely flat. Bellamy licked his lips as he knelt over him. "I'm going to suck your cock, Finn. And you, *nice guy* that you are, are going to return the favor."

Fuck, yes!

Wait, no he couldn't do this. Could he?

A momentary image of Toby sucking him off in his truck flashed through his mind, then Bellamy turned and straddled his face. Seamus almost whimpered as hot, tight balls brushed against his cheek. There was no way this could work.

But he wanted it to.

A second later he was shouting, his hips bucking off the cushion as Bellamy took every inch of his cock in his mouth. "*Fuck.*"

His lips parted instinctively when Bellamy nudged his erection between his lips and he couldn't stop himself from licking and sucking the hard shaft filling his mouth. This was what he wanted Bellamy to do. What he craved. And then he started craving the hot velvet flesh under his tongue. It tasted even better than he'd imagined. *So much better.*

And if Bellamy's reaction was any indication, it gave him back some measure of control.

I'm sucking a cock, Seamus thought as he tilted his head to take more and dug his fingers into strong thick thighs. *Holy shit, finally and it's so fucking good.*

"God, Seamus. *Yes*."

His cock. Bellamy's long, delicious cock that Seamus wanted to fuck him. It was big like the rest of the man.

Could he take it? Did he really want to try?

A long wet finger chose that moment to push inside his ass, and Seamus howled around the steel-hard erection in his mouth but Bellamy didn't stop until he was pressing against Seamus's prostate. The bolt of sensation made him see stars. Fucking stars.

Holy shit, yes. Yes, he wanted to try.

Again. I'll do anything if you do that again.

Bellamy must have read his mind, because he started thrusting in time with his mouth. *Swallow and thrust. Swallow and thrust.*

Jesus, he was way too good at that. He must have had a hell of a lot of practice. The thought made Seamus redouble his efforts, sucking, using his tongue to give Bellamy even a fraction of the pleasure he was receiving.

He jerked when Bellamy added another finger and made a scissoring motion inside him, stretching a part of him that didn't seem to want to stretch. It fucking hurt, but he didn't care. And as soon as Bellamy rubbed that magic button again, the pain disappeared and Seamus pressed into his touch with a whimper. He lifted his legs and spread them, not-so-silently begging for something else he'd never experienced before.

Bellamy lifted his mouth off of his erection and gasped for breath. “Look at you, Shameless. I could do it right now, couldn’t I? No lube, no prep, and your sweet ass would still take me like it’s starving. But you’re still too tight.” He thrust deep and Seamus shouted around him, hardly able to concentrate on what he was supposed to be doing. “Fuck, that’s good. Suck my cock, gorgeous. Suck my cock and fuck yourself on my fingers.”

Seamus pumped frantically against Bellamy’s hand, close and nearly wild with a desperate kind of desire.

“I’ll give it to you, I promise. I’ll always give you what you need, Seamus. I’ll make you come so hard.”

That mouth was on him again and there were no more words as they both fought to get to the finish line.

Deeper. God, yes. Make me come, Bell. Have to come.

Bellamy added a third finger and did something indescribable with his tongue, and suddenly Seamus was done. His mouth opened on a scream that Bellamy took full advantage of, thrusting his dick down his tight throat as he came with him.

Seamus choked, swallowing because Bellamy was eagerly doing the same and it was curling his damn toes.

It tasted like him. Salty and dark and sexy as hell.

Did I say holy shit?

It was a moment of revelation. True awareness. He felt like he was looking down on their bodies and finally understanding something about himself that had never made any sense.

Where was his fire? Right here. No woman had ever made him feel anything close to this. Maybe he wasn't as bi as he'd thought.

No fucking wonder.

He'd never come so hard in his life. He didn't know it was possible to have an orgasm that intense, or that it would give him such a rush. At this moment he was fairly confident he could leap a tall building. If his legs still worked.

When a laugh slipped out, Bellamy rolled off of him and rose up on one elbow. "Did you just laugh?"

"Yeah?"

Bellamy's thick eyebrows lowered suspiciously. "You sucked my cock down your throat and took three fingers in your ass after days of swearing this was never going to happen and that, what—amuses you?"

Seamus felt his face heat. "I haven't had a chance to catch my breath yet and I wouldn't have put it quite like that, but yeah. I didn't expect that at all. It felt pretty damn good." He swallowed hesitantly. "Didn't it?"

"So much better than good." Bellamy's smile was slow and bemused. "I knew it would. As soon as I saw you, I knew we'd fit."

They'd fit all right. Seamus pushed himself up and got to his feet, stretching. Yep. Legs were still working. He moved them back toward the water, desperately needing to cool off. "I didn't expect to be exploring my sexuality at thirty-nine. It's a little early for a midlife crisis."

"I don't want to be your midlife crisis, Seamus." Bellamy was quiet, watchful.

What do you want to be? But he didn't ask. His was the only path forward that made sense. "I'm not sure what it means for me, if it means anything, but there's no point trying to hide my reaction to you now." Bellamy had felt his reactions with his tongue and his fingers. God, he had talented fingers. "If you wanted more of the same until I fly home…I'd be okay with that."

I already want you again.

"That's very evolved, Seamus. And yes, I definitely want more of the same. In my bed. In yours. In the damn larder and anywhere else I can talk you for as long as you'll have me."

Seamus laughed and dove into the water before Bellamy could see his body's instant reaction to those ideas. He wasn't expecting someone like Bellamy, but it was good to know he was capable of feeling that kind of passion and intensity for someone.

He never had before.

It wasn't something he could handle on a day-to-day basis, but for now? He would let go of his control and grab as much fire as he could stand.

Bellamy joined him in the water. "What are you thinking right now?"

Seamus felt the grin teasing his lips. He couldn't help it. He was still flying from that orgasm. "Adjusting to the new paradigm. Now that I'm out, Seamus the Dad's yearly night out might never be the same."

He was joking, but Bellamy didn't find it funny. "You're adjusting too fast, Finn. We've barely started and you're already thinking about fucking someone else? That is *not* what's supposed to happen after something like this." He pointed toward the used lounge behind them.

"Done this a lot, have you?"

"Have I fucked a lot of men? Yes. But what's between us is different. For me…it's different, Seamus."

He hadn't meant to piss him off. "This is all different for me. Give me a minute or two, Bellamy. I'm processing."

"You want to know what I'm processing?" Bellamy leaned into him and kissed his throat, then nipped it with sharp teeth, making Seamus groan and tilt his head back. "That I can still taste you in my mouth." He licked a nipple then sucked it until Seamus shivered and started to moan. "I'm processing how many times I felt you shout against my cock, which means you're a screamer. I love that, by the way."

He reached down between his legs and felt Seamus, his dick already hard and eager for his touch. "I'm processing how hot it was to watch you push against my fingers like a greedy slut, and how mad at me you'll be if I tell you it will be even better this time, because before, I was too impatient to get the lube I snuck in on the food tray."

Seamus loved the touching, the dirty talk, and every single fucking thing about this moment. He wasn't going to question it, he just wanted more. "You're so cocky."

"How long can you hold your breath underwater?"

"And a little crazy, Bell."

"You may be right. Don't worry, gorgeous. You'll adjust."

Chapter Seven

"Bellamy, wait."

"Fuck that." He pushed Seamus against the door of his hotel room and undid the buttons on his jeans. "I've been waiting all day."

"I know but give me a—" Seamus groaned when the hand skimmed his dick, then slid over his hip to his ass, fingers curving between the cheeks possessively.

Bellamy loved his ass.

And one touch was all it took to get him hard. Hell, if their encounter on the massage table was any indication, that's all it would take to make him come.

"I've been giving all over the place. Holding back until you were ready. Letting you set the pace for days. I went with you to that madman's house today and nearly got a concussion. I could have died without ever making you mine."

Seamus laughed, breathless. "I didn't expect our cousins to be crazy. I can't wait to tell Dad."

Bellamy was still grumbling. "And I'm taking you back to the fights tonight so you can meet his grandkids, who'll either love you or steal your wallet. I'm doing my part in this relationship, Seamus. It's time for you to stop talking and take off your fucking clothes."

Seamus helped Bellamy strip him before reaching for the other man's clothes, still shocked at his own behavior. Since the other night, he'd been in a nearly constant state of arousal. Always one touch or kiss or lusty command away from losing control.

You lost it days ago, and you don't even care.

He didn't. Bellamy hadn't made good on his promise to fuck him yet, but he'd done things with his hands and tongue that brought Seamus to his knees. Literally. Just that morning he'd been on his knees with his pants around his thighs, begging to come with Bellamy's tongue inside his ass.

God, Bellamy's tongue had been *in his ass.*

And he'd loved it.

Bellamy turned Seamus away from him, one arm

around his chest to keep him close while his fingers slipped between his cheeks again. “I can’t stop thinking about having you, Finn. I don’t think I can wait much longer.” He rubbed the tight ring of clenching muscles he was so obsessed with and Seamus shuddered in reaction. “I need to see every inch of my cock buried inside you.”

Seamus flushed with arousal, long past embarrassment. He’d never had anyone talk to him the way Bellamy did. The graphic pictures he painted got him so hot he was willing to give him whatever he wanted. Anytime. Anywhere. “Stop talking about it and do it.”

Bellamy froze. “Do what, Seamus? I need you to say it.”

Was that what he’d been waiting for? “What you said. Inside me.”

“This isn’t the right time for subtle. No one can hear you but me. Tell me exactly what part of me you want inside you. Fingers? Tongue? I know you liked that.”

Seamus closed his eyes and groaned when Bellamy pushed the tip of one finger roughly into his ass. *Jesus*. “Your cock. Damn it, I want you to fuck me. Really fuck me. Is that what you want me to say?”

"Close enough." Bellamy tightened his hold and scraped his teeth along one bare shoulder. "I want it all, but for now I'll take whatever I can get."

He pushed Seamus hard, and he fell on his back with a surprised laugh. This bossy bad-boy thing really did it for him. He never expected to, but he loved how demanding Bellamy was. How focused on him. Only him. And he never did anything Seamus didn't ask for. But when he wanted it? Bellamy took over and owned him.

A few condoms and a bottle of lube were tossed on the bed beside him while Bellamy reached for a pillow. "Lift up." He slid it under Seamus' hips and caressed his thighs as he studied the position. "I want you like this the first time. I have to see those beautiful blue eyes when I take you. But I need you to hold your legs high and wide for me."

Seamus cupped the backs of his thighs and lifted, spreading his legs obediently, already short of breath.

Bellamy licked his lips, stroking himself now. "You're so damn sexy, Seamus. I've been imagining this for a while. You, ready and waiting to be fucked. *Asking me.* The first time I saw you, I knew I was either going to fight you or fuck you, probably both, but there was no way I could leave you alone."

He was sexy? Bellamy had it backwards. Seamus had no idea why someone like him was interested in an ordinary bartender from the States. It didn't make sense. None of this did. It was an erotic dream he didn't want to wake up from. Not until he knew what it felt to take and be taken by Bellamy Demir.

Seamus bit his lip and hefted his legs higher, offering himself without hesitation or fear. He didn't care if it hurt. He needed it just as badly as Bellamy did. "What are you waiting for?"

"That, Shameless." Bellamy's eyes were green flames. He reached for a condom, tearing it open and rolling it on in swift, practiced motions. Squirting lube in his hand, he coated his shaft, not taking his eyes from the spread ass and erection that was already dripping with precum. "I want all your attention on me and what I'm going to do to you."

With another word of warning, three fingers pushed inside Seamus's ass and his spine nearly bent in half. "Fuck."

Bellamy was holding the base of his own erection with one hand and using the other to stretch and fuck Seamus into oblivion. His fingers spread and curled inside him, rubbing that spot that ripped him open and took away all his control.

He couldn't hold in his loud moans of pleasure. His pleas. He didn't let go of his legs but he needed more. "Bell, please. Do it. I need you to fuck me."

Bellamy growled as he knelt on the bed, still watching his fingers with hunger in his eyes. "You're so damn hot. Tell me you want my cock."

His cheeks heated. "I want your cock. *Now.*"

"Yes." He felt the tip of Bellamy's thick erection and bit his lip so hard he tasted blood. He wasn't sure he could take it all, no matter how much he wanted to.

Bellamy gripped his thigh hard enough to leave a bruise and guided himself slowly inside. "Push out and breathe for me. You can—yes, like that. You're tight but you can take me. You're going to take all of me."

It was too much. Seamus couldn't catch his breath, couldn't see anything but Bellamy's fierce expression as he struggled to follow his muttered commands.

This wasn't sex. Nothing in his limited experience had prepared him for what was happening inside him. Pain so sharp it felt like pleasure. Desperation and greed and impatience for more. Bellamy was going too slow. Being too careful.

Seamus let go of his legs and reached for the man above him, fingers digging into firm muscle and hot skin as he pulled him closer. Deeper. "Yes!"

"Oh you bastard," Bellamy swore, grabbing Seamus under his knees and lifting until his ankles were resting on his broad shoulders. "You want to make me rush this? In that much of a hurry for it to be over?"

He pressed their bodies together, bending Seamus in half and teasing him with soft, biting kisses. "You really are shameless, aren't you? You're dying for my cock. You couldn't wait for me to cram every inch inside."

Yes, you sexy son of a bitch. He groaned into Bellamy's mouth as the man ground against him, rotating his hips in a way that made them both shake and sweat with need.

God, where did he learn *that*? It felt so good.

His erection was pressing into Bellamy's tight stomach with just enough friction to make him needy, but not enough to find his release. He reached for Bellamy's hips again but his wrists were caught and dragged over his head.

"Stop distracting me. I'm enjoying all those sexy noises you're making," Bellamy muttered against his jaw. "I want to hear more. I want to make you scream my name."

"I'll scream if you stop fucking with me," Seamus gasped, struggling lightly in his hold, close to taking over if he didn't get what he wanted. "All that work you put in and you aren't going to give me what you promised? What I need?"

"Sounds like a dare." Something dangerous crossed Bellamy's expression and Seamus knew he was close to pushing him over the edge.

"Maybe it is."

"It's your first time and I don't want to hurt you."

He wasn't sure what came over him, but it was something stronger than desire. Hotter than lust. Seamus lifted his head and bit Bellamy's neck, sucking hard on the tight salty skin. "Hurt me," he rasped out, feeling raw and completely vulnerable. "Please, Bell. I need it." *Need you to fuck me.*

The words caused a tremor to run through the man above him and then—yes—then he came unhinged. Bellamy's hips began to pound hard and fast against his. The bed shook and creaked beneath them with the force, and Seamus cried out with every deep thrust.

Yes. Yes, Bell, harder. Fuck me harder. So hard I'll feel it forever.

He was shouting unintelligible words, his body struggling to get closer, to reach something he couldn't name that was closing in on him. This *wasn't* sex, it was an instinctual race to the ultimate prize. A struggle to get closer to the fire. To fly into the damn sun. Seamus never wanted it to end. "Don't stop."

"I'm close." Bellamy dropped one hand between their bodies and gripped Seamus tight, stroking his hard shaft. "Come with me."

"No," Seamus moaned. "Don't stop, damn it. Not yet."

Bellamy's laugh was filled with lust and a rough satisfaction. "Stop fighting me. This isn't over. This is only round one. Come and we'll do it again. I need to feel you come on my cock."

With that promise ringing in his ears he let himself go, coming so hard he lost his voice from shouting Bellamy's name. Nothing had ever…it was… *Fuck.* He couldn't find the words or remember his name. When Bellamy stiffened and found his own release, hips jerking and pulsing against Seamus, something inside him shifted. Changed.

It took a while to recover. When he did, Bellamy was rejoining him on the bed after disposing of his condom, the expression on his face so arrogant Seamus wanted to hit him again. Or tie him up and have his way with him until he was the one begging.

I'm starting to sound like Owen.

Bellamy was caressing his chest and he lost his train of thought, moving to get closer. "I think it's safe to say you enjoyed yourself."

What did he say? He wanted to thank him. He wanted to say *Wow!* fifty times like a dumbass. He wanted to do it again and his brand-new erection seemed to agree.

But there was another part of him that wanted to put some space between them. That voice was scared and louder than the others. It might not be a bad idea to take a beat and think. *This was too much*, the voice said. *Too addictive. You'll miss it when it's gone.*

He pushed up onto his elbows and glanced at the time on the alarm clock. "We should shower. I want to stop by Murphy's before we meet the cousins."

"I can see it's been a while since you experienced what happens after mind-blowing, body-breaking sex." Bellamy was kissing his neck and the soft words made his skin heat.

"A long while," he admitted hoarsely. Never. He'd never had sex like that in his life.

Bellamy rolled him onto his stomach and started kissing his way down his spine. The scared voice disappeared, the way it always did when Bell touched him like this.

"I find the best thing to help me recover from great sex is doing it again right away. Just to make sure it wasn't an accident." Before Seamus could respond his cheeks were spread and Bellamy was spearing his still sensitive ass with his tongue.

"Christ!" Seamus rose up onto his hands and knees, and Bellamy's mouth followed. It was good. Better than it had been before because Seamus knew what was coming. "Good plan," he panted, spreading his knees apart so Bellamy could have better access. "Oh God, that's…."

He looked over his shoulder and moaned at the sight of Bellamy's face pressed against his ass. "So good, Bell. Don't stop." His tongue was thrusting like a cock inside him and Seamus was pressing back, riding it helplessly. Wantonly.

He really was shameless.

***

"Thank you for that," Gillian said as they walked

down the hall to his hotel room, arms full of bags that smelled like heaven. "Bess has been asking about you for days, wanting you to come back in before you went home tomorrow. I think she's in love with you."

He got the door open and held it with his hip, letting her through while snagging a chip to pop into his mouth. "The feeling is mutual," he mumbled as he chewed.

Seamus was definitely going to miss Bess and Gillian.

And Ireland.

But most of all, he was going to miss Bellamy. This week had been like something out of a fantasy. Now Owen and Jeremy were meeting him at the airport in the morning to fly back to reality. The reality of his wonderful life with his loving family and beautiful children. The business he'd wanted for years.

So why was he so Goddamn miserable?

"Hey." Gillian dragged him over to the small dining table in front of the window and spread out their feast. "Talk to me. I haven't seen you either, you know. I was starting to think Bellamy had kidnapped you and tied you to his bed."

Seamus felt his face heat. "Only once."

She crowed in delight. "I knew it. When I asked him,

he denied it, but I had a feeling."

"You asked him? When?"

Gill finished chewing and wiped Bess's special sauce off her lips. "You know. When we were finalizing our partnership for Murphy's."

Seamus lowered his fork and stared at Gillian. "What partnership?"

Her cheeks flushed. "He wants to be my silent partner, Seamus. He loves what I've been able to do with Murphy's on a shoestring and he thinks my ideas are promising. That means he's taking on a significant portion of our overhead and boosting our marketing ad-buy with the tourism board." She shook her head, as if unable to believe her good fortune. "My father needed to pass the ownership title over to me, and my brothers are limited in what they can access, financially speaking, but with what he'll do for us in return, it's a small price to pay."

There was a buzzing sensation in his ears. "That was why he was at the pub?"

"No, isn't that crazy? It was fate. He said he had a meeting about a fundraiser with the owner of the hotel you were staying in, and that he just happened into Murphy's. A billionaire wandering in from the street to save the day. It almost makes me believe in fairies."

Seamus shook his head, wanting to be happy for her but wondering at Bellamy's decision. Whether Gill knew it or not, he'd taken over, made demands in exchange for giving her the help she'd desperately needed. "Are you sure your father is okay with signing over the title?"

Gill was still beaming. "Are you kidding? He's been crying for joy on anyone who will stop long enough to listen. Of course, he was sure Bellamy was trying to buy my affections until I told him about the two of you. Now he couldn't be happier. He doesn't have to worry anymore. Murphy's is going to be around for a few more generations yet."

"That's great, Gill."

He must not have sounded enthusiastic, because she reached out to rub his arm affectionately. "Maybe he was too busy planning your next sexy adventure to tell you. He did say that, along with my smarts, he was in my debt for kissing you and proving him right." She chuckled. "Men that rich are usually eccentric, Seamus. Connor says it all the time. Strange ducks, every one. The only reason we have to take them seriously is because at any moment they could impulsively save a floundering business with the change in their pockets. Or feed a village for a year after hearing a particularly moving song."

Seamus couldn't begin to relate to that kind of money. He'd thought Declan's house and the television that took up the entire wall was overkill. Saving a family brewpub on a whim during a vacation was…

Bellamy. It was something Bellamy did without mentioning it at all to the man he'd been sleeping with. The man who was close friends with his new business partner.

He was in my debt for kissing you and proving him right.

"What's wrong, Seamus?" Gillian's cheerful expression had faded. "Has it gotten serious between you? You said it was just—"

"It is," he assured her, pushing his plate away. "A strange duck like that? We'd never work out in the real world, Gill."

She looked so disappointed. "This *is* the real world, Seamus. And you looked so happy a few minutes ago."

He forced a smile. "Great sex will do that, I'm told. You should try it with Connor."

Gillian's face turned a shade of scarlet he'd never seen and his laugh was genuine, if still strained. "You should take your own advice and have an adventure, Murphy. I'd be willing to bet he wouldn't say no."

She whacked him on the arm as his door opened and Bellamy strode through. He took in the mountain of food, Gillian's blush and their close proximity, and frowned. "I didn't realize you had company."

Seamus lifted his chin. "You had a business call that lasted most of the day. I wanted to see Gillian before I left for the airport."

Gillian jumped up like she was spring-loaded. "I should get back to the bar. Give us a hug and promise you'll call or send me an email as soon as you get home."

Was she leaving so fast because of the money? Or was it because of the look on Bellamy's too-handsome face?

Seamus stood and pulled her into his arms, lifting her off her feet. "I'm going to miss you."

She kissed his cheek and wiggled until he set her down again. "I won't give you a chance, Seamus Finn. Be safe."

As soon as she left, Bellamy's shoulders relaxed and Seamus frowned. "Why didn't you tell me about your new partnership."

He flinched and Seamus knew he hadn't wanted Gill to tell him. "I invest in companies all the time. In Spain, Turkey, France. I'm known for leaving places better than I found them."

"Must be nice."

Bellamy sent him a speaking look. "Gillian seems to think so. She was almost your fiancé, remember? I thought you'd be happy about it."

"Which is why you told me."

Bellamy swore and reached for Seamus, pulling him close and burying his bearded face in his neck. "Don't be mad. It was going to be a surprise, that's all. One of many I have in store."

"There's more?" Seamus asked distractedly, leaning his head to the side to give Bellamy better access, his body responding as if they hadn't seen each other in months. "Did you buy Bess up too?"

"I'll tell you after."

"After what, Bell?"

Bellamy tongued the pulse at his neck. "After you say yes."

Seamus stepped back and shook his head, trying to clear the haze of arousal being that close to Bellamy always caused. "What am I saying yes to?"

Bellamy ran a hand through his hair and stared at him with those unearthly green eyes. “Look in your top dresser drawer, Seamus.”

He obeyed suspiciously, knowing it was empty now since he’d packed most of his clothes this morning.

It wasn’t empty anymore.

Four plane tickets lay there next to a decorative red bow. “What is this?”

“I used Tanaka’s example and got you, Owen and Jeremy something special.”

Seamus picked up the tickets, his heart pounding in his ears. Paris. Four tickets to Paris. They left tomorrow and the return flight wasn’t for another three weeks.

Bellamy couldn’t let the silence stand. “I’m extending their honeymoon. They enjoyed Ireland, but Paris is the city for lovers so they’d fit right in.” He came up behind Seamus and wrapped his arms around him. “And you and I can stay at my apartment there. It overlooks the Seine, Seamus, and it’s beautiful this time of year. I want to show it to you. I want to show you everything.”

Seamus squeezed his eyes shut, hating himself because for the space of a heartbeat he was tempted. In that moment, he wanted to go to Paris with Bellamy more than he could remember wanting anything.

More than he wanted to go home.

In his mind he saw Jake, the twins and Sean. Their hopeful faces shamed him. He'd never put them out of his mind, not for a second, until this last week. The knowledge of how much control his feelings for Bellamy had over him was terrifying. "We can't accept these, Bellamy. You know that. I have a business to run and I've been away from my kids long enough."

Bellamy was sliding his hands under his shirt and kissing the back of his neck. "You've told me about your family. Crowded Finn Agains and your sister's men. They're never alone, are they? They spend their days in school and their nights being spoiled by their relatives. Who wouldn't want a few more weeks of that?"

He couldn't understand, Seamus knew. He wasn't a parent. "They need me, Bell. Not my parents or my sister. Me. And *I* need to be with *them*."

Bellamy took his shoulder and turned him around to face him. "I'm not ready for this to be over. I've never felt like this before, Seamus. They have you for the rest of their lives, but I only had a few weeks. Come to Paris with me."

He didn't offer to join him on his flight home. To

meet his children. Seamus suddenly remembered that Bellamy had always made himself scarce during his nightly phone calls to his children. That he'd always changed the subject when Seamus brought up his life back home.

Bellamy didn't want him. Not the real Seamus Finn. He only wanted the one he'd met in Ireland. The one without responsibilities and other people who needed him.

His skin felt tight and there was a lump in his chest that he wasn't sure was going away anytime soon. This was all they had. He'd known it from the start; he just hadn't been expecting it to hurt this badly.

"I can't come with you, Bellamy. My decision is final and I won't spend my last night arguing with you."

Bellamy scowled and crossed his arms, looking every inch the pampered prince Seamus had imagined he was. "Your decision is final, is it? Do you know who you're talking to? I'm not one of your children. You can't send me to my room without supper for saying something you don't fucking like."

"Are you sure?" Seamus let his anger at the situation shield him from the pain he was feeling. "Because you're acting like a spoiled, bored child right now. One who plays with people instead of toys."

Bellamy's eyes narrowed. "What the hell does that mean?"

Seamus couldn't shut it off. He didn't want to. Anger was better than heartbreak. "Gill's bar? These tickets? You always get what you want, don't you? It's always easy for you. And if it isn't? If life takes effort, if a relationship has complications, you throw money at it until it changes or goes away."

Bellamy responded as if Seamus had hit him. "This is about your kids."

"Yes!" Seamus shouted, turning toward the closet to gather up his suitcases. "*Everything* is about my kids. My family. I don't know who you've been sleeping with, but if you don't know that by now? You never will."

"Seamus, wait. Let's talk abo—"

"There's nothing more to say." Seamus dropped his luggage to open the door to his suite. "Goodbye, Bellamy. I need you to leave now."

"Seamus."

The pain in his eyes was too much to bear and Seamus looked away. "Please, Bellamy. Just go."

***

Owen and Jeremy were too exhausted from their last night in Ireland to do much more than sleep during the long flight, and Seamus was thankful for the reprieve. He didn't want to spoil the last leg of their honeymoon with his dark mood and even darker thoughts.

Somewhere over the Atlantic, he left part of his heart, reminding himself that fire was overrated. He hadn't needed it for almost forty years, and he didn't need it now.

Everything he'd needed had always been at home, and a few weeks in Ireland hadn't changed that.

He'd forget. He'd move on.

He'd be alone, but maybe that was better.

It had to be.

CHAPTER EIGHT

Present…

"Happy Birthday to me again!" Wes laughed good-naturedly when Little Sean threw foam peanuts over his head as if it were confetti. Several of the presents for Penny and Wes that had come in the mail had been packed with the stuff, and Sean had been throwing it around for close to an hour with no sign of waning interest.

Seamus glanced at the trash all over the floor, as well as the suspicious pink lumps floating in the punch, and sighed. The stuff was everywhere.

Never a dull moment.

"Hey buddy." He grabbed Little Sean and tickled him

until he screamed in delight. "You and I have cleanup duty! Isn't that great?"

His four-year-old stopped laughing and looked dubious. Seamus couldn't really blame him, but it had to be done. "You know the rule. This isn't our house so we have to leave it as clean as we found it. I bet Gram would be so happy with us that she'd get out the special blanket for you."

That did it. In an instant, he was wriggling out of his father's arms, ready to clean.

Seamus's mother had a soft blue blanket with silky edges in her linen closet, and for some reason every time she mentioned letting Sean hold it, he turned into an angel. Seamus didn't know the entire story behind it, and he didn't really need to. Sometimes a grandmother's magic just needed to be accepted and appreciated.

And that blanket needed to be protected at all costs, because Little Sean was a big handful.

Seamus grabbed a garbage bag and guided his son to every damn packing peanut he could find, even the ones in the punch, and tossed them safely out of reach.

Most of the family had descended on his parents' house for the party, and the twins couldn't have been happier. Penny was showing her new wand and tiara to

Tasha and Jen and the little seven-month-old boys wriggling on the couch beside them. Huck and Ned—*Patrick* and Ned whenever their grandmother was around—got bigger every time he saw them.

Jake was deep in conversation with Wyatt, and Wes was running around like an overstimulated spinning top, making everyone laugh and hold their drinks a little tighter when he passed by. He'd sleep like the dead tonight.

"Need some help?" Noah asked quietly, holding out a handful of packing bits that he'd missed.

"Always." Seamus smiled easily and tilted his head in the direction of the kitchen. "Join us. We're the cleaning crew."

As he gathered up all the paper plates smeared with red and blue icing, tossing them in the trash, he met Noah's troubled gaze. He knew exactly what his cousin needed to talk about, and frankly it was just what he needed to take his mind off his own troubles, so he didn't beat around the bush. "When is she due?"

"A few weeks. Well, her lawyer said it would be a few weeks. Since I agreed to take care of the baby, she's decided we should make sure everything is official and less emotional."

Seamus shook his head. How did you make bringing a new life into the world less emotional? He knew she was young, but this girl was educated, moderately successful and…well, she wasn't sleeping in an alley with no other options. On the other hand, he supposed it was a good thing she'd given Noah a say at all. And hell, she was probably just as overwhelmed as he looked right now. "What are you doing in the meantime?"

Shell-shocked might be a better term for Noah's expression. "In the meantime?"

"To prepare. Are you staying in the townhome with Wyatt after the baby comes? Have you been looking into pediatricians in the area, nanny services, that kind of thing? I have Little Sean's old crib if you need it, and I've kept most of his baby clothes in the basement for Penny's dolls. You should come over and we can pack up whatever you need."

His cousin sat down heavily on a kitchen chair, his expression so lost Seamus stopped cleaning and sat beside him. "It's okay, Noah. You've got family to help you. You aren't alone."

Bartender, heal thyself.

"Wyatt won't." Noah shook his head then shrugged as if it didn't matter. "He's moving in with one of our friends from the firehouse next week. He doesn't think I'm making the right call."

Noah and Wyatt weren't twins, but you wouldn't know it to spend time with them. Barely eleven months apart in age, they'd done everything together for as long as he could remember. They were closer than Stephen and Seamus had ever been. At least, they had been.

"That's his choice, but this isn't his baby, Noah, it's yours. So is the decision to keep it." He remembered Solomon's concern, and it was one he shared. "But before you make things official with her lawyer, be damn sure this is what you really want. Because there's only one person that doesn't have a say in anything right now, and they'll be the most affected by whatever you decide." He felt Little Sean lean against his thigh and cupped his small shoulder with his hand. "I'm not going to lie to you. Your work life will change. Your social life will change, and for a while it might disappear entirely. Every single decision you make, good or bad, is going to revolve around that one little child from now on. Being a father isn't easy, and it isn't something you get to change your mind about in a year or two or eighteen."

He refused to sugar coat it. It wouldn't be fair to his cousin or the baby on the way. But he didn't tell him the worst part. That he could fall for someone who had no interest in his baby at all. That breaking things off would leave a hole inside that refused to heal.

Stop thinking about Bellamy, you selfish jackass.

Noah was watching Little Sean watching him. "What if I'm not good at it? What if I'm more like Elder than you?"

Hell, was that what he was worried about? Sometimes Seamus really wanted to knock Uncle Sol's teeth in for what he'd done to his sons. "Between you, me and the wall? Elder would never have asked that question. Which means, if this is really what you want, you're already light years ahead of him."

"I want it." There was something fierce and full of longing in his voice, something Seamus had never heard from the lighthearted Noah before. "I can't explain it. If you'd told me a few months ago that this would happen? I'd have laughed. But when she showed me the sonogram? I just knew the baby was mine."

"That's a good start. The rest you can learn as you go."

Noah rubbed his face roughly and groaned. "Do you know how strange it is for us to have so many single dads in one family? Tanaka threw some statistics at me the other night and it blew my mind. And don't even get me started on our threesome trend."

Seamus forced a heavy sigh, fighting his smile. "Yeah. Stephen really took the easy road, didn't he? Imagine. Finding that *one* special girl and falling in love *before* she had a baby? Amateur." He met Noah's gaze and they both started to laugh.

He'd almost had that with Gill. But if her last email was anything to go by, she wasn't missing out. She'd decided to take his advice about Connor. Beer and massages all around.

Not wanting to be left out of the conversation, Little Sean climbed right up into Noah's lap and patted his cheeks. "Baby?" he asked, excited. "A boy?"

Noah tickled Sean until he squealed. "I don't know yet. I guess we'll find out soon."

"I'm hoping for a girl," Seamus said, patting his son's back. "Penny needs some company and you, little man, are enough trouble without a partner in crime."

The party was winding down when Seamus finally got to sit again. He was a little depressed he hadn't gotten a chance to hold his nephews, but he may have mentioned Noah's predicament to Stephen and asked if they could invite him over for some quality diaper-changing time. He'd seen Jen, Trick and Declan off, as well as Wyatt, Noah, and a strangely subdued Rory. James had sent presents, but Seamus could see that Solomon was upset he hadn't shown up again. He was still trying to text his brother as he hugged the kids absently and waved goodbye.

He'd cornered Seamus earlier, asking about Bellamy again and reminding him what Ken could do. But Solomon didn't know that Demir and Tanaka were friends. And Seamus didn't know if they were close enough that they'd been in contact.

You could always ask Ken.

Penny crawled over to him and plopped her head on his shoulder with a dramatic sigh, offering a timely distraction. "Am I old enough now?"

He smiled at that. It didn't matter what she was asking for, the answer was still the same. "Not for years, sweetheart. But you are *older*. Which means another quarter in your allowance." She clapped happily. "As long as you keep your room clean at home and your nose clean at school."

She thought about that for a second. "If a dog licks it, is my nose still clean?"

"Maybe?"

"Can we have a dog?"

Interesting segue. Seamus gave her the side eye. "Didn't you get enough presents today, young lady?"

"We loved our presents, Daddy." Penny motioned to Wes, who joined her on the other side of their father. They were basically penning him in.

It's a trap! Run!

"Uncle Rory showed us a picture of his friend's sister's dog, Harmony."

"Her-Mine-Eee," Wes corrected. "Like Harry Potter."

"That's what I said. And she's gonna have babies."

"A lot of them," Wes confirmed with glee.

Seamus's mother chose that moment to walk by the sofa, her hand fluffing her short auburn hair. "Jennifer is already down for two, if you can believe it. One for each wing of that house of theirs, I guess." She chuckled then shook her head. "Even your father is thinking about getting one. You know how jealous he's been of Owen's. They're due in a few weeks, right after school starts. The cruise we're taking the kids on next week couldn't have been timed better. We couldn't have gone if we had new babies in the house, now, could we?"

Right. The cruise. His parents were taking the kids on

a seven-day cruise to Canada. She'd handed him the tickets when the twins were opening all their presents.

Canada. He could drive there in one day, but she'd been so excited Father Drew had called her name as the winner of the church raffle, it might as well have been a trip to Paris.

Seamus let his head fall back against the cushions. "Thanks, Mom." *Thanks, a lot Rory.* "I appreciate the support. Why do I get the feeling you're all ganging up on me?"

Jake appeared beside them then, a small smile gracing his features. "I can take care of it. Walks and stuff. We can get a book on training from the library."

"Guess who has two thumbs and will be stuck with walks *and stuff* while you're at school being a super brain?" Seamus pointed two thumbs at his chest.

"Please?" Penny begged, her tiara dangling precariously from her braid.

"Pretty please?" Wes pleaded, his hands folded as if in prayer.

"Please! Please! Please!" Little Sean had no idea what was happening, but he was one hundred percent behind it, as usual.

"You know I told your brother after we brought Sean

home that we were never getting a puppy."

The look in Jake's eyes told Seamus he'd remembered that, but he'd been hoping his father hadn't.

Hell. "I'm *not* cleaning up the poop."

That was enough for his children. They started jumping on the couch, fist-bumping each other and making such a racket he almost didn't hear the doorbell.

He saw his father heading toward the door and glanced over at Jake. "Where's Owen?"

"They left a while ago."

Of course they did. Lucky deviants.

"Uncle Necky is still here," Penny told him breathlessly, still doing her happy dance as she spoke. "He's making coffee so Uncle Brady can build my dollhouse." She tried to spin and nearly fell off the couch, but Jake caught her.

Bless Brady. And Ken, because coffee sounded amazing.

"Seamus Finn..." His father had a tone in his voice that had Seamus scrambling off the couch. "Something you forgot to tell me?"

"What do you— Holy shit."

There were two small ponies standing in his parents' front yard. A woman dressed like she was on her way to a Renaissance festival was holding their reins while a man in a cowboy hat stood at the door.

He took off his hat, glancing at Shawn and Seamus nervously. "We got a little turned around, but I hope we're not too late for the birthday party?"

Motherfucking ponies. There was only one person in this house who could afford this. And he was still here. Suspiciously making coffee.

Seamus kept his eye on the cowboy and yelled, "Tanaka! Front door. *Now.*"

He caught the children circling curiously from the corner of his eye and held out one hand. "*Do. Not. Move.* Move and I'll change my mind about the dog."

They all froze obediently in place.

"Is someone bellowing for me?" Ken came out of the kitchen, wiping his hands. "I was doing the rest of the dishes while the coffee was brewing." He looked over their shoulders and out the door. "Hey. Who got the ponies?"

Seamus closed his eyes. "You said it. I can't believe you actually said it."

Something compelled him to turn toward his children. Some instinct of self-preservation or imminent Armageddon. Sure enough, Penny's face was turning a brilliant and alarming shade of purple.

And then she exploded. In place, since she believed she wouldn't get her puppy if she moved.

"*Ponies?!* There. Are. *Ponies?!* Right now? Outside? *For my birthday?*"

The cowboy, hearing the ecstatic shrieks, took a wise step back. Good instincts. "We're supposed to ride the twins around the yard for an hour? Were you…um, this is Penny and Wes Finn's birthday party? We're at the right house?"

"Dad," Jake warned him, concern clear in his voice. "I think she's going to lose it if you don't let her look soon."

His father was still studying the cowboy suspiciously when he spoke to Seamus. "I don't think we have another choice, son. She knows they're out there now."

Ken groaned. "I'm so sorry, man. I didn't realize."

Seamus nodded but kept himself between the kids and the door as he faced his daughter. "You need to stay calm, sweetheart. You and Wes both. These aren't kittens or puppies, they're horses. If you make them nervous they could…" He didn't want to scare them. What could he say that wouldn't give them nightmares about hooves, head injuries and stampedes?

Jake knelt beside Penny and took her hand. "It's like the bird outside my window, Pen. The pretty red one you love. When you shouted at it or reached for it, what did it do?"

"Flew away," she whispered intensely, her eyes bright and cheeks feverish. "But when I was so, so quiet, it came closer and stared at me."

"Exactly," Jake said approvingly. "You have to be the same way with the ponies. Breathe the way I told you to, and then Dad will let you ride one."

She nodded, breathing deeply as she tried to calm herself down. Wes, in a show of brotherly support, came up and took her other hand. "I'll help you," he assured her, almost as excited as she was. "Just stay by me."

Seamus wanted to grab his sons and hug them both tight, but he didn't dare ruin the moment. "Okay. Let's all stay relaxed and go out together to see the ponies. Slowly."

It took a while to introduce them to the animals, and even longer to get them both safely in their saddles. Seamus gave Sean to Brady while he and Jake stood by Wes and Penny, on the other side of the trainers.

"Dad?" Wes said calmly. Seamus noticed how tightly he was gripping the reins.

"How you doing, buddy?"

"Is Penny scared?"

Seamus glanced over at his little girl, who was beaming at Jake and looking like she'd been born in the saddle. Like she'd be barrel racing in the next five minutes. But that wasn't what Wes needed to hear. "I think she is a little. But this is the first time either of you have ever been on a horse, right? It's okay to be nervous about it."

"Yeah," Wes breathed out, relieved. "Like the first day of school."

"That was rough," Seamus agreed. "But after that first day, it was easier. Do you think you can let Cowboy Joe here walk you and your pony around the yard?"

Wes nodded rapidly, then frowned. "You'll stay with me?"

"I'm not going anywhere, Wes. I'm right beside you."

Seamus had something in his eye. As he walked by his mother, who was taking picture after picture on her cell phone, he told Wes and Penny to smile.

And that's when he saw the car idling on the corner. Tinted windows and a driver who looked vaguely familiar.

Knots instantly formed in the pit of his stomach and he caught his breath.

Bellamy.

"Seamus? What is it? What's wrong?" His mother looked away from her phone and narrowed her eyes.

"Nothing," he assured her.

It couldn't be him. That would be insane.

Insane or not, he's here. And Tanaka didn't get these ponies.

Bellamy wasn't just sticking his nose into his life; he was in town for a front-row seat after five months of nothing. What the fuck?

"Cowboy Joe? I need to ask you a question."

***

Cowboy Joe—whose real name was Isaac—couldn't get any information out of his agent. Whoever had hired him to give pony rides to the Finn children was determined to remain anonymous.

Seamus knew who it was. What he still didn't know was why.

"Seamus? You okay?" Fiona, his bartender, put her hand on his arm to get his attention.

"What? Sure." No. No he wasn't.

"If we weren't so swamped I'd find a couch to analyze you on, but we are and you're just standing here scaring people and slowing down sales. Why don't you go join Ken at his table? *Away from my bar*."

Seamus looked down at her ruefully. "Sorry. I wouldn't want to scare away the customers."

"Neither would I, boss. I love this job. And the tips I get when your scowl isn't distracting our regulars from noticing my indefinable appeal." She pointed to her cleavage with a wink. "Now go."

He obeyed with a small smile, glad his new hires were exceeding expectations. Fiona was an outgoing, curvaceous young woman with several piercings and tattoos covering her arms and back, most of them lines of poetry in feminine script. Her hair was a fascinating mixture of blue and gray that faded into purple and made her look like one of Jeremy's comic book characters.

He worried she wouldn't stay long—a woman with a master's degree in psychology could make more than *he* could ever pay her—but she'd assured him the experience and human interaction would be worth more. His regulars were already in love with her, and she'd even started emailing Gill, who'd made Seamus promise to never let her go.

And then there was his brewing assistant. Thoreau was the brother of Hugo Wayne, a friend of Solomon and James who'd been a rising star on the police force until an incident on the job had caused him to resign. Solomon was still trying to convince him to come back to the force after nearly six months, and part of that convincing apparently came in the form of nepotistic bribery. When he'd suggested Seamus hire Hugo's brother as his assistant brewmaster, it was as close to begging as he'd ever seen him come. Seamus couldn't say no to that, and besides, he'd needed the help.

Over the last few months he'd gotten Thoreau trained in-house and certified in craft brewing through the new program at a nearby college. The handsome twenty-two-year-old black man worked in the back every day brewing, monitoring fermentation and filling kegs—in the old kitchen and the basement Seamus had refurbished to serve as the brew house—putting the Murphy family's lessons to good use. He seemed to enjoy it as much as Seamus did.

So far, they had an Irish Red named *Little Finn* after his sister, and *Brady's Stout* for his super-sized cousin. There was also the beer he'd initially made for Owen's bachelor party, *Jeremy's Porter*. He'd have to tell Owen how popular that one was because it would drive him crazy.

Rory had suggested he create one called *Elder's Bitter*. It was tempting, but Seamus was worried about how his father, Shawn, might react to that poke at his grumpier twin, despite their falling out.

His customers were in love with his microbrews. They couldn't make the beer fast enough.

He should be in heaven right about now. This was what he'd gone to Ireland for. This was what he'd wanted.

But now all he could think about was what he'd left behind.

Ken Tanaka had been sitting at his corner table with his laptop open all night, ignoring the band, the regulars who recognized him and the strangers who stared at his long braid and beautiful profile in fascination. He said he'd been going stir crazy at home, but Seamus couldn't help but wonder if there was more to it than that. Did he know Bellamy was in town?

Did he know why?

Ask him.

Seamus found a free chair, turned it around and straddled it so he could face his cousin's fiancé. "What are you doing that's so fascinating? You've been at it for hours."

"Multi-tasking." Ken grinned, stretching his arms over his head before slipping his long braid into a loose type of bun. "I've updated your website, added pictures from tonight's band into your gallery, gotten by a few firewalls for something too classified to tell you about, and earlier Fiona was helping me set up a profile for your cousin Wyatt on a dating site."

"Is Wyatt having problems getting a date?"

Ken sighed and shook his head. "No. But he's being more of a tool than usual and I want to enjoy his reactions when the emails come pouring in."

Seamus tried to smile, but he was strung too tightly for it to look genuine. "Is that all?"

"Actually no." Ken studied him. "I was trying to find your anonymous equine provider and researching a business plan for marketing and mass production."

"Any luck with anonymous?"

"Not yet."

Seamus nodded casually, as if it didn't matter. "Me either." He paused. "Mass production of what?"

Ken waved his hand down the bar. "Your beer. People love it, and it's not just the microbrewery experience. It's everything you've done since you took over. You're making something special here. I genuinely want you to think about thinking bigger."

Seamus snorted. That was the last thing he'd expected him to say. "These last few months have been great, but I've expanded so fast I'm not sure how I'll keep up with it on my own. And I wouldn't even know where to start."

Ken shrugged. "Neither do I. That's why I'm putting out feelers about getting you someone who can walk you through the process and see how feasible it is."

Seamus crossed his arms and stared at Ken sternly. "*You* aren't allowed to put out feelers or get me anything else. Ever. If it's my birthday? If I save the world from evil aliens and you just want to thank me? I'll take a card that says, *Remember Little Sean and Ireland?* And we still won't be even."

"Stop."

"I mean it, Ken. I appreciate your generosity and I'm thankful Brady has you in his life, but I'm not comfortable with more. I slept in a damn castle disguised as a hotel and I owe you more than I'll ever be able to repay. Though I'm hoping you'll start accepting the money I've been trying to give you to cover at least half of my trip."

"It was a Christmas present, Seamus. And money doesn't mean much if you can't do something good for your family." His eyes darkened for an instant, as if he were remembering something painful. "I haven't had that in a long time, and I know Brady and I aren't married yet, but—"

"But nothing," Seamus assured him gruffly. "You saved me from losing my son and gave Tasha back to Stephen. You've made Brady happier than I've ever seen him. And you're just as stubborn as the rest of the Finns. You're family."

"As stubborn as you, you mean?"

"I'm not being stubborn when I say this place is finally what I knew it could be. Branching out would take more money. More time. More space and more employees. I have four kids and two parents getting older every year. I'm building this for them. I can't gamble with it."

Ken shut his laptop, but the expression of determination on his face didn't waver. "Is what you have enough for four full rides to college with all the trimmings? Jake is smart, it's likely he could end up with a scholarship or two, but there are no guarantees.

And what about Wes and Penny? Little Sean? You still have to pay for all these changes you've made to Finn's. And that includes your employee health insurance package, as well as salaries for Fiona and Thoreau. The bands people love? The ones you keep hiring? You pay for them too."

"Thanks, Tanaka. I don't worry enough. I needed that reality gut check."

Ken sighed and placed a hand on his arm. "Think about it, okay? The Finn name is good around here and you're putting out a great product. Retail micro-brewed beer is popular and it has more longevity than other trends because…well, beer never goes out of style. If we did this right, you could put all your kids through school, take them on vacations, and build a nest egg instead of just scraping by."

It sounded good. But so did winning the lottery. "So the government hacker thing was just a front, right? You're really a business mogul?"

Ken laughed. "Not me, but my father was. And I might have one or two college friends who know what they're doing. In fact, I got an email from one of them recently and he mentioned investing in a brewery."

And there it was. All his senses went on high alert.

"Really? Murphy's got a silent partner right before I left Galway. Must be a trend."

Tanaka looked down and opened his laptop again. "Must be. Maybe I should think about investing."

He knew something. He had to. "This friend of yours, is he in town? We could invite him over for lunch and pick his brain."

Ken frowned thoughtfully. "His home base is in New York, but he travels a lot. I could call him if you're interested. At the very least he'd have consultant suggestions, and he's always had great instincts about people."

He says the same thing about you.

Tanaka didn't know he was there. Seamus was grateful for that, at least. He liked Ken, and he didn't want to think he was plotting with Bellamy. "We can hold off on that for now. I need to think about this idea of yours first. It's a lot to take in."

"Of course." Ken's expression was enigmatic. "I better get back home. Brady was spending the evening playing videogames with Owen and Jeremy, but he's probably home by now."

"Don't be so sure," Seamus joked as he watched Ken shove his laptop into a beat-up backpack. "Owen takes those games seriously."

After he'd left, Seamus couldn't stop wondering why Bellamy hadn't connected with his old friend since he came to town. Clearly he was avoiding Seamus. If he weren't, he would have called instead of getting the twins that outrageous birthday present. If he weren't, he wouldn't have done what he did for the twin's mother, Presley—which was the whole reason he'd gotten Solomon involved in the first place.

How had Bellamy found out about her when he'd kept her a secret for so many years?

He'd have to go to Parkridge tomorrow. After that? He and "anonymous" needed to have a talk.

For the first time in months, Seamus felt his body come alive again.

Chapter Nine

Seamus walked through the doors of the Parkridge facility and headed straight toward the nurses' station, pulling off his baseball cap and running his hands through his hair. "Can I see her?"

A smiling Cuban woman came around the desk and guided him to a nearby table. "Let's talk for a minute before I take you back. How are you, Seamus? Have the kids had a fun summer?"

"We're doing okay, Camille. They're actually going on a cruise with their grandparents tomorrow, so I imagine they're having a blast. How about Felicia? The last time I saw you she was about to go on her senior trip. Italy, right?"

Camille beamed. "Yes, she fell in love with

everything. She wants to go back as soon as possible, but I told her not until she has her college degree." She braced her hands on the table and sighed. "It'd been a long time since we had a good day. But it's been a few weeks now, so this isn't another false alarm."

He nodded. "It was six months. I wasn't sure Presley would come out of it this last time."

Camille looked sad. "I don't think she was happy when she found out she had. And I'm not sure how long this will last, but she does know who I am and where she is. And she's been asking about you, of course."

Seamus rubbed his forehead. Schizoaffective Disorder. That's what the doctor called Presley's condition. At first, they'd been hopeful she could improve with medication, but she seemed resistant to treatment, and she'd gotten worse in the last six years instead of better. For the past three she'd been slipping into catatonic episodes for months at a time. Now, other than care and comfort, the prognosis was nowhere near as positive.

"I guess I should see her first, then we can talk about the recent donation."

Camille nodded. "She's expecting you."

Presley was standing by the window of her room

when he found her, a wheelchair close in case she needed to sit. She was smiling at whatever she saw outside, her blonde hair freshly washed and braided, though she was still incredibly pale. Seamus purposely shuffled his feet and she turned to face him, her expression reminding him so much of Penny's it made his heart hurt.

"It's good to see you, Presley."

"I was wondering when you would show up." She grinned and held up her hands to show off her hospital gown, batting her lashes. "I'm back and dressed in the latest fashion. Not quite strong enough to go for a walk yet, but I am ten pounds lighter. Being crazy is the best diet I've ever been on. Maybe I should write a book. I'd be rich."

He laughed softly and stepped inside. "I'd read it."

"Sweet Seamus. What have you been up to while I slept my fat away?"

He shrugged. "Not much. I'm still making changes at the bar and that's going well. Brady is engaged to his boyfriend—"

"Didn't Owen just get married?"

"That was back in December, yeah. But they're still honeymooning like it just happened."

Presley's laugh was bright and genuine. "I feel so bad for the women in town. All the good Finns are either taken or gay."

You have no idea, Pres.

"I'll tell Mom you said that. She said something similar at the twins' birthday last weekend."

Presley wrapped her arms over her stomach protectively. "Birthdays are nice. I think I slept through mine. Was there cake?"

Seamus rubbed the back of his neck. "Two cakes. They each got a mountain of presents, then rode ponies and talked me into getting them a dog." He frowned when he saw her shoulders slump. She still didn't want to hear about the kids. He should know better by now. Why was he always pushing? "Do you want me to take you outside?"

Her body language changed in an instant and she lowered herself to her wheelchair expectantly. "It looks like a beautiful day."

"It is."

Seamus pushed Presley to the small enclosed yard of the secured wing. It was full of blooming flowers and she sighed happily at the sight. "It's so pretty here in summertime, Seamus. My secret garden. My mother planted all these flowers for me because she knows how much I love them. She spoils me. She knows you spoil me too. Did you see her when you came in?"

Her mother had been dead for eleven years and Seamus had never met her, but he didn't say that.

"Do you want to see something beautiful?" He pulled out his cell phone and skimmed through his pictures until he came upon a few she'd like. "This is Ireland. Galway."

She didn't reach for it, but she was looking, so he held it up and slowly moved through each shot. The rocky shoreline. The green slopes that had taken his breath away and the colorful flowers scattered throughout that he'd taken because Penny loved flowers as much as Presley did.

"Why do you have pictures of Ireland?"

"I went there on business a few months ago."

Presley looked up at him with suspicion. "You're a handyman, Seamus."

"I'm a bartender now." He chuckled. "And there are a lot of pubs in Ireland. I learned all about making beer."

She suddenly reached for his hand. "You should take me there," she whispered. "For our honeymoon. I'd love to see Ireland with you."

He closed his eyes and swallowed, trying to pull his phone away. "No, Seamus. Show me more."

He was so thrown he didn't realize that the next picture he had was Penny, Wes and Little Sean playing by the lake at Owen and Jeremy's. Seamus watched as Presley recoiled from the image of her children as if they were rats. "That's enough."

He knelt beside her wheelchair and took her hand. "I'm sorry, Presley." And he was. Sorry he had mistaken her earlier symptoms for an active imagination and a sensitive nature. That he didn't realize she was building a scenario for their future after a few short weeks that he didn't share, hallucinating things that had never happened.

He hadn't realized she was jealous of his relationship with Jake, or that she'd believed tricking him into getting her pregnant would solve everything and make him love her the way she needed him to.

Instead it had sent her irretrievably over the edge. The further along she'd gotten in her pregnancy, the more unstable she'd become—a horrible mixture of hormones and her already manifesting illness. He'd managed to keep it, and her, from everyone. He still had no idea how. He'd told them she was working on herself.

That she wasn't ready for a family. That she didn't love him. That she'd left the state and started a new life.

He told them everything but the truth. That Presley wanted to end her pregnancy six months in. She'd wanted nothing to do with the two "beasts" that were trying to kill her from the inside. She'd tried to take pills to get rid of them, and when they were born she wouldn't hold them, she wouldn't eat, and her hallucinations got worse. Dangerous.

During one of her few lucid moments, she'd signed custody over to him, and even smiled when he told her that he'd named the twins after her. Penny and Wesley for Presley. But that was the last time she smiled when he mentioned their children.

He'd never told anyone. Not Stephen, not his parents. No one knew the mother of his children was being hidden in a long-term care facility a half hour away.

No one except for Bellamy and, because of Bellamy, his cousin Solomon.

Seamus had been terrified last year when Burke, the man trying to buy Stephen's loyalty or take him down, had located Little Sean's mother and tried to use her against the family. He'd been sure Presley would come up then, that he'd see a newspaper headline about the senator's twin brother hiding the mother of his children away in a loony bin. That he'd lose all his kids at once. But it never happened, thank God.

His mother would have come to visit if she knew. Maybe she would even convince him to bring the children. Maybe seeing them would help Presley…

He looked down at her as she fiddled with her braids and hummed softly under her breath. No. They were too young to go through this, to understand it, and his mother had enough to worry about. This was a lifetime commitment, and it wasn't fair to put that on anyone else. He couldn't let Presley hurt herself, but he'd never let her have the chance to hurt his children.

They reminded him of her sometimes. Before she got sick. Penny's dramatics and boundless energy, how sensitive Wes was—that reminded him that Presley was their mother. But they had his eyes and his heart. His family to watch over them and make them feel loved and safe. They were *his* children.

Seamus stayed for another hour and listened to her talk about flowers and the doting mother in the other room who didn't exist. He listened, but he was thinking about Bellamy. He and Presley had something in common. They'd both wanted him without his children.

Presley because she was sick, Bellamy because… Well, Seamus still wasn't sure.

You didn't give him a chance.

As he was getting up to leave Presley's eyes pooled with tears. "Who is she?"

"She?" He pushed a strand of hair behind her ear the way he knew she liked.

"I wanted you to fall in love with me, but you never did. I did everything for you, made myself sick because of you, and now you're keeping me here against my will so you can be with *her*."

"There is no other woman in my life," he assured her, cursing himself when his response sent her into a rage.

"There is. I know you. I can see it in your eyes, Seamus. You can't lie to me, you bastard. You're in love. I'll kill her, I swear I will. Like I killed those babies you wanted more than me. And I'll do it over and over. I'll make sure they—"

"Presley? I think it's time for your medicine," Camille interrupted brightly, as if she hadn't been threatening to murder her own children.

At the nurse's voice, the screaming stopped and Presley looked over her shoulder with a playful smile. It always shocked him how quickly her rages could turn off and on. "Will it come with pudding? I'm starving, you know. I think I had a month-long dream all about different flavors of pudding. Roll me inside, Seamus. We'll make her give us a treat."

He decided to leave while she was happy and distracted, but Camille caught up with him at the door. "Are you okay?"

He felt sick to his stomach, the way he always did after a visit here. "I set her off again. I didn't mean to." He didn't know how to *not* talk about his children. Especially with their mother.

Camille took his hand and squeezed it between both of hers. "You're a good man, Seamus. And such a good father that I think you keep hoping—despite six years of proof—that she's going to love those angels as much as you do. But her sickness isn't the kind that goes away. You know that."

"I do."

"I hope you also remember that it isn't your fault. If she hadn't focused on you it would have been someone else. Someone who wouldn't have been as compassionate. And that would have been a shame, because little lights like Penny and Wes make the world a better place."

He smiled weakly at her. "Yes they do, Camille. Thank you. I'm not sure how I'd do any of this without you."

She bit her lip and looked behind her surreptitiously. "About that donation."

Seamus braced himself. "Is there any way to send it back? The director knows I can make my usual payments, doesn't he?"

"I talked to him, but he says it's out of his hands. She's taken care of for at least the next ten years."

Seamus flinched. He knew how expensive it was here. "I didn't realize it was that much."

Camille bit her lip again. "Is it a family member? I thought you hadn't told anyone yet."

"I hadn't, but no, it's not family. It's…well, he either thinks he's helping, or he's making a stupidly over-the-top gesture to get my attention."

Camille's eyes were wide. "He? Oh my. So she was right about you being in love?"

Was she? Seamus sighed. "If she was, I'm an idiot, Camille."

"I hope you're an idiot then, Seamus. You deserve to have someone care about you that much."

That was just it. That much money was nothing to

Bellamy. It didn't mean he cared. Seamus honestly wasn't sure what it meant. Did Bellamy want him, or was he trying to ease a guilty conscience?

"Thank you, Camille. I really appreciate it and I'll see you soon, okay?"

She nodded, but her expression turned somber. "Not too soon, I hope. As good as you are to visit, Seamus, I don't think it's healthy for either of you."

He knew it, but what could he do? "I'm all she's got."

Seamus took his phone out of his pocket as he strode to his car. He found the number he couldn't erase but swore he'd never call and sent a text.

Come to Finn's at two o'clock. I know you're in town.

He didn't wait for a response, just climbed into his car and turned it in the direction of his parents' house. He needed to see his kids and say goodbye, and then he'd head over to the bar so he and Bellamy could hash this out alone.

Maybe he would finally find out what the hell was going through Bellamy Demir's head.

***

"The children are packed, but I'm taking them to the store for a few last-minute items," his mother told him as soon as he walked through the door. "They can spend the night here since we're leaving early. And don't worry, I have copies of all their birth certificates so we won't lose them in Customs or anything."

She had one for Jake too, he knew. They'd called in a lot of favors to find it and the hospital his son had been born in.

His mother was still talking and making lists as she disappeared in a whirlwind and his father grinned, taking a seat at the kitchen table and gesturing for Seamus to join him. Owen had that same grin. It usually meant trouble. "A whole week at home alone. What *will* you do with yourself?"

Confront the man I had an affair with in Ireland and find out why he hasn't tried to contact me in the last five months.

Seamus shrugged with a tense smile. "Same old, same old."

"Well, that's a shame." Shawn stirred his coffee. "Speaking of things that make no sense, I got a phone call today from an irate old man who accused me of stealing his grandchildren. Said his name was Aaron.

Any idea what that was about, son?"

"Oh." Aaron's grandchildren. He had no idea how they'd managed to scrape the money together for airfare, and to be honest he didn't want to think about it too much since it was possibly illegal. "Aaron's the guy I told you about, Dad. The Finn who threw plates at my head when I went to visit?"

Shawn started rocking with laughter, hitting the table with the flat of his hand. "*That's* who that was? Well, he definitely sounded like he wanted to throw a few more today. Why does he think I'm kidnapping his grandkids?" Shawn shook his finger at his son. "Tell me you aren't adopting another child, Seamus. I've already spent the money I won from your cousin's bet."

"It's not nice to bet on your own child, Dad."

"I was being supportive."

Seamus shrugged uncomfortably, his mind on other things. "Their names are William and Matthew. I met them while I was there and I guess they both really wanted to come for a visit."

And by visit Seamus was fairly certain they meant moving in and putting an ocean between them, their grandfather and no doubt several men William owed money to. "They're decent kids who could use some direction."

"Kids?" Shawn frowned. "How young *are* they?"

"William is twenty-three. He's between jobs at the moment, but he's definitely worked in a bar before." Most recently in the back of one, fighting for his pocket money. William, or Billy, as his brother called him, was sure an old flame of his lived near his American cousins. He said it was fate that had brought Seamus to Galway. That it was time he found out *the truth*.

He made it sound romantic but Seamus would keep an eye out, just in case. William was a little intense and the last thing he needed was to help some stalker—Finn or not—chase after someone who didn't want to be caught.

"Matthew is twenty-one. He's good with computers." He was clever and quiet, and his older brother's shadow. "I figured we could put them in the apartment behind the bar if they ever showed up."

"They'll be showing up," Shawn said with a knowing nod. "According to Aaron, they've got started making plans to come in the next few months. For all his bluster, I think he was trying to be polite. Letting us know we had company coming. Though I must be going deaf, because I was sure he said that all three were coming."

"Three?" The little apartment might not be big enough. "He must be talking about Calamity."

"Who?"

"Kate." Seamus tried to recall the conversation about her. "Her brothers call her Calamity. I think she's nineteen? Matthew mentioned something about her looking into colleges. Maybe she wanted to check out a few here."

"Well no wonder he's upset," Shawn said. "Sounds like he had a full house and they all decided to leave him at the same time."

Seamus nodded thoughtfully. "Should I try to invite him again? He's a prickly bastard, but I wouldn't want to be responsible for him being on his own."

Shawn put a warm hand on his shoulder. "Have I told you how proud I am to be your father?"

"I know we look alike, Dad, but I'm not Stephen," he joked. "And yes. You tell me all the time."

"Don't ever compare yourself to anyone, Seamus. Not even your brothers. It wouldn't be fair to them."

Seamus patted his hand with his own. "Thanks."

Shawn sighed. "You don't see it, I know. Maybe that's our fault, because we expect it from you now. And I know we give you a hard time with the jokes about the kids, but you have to be patient with us, son. We haven't caught up with you yet."

He was at a total loss today. "What are you talking about?"

Shawn's face showed his struggle as he reached for an explanation. "Do you know when you and Stephen were Little Sean's age, you spent the summer driving us crazy because you kept running over to the neighbor's house every time we turned around?"

"What? Me?" He had no idea what his father was talking about. Or why. "Are you talking about the Crosby house?"

Shawn shook his head. "No, this was before they moved in. The woman who lived there… Her last name was Ames. Your mother would bring her casseroles and soup several times a week because, well, she was very old and wanted to die in the house where she'd raised her children. Anyway, at some point, we think you must have overheard your mother talking to the home health aide about Mrs. Ames, and how sad she was that it was summer and she wouldn't be around for autumn and the breeze that came with it."

His father smiled, remembering. "She had this collection of wind chimes, you see. So many it was a little horrifying, to be honest. They were all hung outside her bedroom window and, according to your mother, she spent her days staring at them. Waiting."

"Are we going somewhere with this or did you just want to give me nightmares about dying alone?"

Shawn ignored him. "Every day you'd go missing—four-years-old, mind you—and a few minutes after you disappeared, we'd hear all of Mrs. Ames chimes playing in a breeze that wasn't there." His father laughed softly. "Your mother tried to apologize, but the health aide said it was the only time the old woman would smile all day."

"So I was weird and obnoxious?" Seamus tried to laugh, but it felt like something was caught in his throat.

"You were *kind*. Like Jake, you always seemed like you knew a hell of a lot more than you should for your age."

Seamus looked down at his hands and lifted one shoulder. He hoped Jake wasn't too much like him. "We both know that didn't last, Dad. I was the rudderless Finn for years. How many times did you tell me I should go back to school or commit to a goal or direction before I adopted Jake? Can you remember? Because I can't."

Shawn waved the words away as if they blocked his view. "Wanting you to find your passion doesn't mean I thought there was anything wrong with you. And being Jake's father didn't fundamentally change who you were. He was another example of it, and he gave you someone to love, but even before he came along you were always able to see what everyone else needed. You were always taking care of us."

His father's gaze refused to release him. "Some people build impossibly tall skyscrapers, Seamus. And *some* people show up exactly when you need them to and talk you off a ledge. Everyone has their calling." He shook his head. "You're such a good man, you're worried about the old geezer who tried to bean you with his dishes. Not even I can compete with that."

"I'm not that good a man, Dad." Seamus stood up, feeling awkward. "You make me sound like a saint but you don't know…"

"What is it, Seamus? What don't I know?"

Habit and fear kept him from bringing up Presley or Bellamy, but he couldn't accept praise he didn't deserve. There were things inside him that weren't nice. Anger. Lust. Violent, desperate need. He'd just pushed it all down for so long no one knew it was there.

Someone knows.

"It doesn't matter. I should let you get ready for your

cruise."

"Seamus?"

"I'm fine, Dad. Just tired."

Tired of lying. Tired of pretending I don't miss him.

Tired of being alone.

CHAPTER TEN

Seamus started setup early, needing to do something to calm his nerves and busy his hands. The brewery offered no distraction this morning. He had several different styles of beer either fermenting or slowly lagering in the cooler at this point, so they were in the "hands-off" stage. What needed to be bottled had been already. He was seriously beginning to question his decision to take up this side venture that required so much patience. But none of that mattered right now. His mind was too busy trying to solve the riddle of the damn century.

What was he going to say to Bellamy?

For the first few months after Ireland, he'd told himself that the relationship was a case of temporary insanity. He tried to be dispassionate about it. To look at it logically. And logically, he and Bellamy were too different for anything real to happen between them.

Bellamy was spoiled. He'd had the best of everything. Education, travel, and a lifestyle that Seamus couldn't even imagine. When *he* was trying to find his path without his family's help, Seamus had lived above a damn garage and eaten Ramen and diner waffles every day. Bellamy's rebellion was the year he'd stayed at his father's home in St. Barts instead of interning at one of his family's companies.

Was that being a reverse snob? Maybe, but he didn't think anyone could blame him for thinking they had nothing in common.

Bellamy also acted impulsively as a rule and did things for the thrill of the experience without thinking about repercussions. He was proud of that. He'd told Seamus he didn't have to think about them. *He paid other people obscene amounts of money to do it for him.*

Seamus didn't have that luxury. He couldn't travel the world taking dangerous risks because he had a business to run and a mortgage to pay. He had family that needed him to always be there with a shoulder and some good advice. He had a porch roof that was developing more leaks than a political campaign.

And he had pride. Shawn Finn had taught his sons that family should always be there to help each other in times of need, but there were some things a man had to do for himself. Seamus had worked hard to reinvigorate Finn's and introduce it to a new generation of regulars. He was proud of that.

Bellamy, meanwhile, ran a massive corporation with his father, created science and clean energy scholarships, and co-chaired foundations for female literacy and education around the world, as well as investing in private space exploration programs and offering grants to countless small businesses.

Okay, so maybe in a weak moment he'd looked him up. And maybe he'd felt like shit for judging the sexy love child of Bill Gates and Elon Musk as harshly as he had. But even if none of his preconceptions about Bellamy were true…the passionate frenzy he'd experienced with him couldn't be good for the long haul.

Who he'd been for those few days scared him, because things that were supposed to matter hadn't. The only thing he'd been able to think about was touching Bellamy. Kissing Bellamy. Giving himself to Bellamy.

And when they'd fought, it was just as passionate.

Disturbingly so.

How could something like that last in his life? And how could he survive it if it didn't?

He'd seen what that kind of intensity could do when it went wrong. When Tasha had left Stephen to protect his reputation, he'd spent weeks broken at the bottom of a bottle, shutting out his family. Brady'd had a similar reaction after his fight with Tanaka, and Jen hadn't been much better—though to be fair, that was more about their mother's reaction to her relationship than Declan or Trick's.

He'd seen it all from the safe objectivity of his bar. The highs were epic, and while Seamus couldn't deny each of his family's situations had ended well, he knew they could have easily gone the other way. His uncle was bitter and alone because of his broken heart. His cousin James was…well, Seamus wasn't entirely sure what was going on with James, but he was willing to bet it was romance-related. Something was destroying his relationship with his family. Someone. But no one, not even Solomon, had been able to get it out of him.

Meanwhile Noah was about to become a younger version of Seamus, which meant he would soon be faced with the same decisions. Would have to make the same sacrifices for the good of his new family.

Maybe he wouldn't find anyone willing to take him and his baby into their hearts. Maybe he'd have to give up the only person who'd ever made him feel like he was truly wanted and alive. Someone he could never decide if he wanted to punch or kiss. Someone who saw him and only him…

Someone like Bellamy.

What he'd said to Owen was true. Seamus *wanted* a grounded relationship with trust and mutual respect more than he wanted to be consumed by a fire that there was no way to put out. Even if Bellamy had been interested in more than a week or three in Paris, the devastation he would cause when he finally got bored was something Seamus shouldn't risk.

In the end, it always had to come back to the kids. Seamus was it for them and they were why he hadn't let himself lose his head completely with Bellamy.

But he'd come dangerously close.

He heard the knock on the front door of Finn's and sent up a small prayer for strength as he opened it and stepped aside to let Bellamy in.

Five months.

He didn't look that different at first glance. He was

wearing another expensive gray t-shirt and jeans that probably cost more than most people's car payment. He still had the sexy facial hair and those lush, sensual lips. But his usual swagger was gone. He almost looked nervous.

Seamus had a hard time believing anything could make Bellamy nervous. You had to care to be nervous. You had to have something to lose.

Bellamy was watching him through his thick lashes. "Did you want to talk first or should I guess what's on your mind?"

Seamus bunched his cleaning rag in his hand and shook his head, walking away until he was behind the bar. Having something between them was a good idea. A necessity so he wouldn't give in to temptation. "I don't know, Demir. Why *would* I want to talk to you? What could you be doing with your spare time and all your money that might upset me?"

Bellamy winced. "I'm Demir again, am I? I guess I deserve that. I can see I've overstepped my bounds and I apologize."

He wondered if he'd misunderstood him. That had been too easy. "Excuse me?"

Bellamy lifted his chin, arms crossing defensively

across his broad chest. "I. Am. Sorry. I confess it. I'm a monster. A—what did you call me before you left? A spoiled, bored child who plays with people instead of toys?" Seamus winced, but Bellamy wasn't finished. "But you're right. I shouldn't have made your daughter's dream of riding a cheap rental pony a reality. I shouldn't have seen the burden you were carrying on your own and tried to do something to help. To pay the bills for that high-priced care facility you chose to put the twins' mother in to assuage your misplaced guilt. I should have known you wouldn't approve. God forbid anyone tries to help you. Especially someone like me."

The way he said it made Seamus sound like an ungrateful dick. "Help? Is that what you were trying to do? You didn't think that as a father I might be concerned about my kids getting extravagant gifts from total strangers? Or that I've been careful that no one else find out about Presley, and because of what you did, I had to tell my cousin Solomon, or—" Seamus tugged at his hair, his skin buzzing in a way it hadn't in months, his emotions intensifying with every minute that passed. "*No one* does that, Bellamy. No one flies in and starts stalking someone they claim they care about, or digs up all their secrets so they can act like the goddamn tooth fairy, leaving money under their pillow instead of stopping by for an actual visit."

Bellamy's laugh was more bitter than angry. "Would you have let me in, Seamus? Introduced me to your family as the guy you fucked in Ireland?"

I don't know, damn it. He slammed his hand down on the bar's mahogany finish. "You call if you come to town. You face me like a man if you want to talk. And you do not *buy* the affection of my children or me. You fucking *earn* it."

Something flared to life in Bellamy's ridiculously green eyes. "Do I get the chance to try?"

Had he moved closer? "I would have to be an idiot to say yes. I've been standing here thinking about all the reasons I should tell you to fuck off. Reminding myself that nothing's changed since Ireland."

"It has," Bellamy swore.

"My list is long, Bellamy. Almost as long as the one with all the reasons you shouldn't want to be here." *Why are you here?*

"I told you that you'd turned me into a masochist. I wanted you to see my car, Seamus. And I came as soon as I got your message." Bellamy walked boldly around the bar to stand beside him, stripping that barrier away.

He put his hand next to Seamus's on the bar—*he was so close*—and looked into his eyes. "I fought it too. Not as long as you have, but I tried. You are a lot of damn work, Seamus, and I think you know that. But I would rather be here to listen to you lecture me than give up and live with the regret."

Seamus bit out a curse. He couldn't let Bellamy's words affect him. Not yet.

"How did you find out about Presley? Wait, don't tell me. It was the people you pay the obscene amounts of money to."

"Yes." He wasn't apologizing. "And I admit I've watched you. I've seen you with your children and laughing with your family. I wasn't trying to make you nervous, Seamus. I was looking for the dent in your armor. The crack in your story. I didn't want you to be that *good.* I wanted you to have a sordid secret, but instead you were quietly taking care of your children's mother, despite what she tried to do. I wanted you to be an addict I could look down on, but your only addictions are your family and this bar. And British television, which you watch the way other people watch porn."

How could he know *that*?

"I was waiting to see you with someone else. A

woman or a man, it didn't matter. I wanted to punish myself enough that I could move on. But that never happened. You weren't exaggerating when you told me your family was your life. Everyone says that, Seamus. No one ever means it."

"I'm not perfect. Not even close." *Don't let down your guard. Remember what you wanted to say.*

"I'm aware of that too, but I've been everywhere, Finn. And I've known a lot of men. There aren't any like you. And there are none I want as badly."

Seamus looked down, realizing he'd taken Bellamy's hands, his thumbs caressing the racing pulse at his wrists. What was he doing? He needed to let Bellamy know that the payment to Parkridge was unacceptable. That skulking around his family was unacceptable. "You only wanted Paris, not complications. My life is full of complications."

Bellamy moved closer, so close Seamus could feel his arousal against his hip. "I never wanted them before, but that doesn't mean I can't handle them. I might surprise you."

His heart was trying to lodge itself in his throat. "I wasn't expecting you to want to. Not after what I said. I didn't think I'd ever see you again."

"Then you don't know me yet. *Get to know me*, Seamus."

When strong hands dropped to the top button of his jeans, Seamus gripped his wrists and shook his head. "No."

"Please."

Fuck. How many times had Bellamy ever said please?

Seamus slid his hands all the way up Bellamy's arms into his thick, silky hair and yanked his head back roughly. "My bar. My rules."

Bellamy's lips parted and his dark skin flushed. "As long as the rules include touching me, I'm good with that."

A wave of crushing need surged over him when he finally pressed his lips against Bellamy's. It wasn't gentle. It was angry and desperate. Hungry. Seamus felt a tremor run through his body when Bellamy pressed against him, wrapping his arms around him as if he were afraid he'd pull away. Seamus could have told him he wasn't strong enough to try.

Their tongues tangled and they both groaned when Seamus pressed Bellamy back against the bar and started grinding against him. *It's been so long. I need to touch you. Need to feel you.*

He tore off the top button of Bellamy's jeans in his haste, heard the ping of the metal bouncing off the floor as he pushed both their jeans down to their thighs.

"Fuck, Seamus," Bellamy moaned, digging his fingers into his ass and pulling him closer. Their erections were sliding hot and heavy against each other, and the delicious friction made Seamus wild. He reached for one of Bellamy's hands and took two fingers in his mouth, sucking hard. He kept his gaze on needy green eyes as he forced those fingers down and back, between the cheeks of his ass.

"I don't have any—"

"Massage me again," he whispered hotly, his hips jerking when Bellamy instantly obeyed. "*Yes*."

He licked his own fingers and, with one arm pulling Bellamy as close as he could, let his wet fingers press against the tight ring of muscles he'd never had a chance to explore.

Bellamy's reaction was explosive. "Fuck!" He started speaking in what he'd once admitted to Seamus was a mixture of Turkish and French. Dirty, nonsensical demands and prayers that happened whenever he was too turned on to control it.

Seamus's own loud moans drowned out everything else when Bellamy pushed one finger deep inside of him.

"So tight," Bellamy muttered. "It's been too long, Seamus. Come for me, gorgeous."

Not yet. He didn't want it to stop yet. And this time he needed to be the one in control. "Turn around," he demanded gruffly.

Stepping away from Bellamy's touch was almost painful, but Seamus had something in mind. He used his foot to slide a crate from the corner over to Bellamy's boots. "Stand on it."

"What?" Bellamy looked over his shoulder but Seamus didn't have time to explain. He lifted the heavily muscled man onto the crate, pushing his torso flat against the bar with one hand and spreading his ass cheeks with the other.

"Wait, Seamus I— *Christ. Oh God.*"

Seamus ran the flat of his tongue over Bellamy's tight hole. "My bar. My rules," he repeated, remembering how good it had felt when his lover did this to him. *Mine.*

Bellamy bucked against him, crying out as Seamus licked and sucked, pushing inside the clenching hole to fuck him with his tongue. It was so hot he had to grip the base of his cock to stop himself from coming. *Now you know how it feels*, he thought in grim satisfaction. *Now I'll make you scream for me.*

"Fuck, yes," Bellamy gasped, pushing back against him uncontrollably. "Fuck me, Seamus. It feels *so good.*"

When Bellamy shouted his name and started coming all over his bar, Seamus couldn't hold back. He lifted his mouth and straightened, stroking his erection twice before he came all over Bellamy's firm, beautiful ass.

Yes. He hadn't come so hard in months.

Five months, if anyone was counting.

The man beneath him was still shuddering and mumbling against the wood of the bar when Seamus heard the sound of glasses clinking together and whipped his head around.

Thoreau Wayne's naturally large eyes widened almost comically for an instant, and then he turned around, heading toward the back where they'd been brewing their beer.

And the back door that he had an extra key to.

Seamus swore and yanked up his jeans as he strode after him. "Thor? Hang on a minute, man. Wait up."

Thoreau held up his hands and shook his head. "Don't sweat it, man, all right? Seriously, *my bad.* But you should think about putting a bell in back or something for this kind of situation."

"I don't normally…" *What? Have sex? Lick another man's ass on my bar?* Seamus felt his face and neck heat in humiliation.

Thoreau snorted. "I know. *We all know.* You don't normally do anything with anyone. It's Finn topic number one with most of the regulars." He grinned. "I was thinking about getting you a hookup with Hugo. My brother's been messed up lately and you're a good guy, so I thought, why not? But then I realized you have way too much on your plate and he deserves some serious one-on-one attention. Anyway," he gestured toward the main bar. "Looks like you're already taken."

"Hugo's gay?" Seamus frowned. "Wait, why did you think that *I* was?"

That brought a genuine burst of laughter. "Don't worry, I'm pretty sure your family's still in the dark. They're way too busy making fun of *Mr. Mom* to notice how many women you fend off every night. Women you don't bother checking out as they walk away." Thoreau lowered his voice. "I had no idea that owning a bar turned you into catnip, Seamus. *I* wouldn't turn it down, but since *you* don't have time for that, and no one could catch a clue, I figured you were what Hugo likes to call an LBMG."

"Do I want to know what that stands for?"

"A late-blooming, monogamous gay." Thoreau wrote the words in the air with his fingers. "That's a romantically challenged man who walks through life alone and thinking he's waiting for the right woman, when what he really needs is the right dick to show him what he's been missing."

Seamus heard choked laughter behind him and knew Bellamy was listening in.

"Of course, he coined that goodness last year to describe Chief Younger, but I think it applies to you too."

Hugo thought Solomon was gay? "You may be right about me, but I think he's off on that one. I would know."

But would he?

Yes, I would, damn it. Everyone in the family can't be gay. The odds of that are... Just no.

"Whatever," the young man said, shrugging. "The point is I've got your back. I wasn't here, I didn't see anything, and I'll be back in an hour after I eat to give you two some privacy." Seamus opened his mouth but Thoreau interrupted him. "As my sister Bronte likes to say? 'You do you, high or low. If I'm not looking, I'll never know.' So I'll keep loving my job, and when you've got a minute later this week, I've sketched out some new logo designs I thought might work if we're planning on bringing Finn's beer to a larger audience."

Seamus nodded and watched Thoreau head toward the back door, whistling.

"Oh and Fiona was getting here early too," he called out as he turned the knob. "Sent me a text right before she got in her car."

"Shit." Seamus walked around Bellamy and started cleaning the evidence of their frenzied reunion off the bar without saying a word.

"He's funny," Bellamy said behind him, his tone casual. "And hot. The report on him didn't mention that, though I don't think you're the kind of guy to lust after a twenty-two-year-old. Does his brother look anything like him?"

"Fishing?" Seamus glanced over his shoulder in time to see Bellamy's frown. "The Waynes are family friends, so leave them alone. And for God's sake, don't buy them a business or anything." Though Gillian *had* kept saying she'd never been happier.

Bellamy slipped his hands into his pockets and hunched his shoulders. "I don't buy things to win affection, Seamus. I hope you know that. I have more money than anyone could ever spend, and if I can't use it to bring myself or other people joy, it feels like a waste to me."

"Just try to tone it down, okay?" He was still reeling from his recent orgasm and Thoreau Wayne's assumption that he was gay. He was, but he hadn't told anyone. He didn't think it showed.

He sensed Bellamy moving closer and shook his head. It was impossible to be in the same room with him and not feel the tension and heat between them. He would have to keep a tight rein on that in public.

"What's next?" Bellamy asked. "If you give me a chance to *earn it*, that is."

"The kids are gone for the week." Seamus finished straightening up and turned to face him. "You didn't happen to rig a church raffle, did you?"

Bellamy smiled with kiss-swollen lips and shook his head. "You mean the cruise? I'm not that good. And I don't think Father Drew can be bought."

He knew about Father Drew? His people were skilled at their jobs.

Seamus sighed. "I guess I could take off tonight and we could go to my place and have dinner. Talk."

Bellamy wrapped his strong arms around him and gave him a smile that made him shiver. "And I was thinking I could take you back to my hotel suite and pamper you with massages, room service and dirty sex on a balcony overlooking the city. No talking required."

It sounded good, but Seamus shook his head. "My rules this time. We're going to sit on my beat-up couch and eat something I cook on my grill. If you want to spend time with me, we'll have to stick to my reality for now. I need that from you." He licked his lower lip, imagining Bellamy in his bed. He'd never shared it with anyone before. "And then we'll see where we go from there."

Brilliant green eyes took on a predatory gleam. "Done. I'll grab a few things from the hotel and meet you there within the hour. As long as you know I'm expecting to pay for my meal with sexual favors, it's a date."

A date. The impossible man he'd spent half his trip to Ireland being seduced by was coming to his house. It felt surreal. So fucking strange.

And right.

It felt right.

He hoped a taste of ordinary Seamus didn't scare him away. He had a lot of lonely nights to make up for, and only a week before the kids came back.

Chapter Eleven

They'd been trickling into the bar all night. Seamus wasn't sure if they thought they were being subtle, but it was entertaining to watch.

First Jen with Trick, then Rory and Noah. Wyatt came with Stephen and Tasha, and seemed to have the hardest time avoiding the bar. Seamus had a feeling that had to do with Fiona as much as his guilt for spreading gossip about his love life.

Three days. That's how long he and Bellamy had had together before reality came busting through his door in the form of his cousin Wyatt. He hadn't called first, but to be fair Seamus rarely did anything that would require privacy, and most of his family members had a key to the house in case one of his kids had an emergency.

He'd wanted to borrow some tools from his garage—apparently his new place had shower issues—but what he'd found instead was Seamus snuggled on the couch with Bellamy, an episode of *Sherlock* playing in the background.

Bellamy had wanted to understand this particular addiction. He'd never been still long enough to get caught up in a television series. Seamus had admitted he had a thing for accents, especially Bellamy's, and Bellamy had obliged him by whispering dirty, erotic things in his ear, and soon they were both naked and moaning as the sociopathic detective went to his *mind palace*. Seamus had never been so turned on…or so embarrassed to be caught.

Wyatt had been almost hilariously traumatized, but he'd apologized instead of joking as usual or asking for details, and then grabbed what he needed, plus a handful of popcorn from the coffee table, before he disappeared.

Seamus had a feeling he hadn't even left the driveway before he called every member of the family he could reach and told them what he'd seen, because within an hour of that visit, he'd had five new messages on his phone. All casual, none of them mentioning him being caught in the act, but the calls were timed too perfectly to be a coincidence.

Bellamy was fascinated, not only by his open-door policy, but by the speed of big family gossip. "Now I wish we'd been doing something more creative. Think of how difficult it would have been for him to explain you tied up and covered in Jell-O while I spanked you."

Seamus had laughed. "In this family? You'd have to come up with something more out-of-the-box than that."

So he had.

Talk about creative...

Which was why this was his first night back to the bar in a few days. It should have made him anxious. Late summer was a busy season and he needed to stay on top of everything. Band bookings were more difficult and people were thirsty for his in-house brewed beers. If it continued to be this popular, he might have to use the apartment out back to expand.

In spite of that, he couldn't remember the last time he'd felt so relaxed. He and Bellamy had barely left the house or put on clothes in days, and Seamus had come more times than he'd thought humanly possible. He thought the fact that he was still able to walk was pretty good for a man pushing forty.

Last night Bellamy had been the one to cry mercy.

"Enough, you shameless sex god. Tell them I died happy."

Luckily he'd gotten his second wind later.

"You keep smiling at everyone else like that and your possessive new man is going to make a scene." Fiona and Thoreau texted each other on a regular basis, so she knew about Bellamy before the family did. She'd been over the moon since her first good look at him and she'd been giving Seamus random thumbs up and fanning herself all night.

She was right. Bellamy was focused on him in a way that made him feel lightheaded. Every time Seamus tried to subtly look his way, he caught him already staring, possession and desire in his eyes. Bellamy didn't seem to notice that anyone else existed. It was a talent that drove Seamus wild. It also made Bellamy a sitting duck for the gang of Irish thugs slowly surrounding his position.

"My *family* is going to make the scene," he muttered back to Fiona, eyeing each of them in turn. "They don't show up like this unless there's free food or a wedding…with free food."

Or unless they disapproved of something a family member was doing and were throwing an intervention or putting together a posse, he thought grumpily, remembering his trip with Solomon and the others to warn Declan and Trick away from his little sister.

"This is so much better than free food, Seamus." Fiona playfully bumped his hip with her own. "I haven't known you Finns long, but a clear pattern emerged right from the beginning, with you at the center. The on-call friend, advisor and everyone's big brother has a sexy secret. You think they'd be able to resist finding out about the man who could tempt Seamus Finn from his status as family paragon?"

"They might scare him away." He tried to sound as though that was the first time that thought had crossed his mind. "He has *people* and a few scattered cousins, but he doesn't have much experience with family. Mine are more involved with each other's lives than most. It's not for everyone." And the children weren't even back yet.

"I spent last summer in a yurt with ten other people. Talk about having no secrets."

"You did?" Seamus narrowed his eyes at her, genuinely perplexed. "*Why?*"

"Let's not make this about me." Fiona swirled her lip piercing thoughtfully with her tongue. "If he hasn't had experience with family living, I suppose they're actually doing you a favor by coming tonight."

"You think?"

"I know. You have home and hearth written all over you with neon paint and shamrocks, old man. Like I said, you're the center. The sooner we see how Beauty handles that the better."

She had a point. He just wished he'd had a few more days to spend blocking out the world before he had to find out how skittish Bellamy was. "Fiona?"

"Yes, boss?"

"Beauty?"

"I heard you call him Bell, and he has a perfectly luscious French accent that sneaks out when he isn't paying attention, so now I'm visualizing him as an erotic Disney prince in an all-male version of *Beauty and the Beast*."

"Am I the beast in this scenario?" She obviously didn't know what Bellamy could be like in bed.

"The beast *was* lonely and sexually repressed, which is you all over. He was cursed to remain hidden from the world until someone saw him and loved him for who he truly was. Oh my God," she gasped dramatically. "Why am I not writing this down? I'm a genius and you are *so* the beast. Would you say Wes was the chipped teacup? Or is it Little Sean?"

Seamus huffed out a laugh. "You have a rich and twisted imagination."

"I chose to study psychology, Seamus. That should have been your first clue I had some issues." She blew him a kiss. "Be happy I didn't go with my first nickname. Because, look at him, you know it was filthy. And after you look, you should go save him. Owen has finally arrived, and it appears that he was the one everyone else was waiting for. At least, that's what Wyatt seems to be suggesting to me with his hand signals. He's a flirt, but I do love a man with a big…guilty conscience."

"Hell."

Bellamy's lips curved when he saw Seamus moving towards him, and Seamus's pulse sped up in reaction. Before they met, he'd never experienced lust. He'd never had greedy, hungry marathon reunion sex that lasted for two days. He'd never spent months with the knowledge of what he'd been missing and what he craved, which only made his need stronger now than it had been in Ireland.

He stepped out from behind the bar, but before he

could get to the others, a regular in a Finn Club tank top threw herself into his path and grabbed his arm. "Seamus Finn, you sexy thing, when are you going to name a beer for yourself so I can order you every night and wrap my lips around your bottle's long neck?"

It wasn't the first time he'd been asked that question in the last few months, but it *was* the first time he'd had an audience for his answer. "I don't think anyone wants a beer named after me, Mindy. Now if you'll—"

"You could call it Big Daddy," she continued as if she hadn't interrupted him. "Or Hot Irish Beef—"

"Shameless," Bellamy said as he appeared beside him to smile wickedly down at Mindy. "It would have to be called Shameless."

She was too tipsy to understand that Bellamy was carefully removing her hand from Seamus's arm because he was jealous. As his family looked on, Seamus felt his face heat.

"Oh I like it," she said, matching Bellamy's grin. "Shameless. I bet you are, aren't you, honey? All the quiet ones usually have the kinkiest secrets."

"You have no idea," Bellamy said, before he lowered his head and whispered in her ear.

Son of a bitch. What was he doing? "Bellamy."

But it was too late. Mindy's mouth opened in silent surprise and she stared at Seamus as if intrigued and disappointed at the same time.

"On the bar?" she asked uncertainly.

"Oh yeah," Bellamy replied, straightening before settling his hand low on Seamus's back.

"Well…" Mindy took a drink and cleared her throat, her own cheeks flushing as she studied the two of them. "I guess it *does* need to be called Shameless."

And then she turned and hurried back to her crowded table.

"That wasn't necessary." Seamus was trying to keep his voice down. "Mindy is a regular."

"Now she's a regular who knows you're taken."

"She didn't need to know *anything*. My private life is private, and she's just here to drink and hang out with her friends."

Bellamy's lips tightened. "She's here to stare at your ass and try and take you home."

"*Everyone* flirts at a bar."

"That wasn't flirting. She wanted to drag you outside and blow—"

"*Blow* me down." Trick Dunham appeared right in front of them, his eyes brimming with laughter. "Not to interrupt, because this is entertaining as fuck, but we'd all like to meet your good friend, *Whotheheckareyou*?"

"I already told you his name was Bellamy," Owen answered, frowning at Bellamy's hand on his brother. "He's Tanaka's old friend."

"Where *is* Ken?"

Seamus studied all of them, seeing a glint of hurt in Stephen's eyes that he tried to hide by pulling his wife closer. Shit, he knew he should have called and talked to him privately. He just didn't know what to say.

"He and Brady are protesting," Tasha answered with a wicked grin. "They disagreed with Owen's battle plan. So do I, for the record, but you know how voyeuristic I am."

"Is this a battle plan?" Seamus asked. He noticed Jeremy wasn't around either. Knowing him, he was protesting too, and his brother would have a lot of making up to do tonight.

Owen looked uncomfortable. "It's a small family meeting. If you'd answered your messages, you would have known that."

Seamus glanced around the bar, feeling eyes on them. "Let's take the introductions to our usual table by the dart board, yeah? I have kids to feed."

He gripped Bellamy's elbow and followed his family, muttering under his breath the entire time.

"Don't worry, gorgeous. I've been to tougher meetings than your Finn Club's."

"Don't get cocky."

"You love my cocky."

"Hush."

It wasn't that he didn't think Bellamy could handle himself. But Seamus still wasn't sure where this relationship was going. It felt way too early for a group interrogation. Bellamy was just visiting, for Christ's sake. What the hell was wrong with that?

Jen came up beside him and winked, holding a pitcher of margaritas. Trick was at her side with beers and bar snacks.

"You might need to hire a server soon, Seamus," she said as they handed out drinks around two tables that had been pushed together. "Fiona is the best, but she's only one woman, and this place is getting crowded. I'm so proud of you, but I'm definitely glad I don't work here anymore."

"I'm proud too," Bellamy whispered in his ear. "I can show you how much if you want to ditch these guys and come home with me right now."

Seamus bit his lip hard to control his reaction. He couldn't believe, with everything going on, that he was actually tempted.

"What's this about, Owen?"

"It's called shock and awe," Tasha said, her hand on the back of Stephen's neck, playing with his hair. "All the men appear to be in shock, while Jen, Rory and I are firmly in Camp Awe."

"They were so outnumbered, I thought I'd help out." Rory shrugged with a lazy, distracted smile.

Seamus's gaze found Wyatt. "I'm so glad I let you have a key," he said a little sarcastically. "And that I can trust you to keep things to yourself."

"Yeah. Wyatt's the poster child for family loyalty," Noah snorted. "No wait. I mean the male calendar model for being a judgmental dick."

"Fuck off, Noah. I'm not the one making stupid decisions."

"Debatable."

"Okay guys," Stephen interrupted, sending them warning looks. "This isn't about you two. We're here for Seamus."

Bellamy pulled up a chair and sat down near the table, appearing so relaxed that Seamus couldn't help but admire him. "Really? I was sure you were here about me." When they were all looking at him he clarified, "Because I'm fucking him."

Seamus had to find a chair or he'd embarrass himself by trying to curl up in a ball on the floor. "Nice."

"I keep telling you I don't do nice. That's your department."

Tasha laughed so hard she spilled some margarita onto her low-cut blouse. "I like this guy. Straight to the point."

Tasha was never afraid to say what she was thinking either.

Bellamy gave her his most charming grin and then his gaze shifted to the somber Stephen. "You're his twin? You don't look much like him to me."

Seamus imagined his confused expression matched everyone else's. They were identical. They had different haircuts and lived different lives, but still. "It must be the suit. Stephen's always been the better dresser."

Seamus smiled at Tasha when Stephen wouldn't meet his eye.

"It's not the suit."

Tasha gave Bellamy a strange look. "I agree. But most people would have a hard time telling them apart. I keep asking to give Seamus a haircut and a tie and stick him in Stephen's office. Imagine the hijinks."

Something was definitely bothering his brother. Tasha usually made him smile. "Stephen?"

"How long have you been keeping this a secret?"

Why was he staring at him like he'd kicked the damn puppy none of them had even gotten yet? "Nowhere near as long as you kept your relationship with Tasha a secret from me, Stephen."

His brother's lips tightened but he dipped his head in acknowledgment. "What about the Scott debacle? When Owen and I both had to come clean? Wouldn't that have been a good time to put it out there?"

"I didn't *know* then," he told them all honestly, feeling bad when he saw Jen pale a little at the reminder of her ex. "I mean, it's never been an issue. I wouldn't have hidden it from you if I had."

"Believe it or not, he was still oblivious for half the Galway trip until I showed him the error of his ways," Bellamy offered. "Even Gillian knew before he did. He's good at seeing what other people want, but blind when it comes to anything about himself."

"You gets points for that," Jen said with a small smile. "And for being smart enough to follow him home."

Owen finally chimed in. "But when we saw him that night, he was asking Gillian to marry him and saying Bellamy was an entitled, arrogant—"

"Shut up, Owen," Seamus growled while Bellamy chuckled.

"Let him speak, gorgeous. You've called me worse to my face."

"He *has*?" Tasha leaned forward, intrigued.

Owen sent Tasha a silencing look. "I'm just saying he's been alone for a long time, and now he's bouncing from one big decision to another, and it's all a little fast for him. I'm worried he hasn't thought it through. Younger is worried too, which is why I think he wouldn't—"

Owen stopped talking abruptly and Seamus felt his stomach clench. Why he wouldn't come? That actually hurt. He and Solomon had grown close this year and he'd expected his support for something like this.

"Let's not be hypocrites, Owen." Rory looked amused. "You were a hetero-manwhore until a little birthday tequila, and you flipped fast enough. Also for the record, you didn't *invent* switching teams for love. Or lust for that matter. I've lost count of how many men

I've—"

"It isn't the same thing, Rory. Jeremy was someone I'd known forever. Someone I trusted. We don't know anything about this guy, and Seamus genuinely wanted to beat the shit out of him the entire time we were there. He had his *Hulk* face on."

"It's true, he did," Bellamy joined in, green eyes sparkling. "He still does on occasion. He's got a temper, this one. It's very sexy."

Tasha's jaw dropped as if they'd just revealed something fascinating. "Stephen, they *fight*."

Seamus rolled his eyes. "Only when he's being irritating."

"Or you're being stubborn."

"I wanted to hit Trick every day for the first few months," Jen said with a sappy grin. "And he loves to rile Declan up. It does make the sex pretty explosive."

Seamus put his head in his hands and groaned when his family all started talking at once.

"Whoa. That doesn't help at all."

"Jesus, Jen. We told you no details. Ever."

"Are my ears bleeding?"

Tasha lifted her glass to toast her sister-in-law. "*I* love hearing about your man sandwich, Little Finn, but these cavemen never will. You'll always be the baby girl to them."

"I'm fine with it," Rory protested, sending Jen a wink.

"We really need more women in this family," Jen muttered, letting a laughing Trick pull her close to his side.

"Here, here." Wyatt raised his beer. "Don't worry, Jen. I'll get to it eventually. One of us has to."

Noah muttered something only Wyatt could hear and Seamus saw him react like he'd been sucker-punched. The last thing he wanted was for those two to come to real blows or say something they could never take back, so he started talking. Telling them what they came to hear. "I don't have an explanation, if that's what you're waiting for. I…I had an experience in high school and I thought I had to choose between that and having a family. I chose. But since then I've never—well, I haven't been in the closet for years or sneaking guys in through the basement or anything like that. This just happened, and I'm still not entirely sure what it is. Beyond the obvious," he added swiftly when Bellamy opened his mouth to respond with something graphic. "Thoreau says I'm something called a late-blooming gay."

A wave of surprised laughter washed over the full table, breaking the tension.

"I think we need new t-shirts," Rory said, still chuckling.

Bellamy put a supportive hand on his thigh and squeezed. "Saw what you did there, peacemaker" he murmured. "But you forgot the M for monogamous."

He didn't forget it. But using that word in this company would only prolong the torture. "I hope you're satisfied now and we can all move on."

"What about Mom and Dad?" Stephen asked. "Do they know? Have you introduced him to the kids?"

Anxiety instantly tightened his chest and Bellamy must have sensed it. "I only showed up a few days ago and we didn't leave things on the best of terms—my fault—so I'm thinking he didn't want to talk about me with anyone."

Was Bellamy trying to help smooth things over with Stephen?

"As for your parents and the kids, I'm sure he would prefer to talk to them himself when they get back from the cruise. In his own time and without any help."

Seamus saw the rest of them nodding in agreement

and felt stunned. Bellamy was helping. Being protective. *I'll be damned.*

"When do you go back to New York?" Owen again. Why was he being such a shit?

"He goes back whenever he wants to," Seamus said in a tone that warned his brother not to argue. "It's not my business and it's none of yours."

"Wrong," Bellamy corrected, sending Seamus a look so hot it made him shift in his seat. "It's entirely his business, and I'm not going anywhere unless Seamus runs me out of town. That means you can all expect me at the next Finn Again."

"How do you know about… You know what? Never mind." Seamus shook his head, frowning. "But stop saying things like that. They'll take it out of context."

Trick laughed. "You mean we might think you want something serious instead of a long-distance fuck buddy? That's so out of character. You're usually such a player."

"Enough, Trick," Stephen said, his lips quirking. "We wanted to make sure he was all right, not get kicked out of his bar."

He wasn't used to being the center of so much attention. Stephen thrived on it, Owen sought it out, but

Seamus preferred being in the background. It was where he'd always been. Anything else felt off and he didn't know how to handle it.

He stood up. "I should check on Fiona. Like Jen said, it's a busy night." He glanced down at Bellamy. "Let's go."

"Not a chance." Bellamy actually batted his eyelashes. "This is the part where you leave and I let them ask me personal questions I may or may not answer in exchange for stories about your childhood. It's what normal people do when meeting the family. I looked it up online."

"That's exactly what I'm trying to avoid here," Seamus growled, unable to stop his hands from clenching at his sides. "Stop enjoying this so much, damn it."

"I can't help it, and you can't avoid it, so go back to work. You have kids to feed and I'm not allowed to buy their affection with ponies or, I'm assuming, well balanced meals. Go."

Seamus was genuinely tempted to physically drag Bellamy out of his chair and out back to finish this conversation, but he could feel his family staring at him with varying degrees of shock.

"Is that the *Hulk* face you said you saw, Owen?" Tasha whispered loudly. "Because you might need glasses, hon. Or a mirror to look into when you paddle Jeremy's ass. I've never seen Seamus so toppy."

"Paddles? Tell me more."

"Forget it." Seamus spun on his heel and strode back to the bar, restocking for Fiona and serving drinks so roughly he broke three mugs in the process.

Fiona gave him a wide berth, but she couldn't keep the teasing smile off her face. His regulars were giving him curious looks and following his gaze, which kept returning to the table full of Finns and a very relaxed and irritating Bellamy Demir.

His family had taken it well. Or well enough, he supposed. It was clear they had more questions about the sudden appearance of a man in his life, but then so did he.

Bellamy was staying until Seamus told him to go? What did he mean by *that*? He knew the man worked, despite his bank account. Sure, he had assistants and more money than God, but he couldn't just hang around indefinitely. Could he?

The point was moot, because once the kids got home and life got back to normal, Seamus was sure he wouldn't want to stay long. Not because his children weren't amazing, but their life was full of tiny, boring details and to-do lists that a man like Bellamy wouldn't have any interest in being a part of. Doctor visits, dental visits, clothes shopping, shoe shopping, food shopping, bill paying…a continuous stream of things that had to be done for growing children on a regular basis and were not—in any way, shape or form—sexy.

There was no scenario where he could see a man like Bellamy sinking into domestic bliss and deciding to stay.

Then again, it hadn't seemed possible that he'd show up at all, so…

"Can I talk to you in private?"

Stephen.

Seamus nodded and followed his brother into the hallway leading to the back exit. Stephen was still in his work suit, but his tie was missing and his jacket long gone. He stuffed his hands into his pocket and leaned against the wall, looking at Seamus with a sigh.

"I'm sorry I didn't give you a heads-up after Wyatt dropped by and saw us."

"*I'm* sorry I'm not someone you think you can turn to when something this big happens in your life." Stephen gestured back to the main bar. "And I'm sorry Younger got weird and didn't show. That's a first for him, so I want to give him the benefit of the doubt, but I know you two are close."

He definitely needed to call Solomon tomorrow. "The Waynes think he's a late bloomer too." He swore as soon as he said it. "Don't tell Tasha. I love her to death but you know she'll start trying to fix him up right away."

"You're probably right." Stephen frowned thoughtfully. "As far as Solomon goes, I couldn't begin to guess. But you two are a lot alike. Neither one of you were ever short on responsibilities, and you both took the brunt of the family's as well, so we could be free to follow our dreams. It didn't exactly give either of you much time to think about what you wanted."

"Everyone needs to stop with this. You, of all people, know what a mess I've been." He snorted. "If I were the angel everyone thinks I am, I wouldn't be in this situation with someone like Bellamy."

"An incredibly successful businessman? A guy Tasha said looks like a romance cover on steroids? Someone who seems smart, funny and determined enough to push past all those protective walls and bubble wrap you've placed around you and the kids? Someone like that?"

Someone who is so out of my league it's frightening. Someone who should never have noticed me. Someone who has no idea how to live an ordinary life.

Stephen had been the captain of the debate team. Seamus, sadly, had not, so he didn't bother going into it. "The point is, I know my strengths. I'm a good dad and some of my ideas here are taking off. I may not have the right balance yet, but I'm getting by."

"Jesus, Seamus, is that—" Stephen cut himself off and gripped Seamus by his shoulders. "I used to worry about you, I'll admit that. I worried you were too nice, too easygoing and you'd let people take advantage of you. People like Mira. I worried that because you cared so much about making other people happy, you weren't doing what you loved as much as what was expected. And sometimes, if we're being honest, I worried that your uncompromising focus on the kids would ensure you ended up alone."

Eyes his exact shade of blue darkened with emotion. "Now every day when I look at my sons? I'm more in love than I thought possible, and terrified that I'm going to make a mistake or a wrong decision. I worry about their future and school and whether or not they'll resent me for giving them a curfew. I honestly never understood what you went through until now, and I don't care if you hate hearing the praise. *What would Seamus do?* is the new house mantra. I've even got Tasha saying it. I don't see you as a martyr or a saint, Seamus. You're my Goddamn hero."

Seamus rubbed the back of his hot neck and took an embarrassed step back. "Okay, that's enough now."

Stephen smiled. "You never could take a compliment."

"You always got to them first."

"I love you, brother."

"I love you back," Seamus mumbled. "And about Bellamy—"

"I was being oversensitive, but that was about me, not him. I'd never judge you for who you wanted. It took years for me to finally fight for my relationship with Natasha. Hell, I might still be going home every night to an empty house I hated if it hadn't been for that kinky party. And you," he added softly. "You took care of me when she was gone. Never left me alone."

Seamus grimaced. "This isn't exactly the same thing. You and Tasha were in love. I don't know what's happening between Bellamy and I, but I don't think these feelings are the forever kind. They're too intense, and not always in a good way. It's definitely not the type of relationship I ever thought I'd be in."

I didn't know I could want someone so badly I ached when they weren't around.

"It makes perfect sense to me, Seamus. You've had your finger in that dam for years. That kind of pressure has a tendency to explode when it's finally released."

"Do me a favor and don't share the finger analogy with Owen." He hesitated. "Why do you think he's pissed off about this? We weren't this bad with him, were we?"

"No, and he knows it, the spoiled brat." Stephen chuckled. "He's not that pissed. I think he's just upset he didn't see it. That he was basically with you on vacation and he didn't know you were going through something he'd gone through. Something he might have been able to help you with." Stephen's smile took on an evil tilt. "And he could be jealous that he's no longer the most interesting brother."

Seamus barked out a laugh. "I think his title is safe."

"I don't know, Seamus. You're on your way to being a beer tycoon, and a sexy billionaire followed you home from Ireland… Owen's just a married construction worker with a cute dog."

"Well, he'll always be the first," Seamus said with a proud smile. It was true. Owen was out there being brave before the rest of them even knew they were hiding. "Let's hope our parents have your reaction instead of his."

"They will. And the kids will love anyone who loves you. The only problem I could see cropping up is that they're not used to sharing you every day."

"No, they're not."

But Bellamy had asked for the chance to spend time with them, and Seamus couldn't find it in him to say no. He didn't want to say no.

He wanted it to work. He just had to find a way to make the ending as painless for his kids as possible if it didn't.

If a heart got broken, he wanted it to be his. Not theirs.

Chapter Twelve

"Daddy says this is your favorite movie." Penny was holding the iPad her grandparents had given her for her birthday. They'd had it loaded with every princess movie they could find. Most she already had recorded on the DVR *and* owned on Blu-ray, but this was easy to use and portable, so she loved it.

It was currently playing *Beauty and Beast*. "Yes, different with a mess of us is Belle!" she sang, swinging the device around wildly as she danced.

Seamus was pretty sure she was getting the words wrong, but he didn't think that mattered to Bellamy as much as the potential for brain injury when the iPad swung so close to his head he had to slide down the couch to take cover.

Little Sean copied his every action, laughing in evil delight, while Jake was watching it all subtly over his history book. Wes had decided to help Seamus in the kitchen, which meant coloring at the table while he cooked dinner.

He should go save him. Bellamy wasn't used to children, and Penny and Sean had *a lot* of energy. Jake still had an alert look in his eyes that meant he wasn't quite won over yet. Bellamy was a stranger to him, and Seamus had never had a friend Jake didn't know sleeping over on the couch before. The teenager's protective instincts for his siblings had definitely kicked in.

He still couldn't believe Bellamy hadn't gone back to his hotel after the kids came home. He seemed fine camping out on the couch bed, or pretending to, so the children wouldn't be shocked with the sleeping arrangements before they got to know him. He just snuck into the master bedroom every night after the kids were asleep and left again before dawn.

Neither one of them was getting much sleep, but Seamus wasn't complaining. It had been the best few weeks of his life.

"This is *my* song!" Bellamy announced to the living

room at large, standing and placing Penny on the couch with Little Sean as he started to perform the part of the arrogant Gaston. By the time he flexed his biceps and got to, "As a specimen, yes, I'm intimidating!" Penny and Sean were screaming at rock concert decibels, and even Jake's lips were twitching.

Wes tugged at his hand three times before he managed to look away. "What's up, buddy?"

"Something's boiling." Wes's blue eyes were saucer size. "What's he *doing*?"

"He's singing with your sister. You want to join them?"

His son shook his head, clinging to his fingers and tugging him back to the kitchen. "You sing like that all the time," he said thoughtfully. "Is that why you're friends?"

"It is today," Seamus laughed, going to the stove and stirring the sauce he'd made to go with what Wes liked to call his veggie spaghetti. Getting Wes and Little Sean to eat vegetables was not an easy job, and he wasn't ashamed to say he cheated. His life-hack, or whatever the heck the mothers were calling it the last time he helped with a bake sale, was the sauce. Cheese sauce, tomato sauce… Hell, he'd use chocolate sauce if he had to. It didn't matter. As long as the vegetables were hidden, they'd be eaten.

"He looks scary."

Seamus paused and looked over his shoulder with a gentle smile. Wes's anxiety was worse these last few months. He'd taken to Ken Tanaka right away, but there was something very centered about him. Something that made Wes feel safe. Bellamy, however, was a force of nature. And sometimes he scared Seamus too, but for an entirely different reason. "That's because you don't know him yet. But do you want to know what Uncle Jeremy said as soon as he saw him in Ireland?"

"What?"

"He said Bell looked exactly like Vini's new best friend. The Dark Prince. Vini thought he was scary too, but he was actually very kind." He didn't really have any idea if Jeremy's prince was kind, but it sounded good and Wes was obsessed with pictures of Vini. He'd never read the comic, though, so Seamus figured it didn't matter if he exaggerated.

Wes dropped his crayon and stared at his father with big blue eyes. "He's Vini's *best friend*?"

"That's what he said. They'll be having a lot of adventures together."

"Can I bring down the picture of Vini and *me* having adventures? The one I got for Christmas?"

Gotcha. "I bet he'd love to see that. After dinner."

"*Dad.*"

"After," Seamus repeated firmly, hiding his grin. "Go tell everyone it's time to wash up."

"So I'm a misunderstood dark prince?" Bellamy walked toward him, a sensual twist to his lips. "You know, I didn't think seeing a man cooking spaghetti would get me so hot."

Seamus glanced swiftly at the door and shook his head. "Keep your voice down and I'll make an adult meal for us tomorrow. We ran out of time today and this is what I make for growing children with stubborn taste buds. Now about that singing…"

Bellamy laughed and slid his hand quickly across the back of Seamus' jeans, making him gasp. "*That* is a classic French story, my friend. If I didn't know all its iterations, including the musical numbers, my mother might have disowned me. Elle is convinced it was written about her. In fact, I'm not sure that isn't how I got my name."

Fiona might be psychic, Seamus thought with a silent chuckle. He'd have to tell her the next time he saw her.

"What's your mom like?" Bellamy's bulk and close proximity forced him to brush against his body in the small kitchen. He rinsed the pasta, waiting for him to speak.

"Beautiful. Ageless. Romantic."

"Are you talking about a skin cream or the woman who gave birth to you?"

Bellamy's lips twitched. "Oh, you want specifics. In all honesty, I adore her. Everyone does. When Elle is focused on you, the world is full of color, anything is possible and you feel so loved you think you might burst. It's genuine and joyful and…" He lifted one shoulder, as if he'd long ago come to terms with who his mother was. "And then something or someone distracts her and she has to go chase it down."

Something about that description sounded familiar. It made Seamus uneasy. "Is she easily distracted?"

Bellamy's smile was tinged with something Seamus couldn't name. "She's on lucky number seven now. He's a nice guy. We've gone rock climbing together. Twenty years younger than she is, closer to my age, so he might be able to keep up with her."

"Seven?" Seamus couldn't imagine that. "At least she sounds like she's coming from a hopeful place. I never understood why my Uncle Sol kept getting married."

"Why?"

He frowned thoughtfully. "He never looked at any of his wives the way Dad looked at Mom, I guess. It sounds simple, but they've been together well over forty years and they're still crazy about each other. My uncle knew going in he didn't feel that way about any of them, but he still did it. He wanted children and he didn't want to be alone. That's not a good enough reason to promise someone forever."

That made him think about Gillian, thankful she never took him seriously. He wasn't like Sol. He didn't want to be alone either, but he'd cared about Gill. He could see her in his life forever…as a friend. He hadn't understood, not really, what he would have missed until Bellamy came along.

Bellamy wandered over to the Popsicle frames and artwork held up by refrigerator magnets. "She *is* hopeful," he said quietly. "But she can't be still. I think forty years would frighten her."

"I didn't mean there was anything wrong with—"

"I know." Bellamy's smile was beautiful. "When I was five, she told me there are two types of people in the world. Trees and birds. I was wondering why she was leaving again, so I'm guessing she was simplifying too." He laughed softly, almost as if he were speaking to himself. "She said trees put down deep roots. They were big and strong and solid, but they could never move. They were cursed with one perspective, one point of view for their entire lives. Birds, on the other hand, have to fly to survive. They might make a temporary home in the tree, keep it company and tell it stories about its travels, but when the seasons change they'll need to take off to a more exciting destination. And the tree will still be stuck. Unable to follow, even if it wanted to."

"Are you trying to say I'm a tree?" Seamus kept his tone light as he set the table, but he couldn't help feeling for young Bellamy.

"I believe *she* was trying to say my father was a tree and she was a bird, but she didn't know what the hell *I* was yet so she was leaving me with the nanny." Bellamy chuckled. "I think. Or it was just nonsense so I'd stop crying. Whatever the case, it worked. I finally thought I understood why she was always leaving, and that it wasn't because of me. It made it easier."

Seamus glanced at the kitchen doorway before reaching up to cup Bellamy's cheek, unable to resist the need to touch him. He leaned into his hand like a cat, his beard scraping against Seamus's palm.

"Jake did a book report once about migratory patterns that says for all their traveling, birds are actually pretty predictable and loyal. Something inside, like a homing beacon, always brings them back. So she may not have left because of you, but I'd bet you're why she always came back."

"I've told you before I don't need you to take care of me, and still you can't resist." But the look in his eyes was warm and open.

"The bartender's curse. Sticking my nose into other people's business."

"Your family's curse, I think. You're all busybodies."

"I can't deny that."

Running footsteps had Seamus taking a step back and dropping his hand guiltily.

Bellamy stopped smiling.

***

It was after midnight when Seamus realized Bellamy wasn't coming to his bedroom. Why? Had opening up about his mom and having Wes go from hiding to climbing his lap so he could tell him all about Jeremy's comic book character, Vini the demon, made him realize that this relationship was a stupid idea? Too complicated?

Maybe he was already back at his hotel. Or he'd headed straight to the airport, longing for his exciting life in New York and telling himself no piece of ass was worth this kind of headache.

Seamus checked his phone, but when he saw no new messages he threw off his blanket and sat up, suddenly and irrationally angry. He deserved a hell of a lot more than that after trusting him enough to let him into his home with his children. If he couldn't handle the pressure, that was fine. If he'd had enough of the sex that was still blowing Seamus away every night? The sex that kept getting better every damn time? Great. But the man should have had the guts to tell him.

He quietly made his way downstairs, scowling when he saw the rumpled sheets on the pull-out couch bed. It was empty. He padded softly to the kitchen, looking out into the backyard, seeing nothing. He was ten seconds away from throwing something against the wall when he heard noises coming from the basement.

Locking the door behind him, he walked down the basement stairs and felt some of his anger dissipate. He was still here. Not in bed where he belonged, but he hadn't left the house.

Why the hell hadn't he left yet?

He seemed just as angry as Seamus was, only he'd found the makeshift gym and was taking it out on the punching bag. He must have been at it for a while. He was in a pair of boxer briefs and nothing else, his dark golden skin glowing with sweat.

"Bellamy? What are you doing down here?"

Why aren't you in my bed?

He didn't even slow down. "What does it look like, Seamus?" He punched the bag so hard the stand it was dangling from shook. "I'm wondering why I'm turning my life backwards and inside out for a man with no balls."

"Excuse me?"

He hugged the bag and finally met his gaze, green eyes blazing. "You heard me. I've been here a few weeks now and you're still treating me like a dirty secret. You turned down the Finn Again, and I know it was because you didn't want more questions."

"We were busy." *Liar.*

"We're always busy. Since the kids got back it's been like a colorful circus. Preparing for the new puppy and the new school year, shopping and singing and wearing tiaras, and that's fine. I've had a great time and I have no problem with any of it. What I don't like is you introducing me as your *friend* to your parents and children. So I can live with you and eat with you, spend every day beside you—but my pillow is on the couch every night and I have to keep my distance during the day. Not touching you when I want to. Not kissing you when I want to. Watching you tense and jump away whenever you forget yourself for a second. Like we're doing something we should be ashamed of." He stalked toward Seamus, frustration transforming his expression. "How long do you think it can last?"

Seamus felt like a knife was twisting in his gut. Bellamy was right. He'd always known this wasn't going to work. "I understand."

Bellamy frowned before shaking his head and dropping it momentarily into his hands. "God, no, that isn't what I meant and you really don't have a clue how to be in a relationship, do you?" He blew out a rough breath. "I mean the secrecy. Your siblings and cousins know about me and they talk all the time, so keeping them from coming over and refusing invitations is pointless. And forcing *them* to keep quiet with your parents is unnecessary. How long are you going to ignore your their calls and avoid touching me in front of your children? I don't want to be the guy sneaking into your bedroom for the next thirty years, Seamus. If we're giving this a shot, you should give it a fucking shot."

The next thirty years?

"I will." He stepped back and crossed his arms over his bare chest. "When the time is right, I will. You said it yourself, the kids are nervous about school starting and excited about their dog. And I can't tell them we're dating without answering a million questions that you and I don't have the answers to yet. I don't want to confuse them." *Or pressure you into making promises you can't keep.*

"You tell them the truth about everyone else. In fact, you've been great with them from what I can see. Your sister is living with two men who take turns fucking her *and* each other, and while they don't get the details, the kids understand they're all in love. They even call them Uncle Declan and Uncle Trick. Rory—"

"It's different. I'm their father."

"And tonight Jake asked me if I knew someone who might want to date *his father*."

Shit. "He did?"

"Since I'm your *friend* who sleeps on the couch, he thinks I can help," Bellamy growled. "Don't ask me to do that, Finn. I won't stand by and let anyone else touch you, even to put his mind at ease."

"That won't happen." Seamus ran a hand through his hair. "I've never done this before. Presley was the closest I came to—"

"I know." Bellamy had come up close and slid one hand around to cup his ass through his pajama bottoms, his other hand caressing his flat stomach. "I know I'm the only one you let in the door, and I heard the stories from your family. Not to mention my reprehensible snooping before came to the States to find you. I'm starting to put it together in my mind."

"Put what together?"

"The Seamus puzzle. The greedy man who begs for my cock and has to have his mouth covered every time he comes was practically a virgin before I seduced him. He's never had a chance to really fuck someone himself. To know what it feels like to truly let go."

Seamus tensed. "I had sex before you came along, asshole. I was talking about being in a relationship."

"Four times before I came along. Maybe five. Most of them before you adopted Jake. Yeah, a true sex addict." Bellamy's expression dared him to prove him wrong.

"You don't know everything about my history, Bellamy. Maybe I'm just good at keeping my sex life to myself."

"I know about Homecoming."

He was blushing and pissed. "Is that what they were telling you about at the bar? I'm going to kill them."

"Why? It was inspiring." He changed his tone until he sounded like he was telling a story around the campfire. "Our hero, Seamus Finn, goes to the dance with one of the hottest cheerleaders in school—the best friend of his brother's date, so they could go together. He was destined to get lucky that night. The cheerleader was a well-known freak in the sheets and she'd never been with a twin before, but her luck ran out when he caught her outside with a few fellow jackasses, laughing at that nice girl from the science club."

Seamus shook his head, trying to hold on to his irritation. "Are you narrating my life, Bellamy? Because no one else is here and I already know what happened."

"I don't think you do." Bellamy slid his fingers into the waistband of his pants, knuckles brushing his stomach lightly. Teasing him. Making him hot. "Not the way other people tell it. Now let me finish. Heedless of his own reputation, our hero rejects his date in front of her friends and takes Science Club back inside for a slow dance or two, and then he drives his damsel to a romantic spot to watch the stars and…talk."

"My date was a bitch." Like something out of a stupid teen movie, they'd ridiculed Tyra about her dress and the fact that she'd come to the dance without a date. It was cruel and pointless bullying and Seamus couldn't stand seeing it. He'd never been able to. So he'd left the cheerleader, whose name he couldn't remember now, and spent the rest of the night with Tyra instead. She was cute and smart and he had a feeling she'd leave them all in the dust after graduation. He'd been right. She was happily married and working for NASA now.

"She was your first. A girl you rescued. And she made the first move too, didn't she?"

"A friend," Seamus corrected. "But yes, she was my first."

"I'm assuming you were gentle and kind and gave her a beautiful memory that changed her for the rest of her life."

Seamus rolled his eyes at his mocking tone. "I was awkward and clumsy and it went about the same way most first times go. Very quickly. Is there a point to this beyond personal embarrassment?"

"The point is you. You rescue children and victimized women. You give advice and help people open up about their childhood or face their fears. Super Seamus, always saving the day." Bellamy tsked and his fingers tightened on his hips. "No one knows what a hot little fuck you are under that cape. How greedy you can be. I'm the only one who gets that part of you. The only one who can take care of you and give you what you need."

Seamus licked his lips and reached for him, but Bellamy pushed him away. "What now?"

"I know about Presley and Science Club. Tell me about the other women."

"Fuck off," Seamus growled, unable to stop himself from following Bellamy as he moved further into the crowded basement. "I don't want to hear about your old flames and I don't want to talk about mine."

Bellamy gave him a look that nearly had him coming in his pants. "No one else mattered, Seamus. I don't even remember their names."

"Bullshit." He wished that were true.

"With a mother who thinks she's a bird and a father

who has a penchant for marrying barely legal runway models, I was firmly in the *relationships are for suckers* camp. I fucked when I wanted. Who I wanted. And for the most part, as soon as I was done I moved on."

What he was saying didn't make sense. Bellamy was brilliant, charming, stunning and rich. People had to be crawling over each other for the chance to spend time with him. "You've never been in a relationship?"

"Not the kind you're talking about. Once or twice I've made arrangements. If I was in town and had an urge, that kind of thing."

It sounded so cold. He couldn't imagine this passionate man being satisfied with something like that. Bellamy needed touch. Constant contact. When they were together in bed he couldn't *stop* touching him, tangling their legs together and rubbing against him like a contented feline. Whenever he woke up in the night, it was always to Bellamy using him like his own personal security blanket.

He'd never dated anyone before?

"So this stalking someone and sleeping on their couch is new for you."

Bellamy's expression changed to fierce need and frustration again in the blink of an eye. "Yes. And I don't like it, Finn. This house isn't big enough for six and it needs too many repairs. Your bed is too small, this gym is a joke and you don't have a pool, even though I know you love to swim."

"I love to pay my bills more."

He was working himself up. It shouldn't be turning Seamus on, but it was. It was also making him angry. "That's right, you can't afford a pool. And what about bookshelves? You have mountains of books in this basement and under your bed. I even saw some in the kitchen pantry. But you don't have your own shelves. The kids do, but you don't."

He was upset about his lack of bookshelves now? "I can make some if I need to. When I have time. Until then I have a system."

"The system is flawed. You're too proud, Seamus. Meanwhile I have to swallow mine, because I'm not allowed to pay for anything, even for myself, while I'm here as your *guest.* So I eat vegetables slathered in spaghetti sauce and strawberries, flavors that should *never* go together, and then I shower in the narrowest bathroom on the planet that happens to be covered in *duck* wallpaper, because you only have one full bathroom that everyone shares, and Wes used to love ducks."

Seamus grit his teeth, feeling like he was riding a damn rollercoaster. "If it's so uncomfortable, then leave, Bellamy. This is my life, not yours. So why don't you just—"

Bellamy claimed his mouth and Seamus instantly grabbed the back of his head, holding him closer as their mouths ate at each other hungrily. *This.* Every day he counted down the minutes to this. He loved the way Bellamy kissed him. Like he needed Seamus in order to breathe. Like he'd die if he couldn't have him. Everything else disappeared until all he could feel were his soft, bruising lips and biting teeth.

His pajama bottoms were pushed to his thighs so Bellamy could grip his erection and stroke it with rough, impatient hands. "I'm not leaving because this is mine," he growled, dropping to his knees. "And I'm nowhere near done with you yet."

"Jesus, Bell." Seamus sifted his fingers through thick hair, his shoulders hunching and whole body shuddering when Bellamy deep throated his cock. They usually did this together in his bed. But down here in the cramped basement, with Bellamy on his knees, it felt wicked. *Like a dirty secret.* It brought Seamus too close to climax too fast. “Oh fuck, give me a minute.”

He tried to pull back but Bellamy sent him tumbling on the mat he’d placed on the floor. He smiled as he pinned Seamus to it with strong hands on his shoulders. “Make me.”

“What are you, five?” Seamus nudged him off, trying to sit up, but Bellamy flipped him over, holding one arm around his neck, his free hand gripping his erection again.

“Wrestling is a man’s sport, Seamus. My family has been doing it for centuries…you’ll never win.”

Wrestling. He remembered the video of Bellamy he’d saved to his computer. The one that never failed to turn him on. “Wait,” he moaned. “Can we… We need oil.”

Bellamy’s hips jerked against his. “Damn,” he growled. “You have a dirty mind, don’t you, gorgeous? Is that what you want? You want to wrestle with me? Do you want me to pin you right here on the mat and make you give in?”

God yes.

He knew he had some oil down here somewhere. Seamus slid out of his hold, pulled up his flannel bottoms and went to the shelf where he’d kept things for the lake. Floaties and goggles… Sunscreen... “There.”

"Baby oil? You know that's not what we use, Seamus." But Bellamy's voice was huskier than ever, closer to a growl. "And there's definitely not enough to cover us both."

He made a note to buy more olive oil. "It's hypoaller—*Bell*!"

Bellamy had taken the large bottle and tipped it over Seamus' shoulders without waiting. His free hand was rubbing and touching, coating his skin in the slippery unscented liquid. "You are so gorgeous, Seamus. Your skin. I could do this for hours and never get tired of how it feels under my hands."

He emptied out the bottle on himself, letting Seamus help and practically purring when he rubbed it in. "I used to think I wanted to box a few rounds with you. But this will be so much sweeter."

Seamus tried to laugh but he was too turned on. "We can go a few rounds next week at Brady and Ken's gym. But I'll win. I might even pin you tonight."

He doubted it. He'd never actually wrestled before, and Bellamy was too strong.

Green eyes singed him with need. "If you pin me, you'll have to fuck me. And you can't go easy on me, Seamus. I'll need it rough. I haven't let anyone top me since I started college. But I'd let you tonight. I'd let you fuck me as hard as you wanted to."

Fuck. Jesus. Fuck!

If this was a strategy to distract him, it was working.

They walked back toward the mat, neither one taking their eyes off the other. "I need to get you in a *kispet* soon so we can do this properly." Bellamy looked at his body as if he were imagining him in the leather pants.

Seamus was already sweating, his heart racing in his ears. Bellamy was stunning like this. Muscles gleaming with oil and an almost feral expression on his face. He was a fighter. Seamus wanted to beat him and take him down. He wanted to lose and submit.

Either way they'd both win.

Bellamy described a few of the moves and holds to Seamus, his dark skin flushed, eyes wild. Then they came towards each other, arms locked in place. The oil made it a challenge. Hands slipped on shoulders and feet dug into the mat as Seamus struggled to remember what they were doing.

"There are rules against doing what I'm going to do to you," Bellamy muttered hotly, accent thick with need. "We might need to find something to gag you with. You might wake the house when you start screaming my name."

"So cocky," Seamus said, struggling for breath and a handhold. "You'd think you actually wanted to win. But you don't. I can tell. You want me inside you for once. You want me to make *you* scream."

Seamus bit back an angry shout as Bellamy took him down with an arm wrapped around his waist. The other slid slickly down the back of his pants, one finger pushing forcefully into his ass.

"Oh God." *Fuck me.*

"*Who* doesn't want to win? I'm inside and I'm not letting go unless you make me." He added a second finger and started to fuck him slowly. Too slowly. "Tap out and I'll give you my cock."

No. I have to win. Need to win. Have to...

Bellamy grunted when Seamus bucked and sent him slipping off his body. He stood and quickly stepped out of his pajama bottoms, revealing an erection so painfully sensitive that the fabric brushing against him had been too much.

It distracted Bellamy, Seamus realized, feeling the need to dominate growing inside him. "You said when you met me you knew you were going to fight me or fuck me, or both." He stroked his dick, the oil on his hand coating it as he pumped his hips forward seductively. "At first, I only wanted to fight you."

"Now?" Bellamy was watching his movements, his lips parted hungrily.

"I think you know what I want now."

Seamus came down, pinning him and reaching for the waistband at the back of Bellamy's briefs. The cloth made a tearing sound as it stretched and Bellamy struggled, but Seamus covered him in the hold he'd seen every time he watched the video.

Oiled up and pinned. Ready…

"I don't think I can wait to finish this match. We'll try again later," Seamus rasped as he yanked the underwear to Bellamy's knees. "I need to—" He'd pressed the head of his cock between Bellamy's cheeks when he realized what he wasn't wearing. "Son of a bitch."

"What's wrong?"

Seamus bent over Bellamy's back and let out a shuddering sigh. "No condom. They're in my bedroom."

"Do it," he said, his voice raw and needy as he pressed his forehead into the mat. "I want you to. I *need* you to."

He hadn't thought it was possible for him to get any

harder. "Are you sure?"

"Do you want me to beg? I want to feel your bare cock in my ass. Want you to come inside me and fill me up. No one's ever done that to me before. Be *my* first, Seamus. *Please.*"

Fuck yes. "My first too. I've never…"

Anything. I never did anything, never felt anything until you.

He should have kissed him again. Should have used his fingers and tongue to get him ready, but Seamus couldn't wait. The drive to claim the man beneath him had taken over. Seamus spread his cheeks, fingers slippery and shaking, and then he was there.

One strong thrust forced his dick past the resistant muscles until he was buried to the hilt in Bellamy. "*Christ*, Bell. Fuck, that's tight."

He bit his tongue to stop himself from shouting in pleasure, his hand skimming damply over Bellamy's shaking back. He was too quiet. "Did I hurt you?"

Say no.

Bellamy shook his head, his whole body trembling, and Seamus had to strain to hear his whispered, "Don't stop, Seamus."

He groaned as he dragged his hips slowly back before

pressing deep again. God, he'd never felt anything like this. *So damn tight.* Adrenaline and desire pumped through him, but he tried to hold himself back as long as he could. He needed it to last.

This was where he wanted to live. With Bellamy's ass clinging to his cock, his body pushing back against him every time he withdrew, as if he couldn't stand the loss. He was making his Bell moan and shake and beg. Taking control of his pleasure for once. His. Bell belonged to *him*.

He tried to dig his fingers tried into Bellamy's side and shoulders but the oil made it impossible. When Seamus leaned forward and gripped the thick hair on the back of his head, Bellamy's groan was loud and desperate. "*Yes*, Seamus. Harder. You can't hurt me. Fuck me like you want to. Let go."

Those words stole the last of his control. He tightened the fingers tangled in Bellamy's hair and started to ride him hard and wild. He could feel every clench and shiver from the body beneath him and it was so good his eyes wanted to roll back in his head.

It's so good. Can't stop. I never want to stop.

The rougher he got, the more Bellamy pushed him. "Harder, Seamus. Fuck, just like that. So good. *Deeper.*

Oh, God, your cock feels so—" He started muttering in Turkish and French and it turned Seamus on. So much he didn't notice they were sliding across the mat with the force of his thrusts. So much he didn't realize his grip was pulling Bellamy's neck back too far so he could kiss him as their bodies slapped wetly together.

This is mine. I want this so much.

"Please," Bellamy moaned against his lips. "I can't last much longer."

"You like it?" Seamus heard the gravel in his voice. "You like my cock in your ass this time?"

"Yes," he said instantly. "Only you, Seamus. Pin me down and fuck me. Only you."

A possessive need curled around him. "Only me," he repeated darkly, his hips pounding so hard he could feel it in his bones. "You've taken everything, Bell. All of me. Now tell me this is mine."

Bellamy was groaning with every breath now, widening his thighs for more. "It's yours. I'm yours. Anytime you want me. Any way you want me. Oh God, Seamus. *Fuck, yes* like that."

Jesus. It was too good. He couldn't get deep enough. Couldn't go fast enough. He felt completely out of control. "I want it all, Bell. All the time. I can't stop wanting you."

"You have me," Bell whispered, hissing when Seamus tugged on his hair again in response. "Please."

Seamus was wild. Close. But he had to wait to send Bellamy over. "Come all over this mat like you come on me, Bell. I want to feel you tighten around my cock. I need to see what I do to you."

The words had Bellamy shouting hoarsely with his release, his body jerking and quaking beneath him. "*Seamus.*"

"So fucking good, Bell. You're taking it so good. I love it. I love your ass so much."

Seamus heard the nonsense coming out of his mouth but he couldn't stop it, any more than he could stop himself from responding to the clenching muscles around his cock. "Have to come inside you. Need you to fill you up, Bell. Love you—*Bell*!"

Everything went black before coming back in bright, brilliant color. His body was a lightning rod in a storm and electricity was arcing off and through him with every jolt of his cock as he found his release. He looked down and saw it leaking out of Bellamy's ass and he wanted to run a victory lap and plant a damn flag. He wanted to howl. He would as soon as his body stopped trembling.

When they collapsed side by side on the mat to catch their breath, staring up at the ceiling of the basement in stunned, satisfied silence, Bellamy started to laugh.

"Are you trying to get back at me for the first time we did this?" Seamus panted, unable to stop his answering smile. "Let me apologize now, because it's not great for my ego."

Bellamy gasped, his hand flopping down to reach for his. "I'm laughing because I came so hard I thought I was going to die. I think I saw the light, Seamus, I swear to you. And then I realized that this was perfect. This is how I want to be found when I finally go in my late nineties."

Seamus sent him a dubious look. "On the floor in a basement, covered in baby oil?"

"Exactly."

"You're a lunatic."

"You may be right. But you love it. You said so."

He did?

Shit. He did.

Chapter Thirteen

Landing in an hour. Get the kids and Vini ready. I have a surprise.

Seamus put his phone down carefully, chastising himself for the excitement that swamped him with Bellamy's text. He'd only been gone for a few days. It was no big deal.

Except it was.

They'd been inseparable for three weeks now, mostly because the man refused to leave and kept claiming squatter's rights or ignoring him or—even better—distracting him every time he suggested it.

Bellamy had been there for the first day of school, he was already helping Jake with his more advanced math homework and he'd sung every song from *Beauty and the Beast* at least twenty times at Penny's command. A lesser man would have run screaming for that alone.

And then there was the dog. The strange-looking puppy the kids decided to name Vini after Jeremy's creation had waddled over to Bellamy right away, curling up on his chest as he hummed it to sleep. Wes had been fascinated, and Little Sean had been upset that he was still too small to chase or hug too tightly, but Seamus had been fucking enchanted.

The last two days that he'd been in New York for business had been harder than Seamus was willing to admit. He was still just as busy with his own life. Still surrounded by children and to-do lists that never seemed to end. But now he knew what it felt like to share it all, to have someone to curl up with at the end of a long, demanding day. Someone who couldn't stop touching him. He'd felt Bellamy's absence more than he'd expected to.

But he'd used the time wisely. While he was gone, Seamus had told his parents about him. It had been incredibly anticlimactic because, just like Thoreau, they already seemed to know what Seamus had only discovered about himself in Ireland.

"Owen was a surprise to everyone because, well you

know how he was with the women." His mother had blushed when she said that. "But you were different from the beginning. If you weren't with the family, you kept to yourself, reading a book. So sensitive and kind."

Shawn nodded thoughtfully. "And you never dated unless your brother talked you into it."

"Or spent too much time in the shower."

His father snorted. "Yeah, the shower was really a dead giveaway. Owen and Stephen both lived in there as soon as they hit puberty. Went through conditioner like you wouldn't believe. Like we didn't know what they were up to."

"Shawn, stop. Look how red his ears are getting," his mother scolded lightly.

Seamus scowled at them. He'd "showered" more than they knew. Not that he *ever* wanted to talk about that with his parents. "You didn't know anything. You tried to get Mira to date me and you were thrilled when I told you Presley was pregnant."

"Well, of course," his mother seemed surprise. "You're an amazing father. Everyone who saw you with Jake knew that."

"You're right. We never knew for sure, son, but the point is, we support you now. I'm just glad you're finally having some fun. Whoever it's with. It's never too late to enjoy your life."

"Thanks Dad." Now he felt old *and* predictably gay.

Bellamy's reward to him for finally following through had been an unforgettable phone sex session that had made him impatient to see him in person.

Everything seemed unforgettable now. Every day felt like it needed to be saved and put on a shelf so he would be able to look at it when he was alone again.

The special Finn Again he'd asked for to make up for the one they'd missed had been full of laughter. Bellamy had entertained them all with stories of his experiences in other countries, and his lifelong goal to try something new everywhere he went. The only people missing had been Ken and Solomon. But Bellamy didn't seem to care that he hadn't seen Tanaka since he arrived, so Seamus let it go, hoping he was just busy and not avoiding them.

Then the other night he'd placed another memory on the shelf when he'd come to tuck in a grumpy, crying Sean, only to find Bellamy already there and singing a lullaby in French that had put the little hellion right to sleep.

It was too late to protect himself. He was deep in love and he knew it. Bellamy knew it too, though Seamus hadn't said it again since their basement wrestling match.

Bellamy hadn't said it at all.

It didn't matter. He was coming back today. He'd escaped the madhouse and was *voluntarily* checking back in. That had to mean something.

The knock at the door stopped him on his way to the shower. He glanced over at the kids through the patio doors. They were all outside with Vini, enjoying their Saturday romp with the dog.

When he opened the door he frowned. "Why didn't you just come in? You have keys."

"Long day," Solomon said simply as he headed into the living room and sat down heavily on the couch. "Can I have a drink?"

Something was wrong. "Sure. You want tea or water or—"

"Beer."

Seamus turned toward the kitchen, got them both a bottle of his Irish Red and took a seat next to him, knowing he'd talk when he was ready.

"I'm sorry I haven't been around lately," Solomon started at last. "And I wanted to thank you for helping Noah get ready. He got a call around four this morning letting him know she'd given birth."

"*What?* Why didn't he let the family know?"

Solomon shook his head. "I found out on my way over. That woman has a lot of conditions. She didn't want to see all of us hovering. Thought it would be too hard on her. But Rory and I are heading over to help Noah pick him up and take him home as soon as the hospital says it's okay."

"It's a boy? Do you need my help?"

"No. We've got this. Aunt Ellen is already planning a late baby shower for Noah, to give everyone a peek at baby Zachary."

"Zachary Finn. Good name."

As they sat there, Seamus could feel the tension coming off his cousin and hoped it wasn't about him. "That's one big cloud over your head, Younger. You know you can talk to me. What's wrong?"

Was he still worried about Noah's decision to keep the baby?

Solomon's laugh was tired. "That's a loaded question, Seamus. There are so many things, I'm not sure where to start."

"Alphabetically, by order of importance… Wherever you need to."

"Okay then. I've been in a constant state of pissed off for a few weeks now. I'm pissed that Officer Wayne is still insisting he isn't coming back. He's actually recertifying for his old job."

"Old job?"

Solomon shook his head, bemused. "RN. I guess he and his older sister Bronte got their nursing degree at the same time, but then Hugo decided he wanted to be a police officer instead and joined the academy with James."

"Is that all?" Seamus wasn't sure why Solomon had been so upset about the Hugo situation, but it didn't sound that bad now. Healing people was just as good a calling as protecting them. Like Rory, Hugo would be saving lives. And he wouldn't have to carry a gun.

"Not even close," Solomon said grimly. "I'm also pissed that Wyatt is being such a jackass to Noah, that James is still doing his MIA routine, and that Donna is showing up around the precinct, asking about him and acting suspicious."

"Your *mother*? Holy shit." James had reconnected with her recently, but Solomon hadn't seen her since the divorce.

His cousin shook his head as if fed up with the entire

situation. "Exactly. And to top it all off, Rory's friend's sister ran out of damn puppies before I could get one."

"Damn." Seamus took a healthy swig of his beer. "*That* is a shit-ton of pissed."

"I wasn't that pleased about you keeping your thing with Bellamy quiet either." Solomon glanced at him quickly and then lowered his gaze to his bottle. "You should have come to me. I might have been able to commiserate."

Seamus narrowed his eyes. Had Thoreau's brother been right? "About anyone in particular?"

Solomon tightened his lips and pierced him with a look that told him not to dig. "Then again, I might not have helped you at all. I've recently been told that I'm so busy telling other people what they need to be doing that I don't stop and think about how they feel or what they really want."

"What's going on with you, Younger? Are you okay?" *Are you an LBMG?*

Solomon ran his hand over his short hair and shook his head. "I don't think so. I don't want to be as bitter as Elder, Seamus. None of us do, but I think I might be the one walking that line. I'm in his chair and at his desk every day, working the job that passed to me when he retired. I love what I do, but not as much as I used to. And lately it seems like I can't make a difference to the people that matter. I'm watching the things and people I care about slip out of my hands and there's nothing I can do about it." He took a deep breath. "I don't want to be *the last single stick-in-the-mud of the family*."

"I should never have said that. And you do make a difference. You're the best police chief we've ever had, Younger. You care about the city and you're constantly working to make the police force a part of the community. Get a new chair if you need to, but never believe you're anything like your father."

Solomon shrugged. "Maybe you're right. But I feel…stuck. And what's been going on with you in the last few weeks has helped me come to a few realizations. It's never too late, right? Which is why I wanted you to be the first in the family to know that I'm taking a six month leave of absence from the force."

"*What?*" That was the last thing he'd ever expected to hear from his cousin.

"I think I need to be just Younger for a while, instead of Solomon Jr."

"That's big." Seamus was having a hard time believing what he was hearing. Solomon loved his job.

He *was* his job. “That’s really damn big, Younger. I didn’t know you could do that. Six months?”

“Yeah, well, the mayor would rather have that than a letter of resignation, and those were his only two options. I have a feeling I’ll be having words with my father by tomorrow. But my mind is made up.”

When Solomon said that the matter was closed, he rarely left room for negotiation. All Seamus could do was support him. “Then let me be the first to say congratulations. As someone who just took his first trip this year, you know I think it’s a good idea. And God knows you deserve a break.”

“Yeah?”

“Yeah.”

Solomon leaned back against the couch and smiled, as if he’d been waiting for permission or approval. “A vacation. Maybe I’ll grow my hair out. Get a tattoo.”

“Don’t go nuts all at once now. What about Ireland?” Seamus joked. “We have a grumpy old man there just waiting for someone to hit with a salad plate.”

He shook his head. “I’m staying close to home. I’d like to spend some time with Noah and the baby if he’ll let me. Finally find out what’s going on with James. Get to know this man of yours and help convince you to market your beer."

"I'm already convinced. But don't tell Tanaka because I don't have time to think about all the details right now."

Solomon nodded and then sucked his lower lip between his teeth. Seamus narrowed his eyes at the action and swore. "You're leaving something out."

"What do you mean?"

"You do that every time you're holding something back." Seamus set his beer down. "I've played cards with you and I know your tells. What aren't you saying?"

Solomon didn't look eager to share. "Before I filed my LOA, I got a call. Apparently a woman had been caught near your old garage apartment, and witnesses said she was barefoot and dressed in a robe, asking for a man named Seamus and threatening everyone who came near her. It was Presley, Seamus."

Icy tendrils of shock climbed his spine. That wasn't possible. He stood so fast it made the room spin. "Is she in custody?"

His cousin stared at Seamus apologetically. "After I realized who she was, we took her back to Parkridge. She didn't do any damage, just scared a few people."

He needed to call Camille. To get details. "How did she get out?"

"Apparently her primary caregiver was out sick for the week and Presley was doing so well that the new doctor—one who hadn't been working there before she'd slipped into her last catatonic episode—decided to move her to a less secure wing so she could work in the garden. She ran the first chance she got."

"Jesus." How long had she been missing and why hadn't anyone called him? He was listed as her emergency contact for a reason.

"There's more, Seamus."

"How can there be more?"

"Before she was restrained, she must have found a phone. She called your mother. Aunt Ellen said she told her that you'd locked her up against her will. That you were trying to kill her so you could be with another woman."

"Son of a—" This couldn't be happening.

"I didn't know until I brought Presley back to the facility myself." Solomon grimaced. "Your mom was already waiting there with her nurse—Camille? They were talking for a while and I may have listened in, just to find out what the hell was going on. I think she got the gist of the situation."

His hands were shaking. "Jesus, is Mom okay? I wanted to tell her. I know I told you I was going to, but I knew she'd feel obligated to visit and…Presley's bad days are disturbing to *me*. The things she says? I didn't want to put Mom through that. I didn't want to put *anybody* through that." And Bellamy's arrival had distracted him.

"I just threw a list of my grievances at you and you didn't bat an eye, didn't judge me at all. But no one in the family—not even Stephen—knew about what you were going through. The only reason I did was because of that payment Demir made. We didn't know what happened in Ireland. We had no idea that you were gay—"

"I wasn't sure until now." Seamus buried his face in his hands. "God, this is my nightmare. I was trying to protect the kids. Our family."

"By hiding it? Seamus, if you can't talk to us or ask us for help, who else is there?"

Bellamy helped. He was sneaky as hell about it and that wasn't okay, but he'd helped. And he understood why Seamus hadn't told his kids.

You won't always be able to count on him. He's a

bird, like his mother.

"I think I felt like I used up my quota, you know? Everyone helps me with the kids. Any more would just be taking advantage."

Solomon socked him in the arm.

"Ouch."

"We help with them because we love them. They aren't favors, you dumbass. They're family."

Seamus scowled at him. "Vacation Younger is kind of a dick."

Solomon's lips curved. "Maybe. We'll find out." He stood. "I need to get to Noah, but we'll talk more about this later. I just thought I'd give you a heads-up. Your mom wants to call you tomorrow, but she does plan on telling your father tonight and I'm not sure how he'll react."

"It's always good to have something to look forward to."

Solomon startled him by pulling him into a real embrace. No manly back pats. A genuine hug. "I am *so sorry* you were dealing with that on your own. If I'd known years ago… If you'd told me she'd tried to hurt Penny and Wes, I'd—" He pulled back and shook his head. "I'm just sorry."

Seamus's throat was tight. "Thanks, man. I mean it. And if you ever want to *commiserate* again? I'm here."

He was still staring at the closed door, wondering what the hell he was going to do, when Penny tapped on his leg to get his attention. "Daddy. *I said* is Bell back yet? He said he was coming."

"He'll be here soon." He picked her up in his arms and held her tight, burying his face in her blonde curls. Horrible scenarios were running through his head. What if Presley had known where they lived now? What if he'd been in the shower and she'd found the kids playing in the backyard?

The possibility of her leaving Parkridge on her own had *never* occurred to him. She'd never shown any signs of that kind of behavior. Not in the six years she'd been there. Now everything had changed. Now the decision he'd made to take care of his family and minimize their suffering seemed like an unacceptable mistake. A selfish lie that could have endangered all of them.

They were all inside now; all his children and their strange little dog, watching him hug Penny and wondering why their father was so upset. He met Jake's gaze head on, knowing he'd have to tell him too. He would take it in stride, like he always did. They were a team.

He'd lied to him too.

He didn't think he could feel any worse.

***

"Is it Disneyland?" Wes asked with wide eyes.

"Guess again." Bellamy shook his head.

"The North Pole?" Penny scrunched up her nose doubtfully.

"Guess again."

"The moon?"

Seamus leaned his body against the door of Bellamy's car and met the driver's eyes. Dan. That was his name. He was smiling, obviously enjoying the mystery as much as everyone else. Bellamy was driving the kids crazy with their surprise destination, but part of Seamus wished they'd stayed home so he could figure out what he was going to do next.

Before he could process what Solomon had told him, Bellamy had burst through the door getting the kids riled up for a big surprise and demanding they all go for a ride. Even Vini.

Seamus had wanted to drag him upstairs and pull him into his arms as soon as he saw him. He wanted to tell him everything so he'd have someone to talk to about what had happened. Someone to tell him everything was going to be okay. That he wasn't a horrible person. A horrible father.

But in this car, with the kids around, he couldn't do any of that. It wasn't fucking fair, and he knew it, but he resented the surprise before he'd even found out what it was. Couldn't Bellamy see how upset he was? Didn't he care?

Jake was looking out the window carefully. "It looks like we're close to Aunt Jen's house."

"Because we are."

Seamus stared at Bellamy suspiciously. "Where exactly are you taking us?"

He winked as the car slowed. "You'll find out in a minute. We're here."

He watched Bellamy cuddle little Vini to his chest and help Wes out of the car to stand in front of a house that could give Declan Kelley's a run for its money. "The door is open. Why don't you guys go ahead with Dan and we'll meet you inside?"

Penny, Wes and Little Sean started running to catch up with the driver while Jake followed at a slower pace.

"Is this a friend's house?" Seamus asked wearily. "I

don't mean to be a dick, but I've had a really bad morning and I don't think I'd be the best company right now."

"Kiss me." Bellamy didn't wait for him to agree. He faced him, hiding them from the front door as he took his mouth hungrily. Seamus moaned, leaning into his touch.

"That's all for now," Bellamy sighed when he lifted his head. "But we're getting back to that later. I missed you, gorgeous. Two days is too long."

"Are you going to tell me where we are now?"

Bellamy glanced away almost nervously, cuddling Vini. "That depends. Are you going to keep an open mind?"

Before he could answer, he heard his daughter scream and started to run. His first thought was Presley, but as soon as he walked through the door he realized Penny wasn't screaming in fear. She'd just realized she'd found heaven.

Holy shit.

If he'd never seen Declan's house, he would probably be breathing into a paper bag right now, but even with that as a benchmark, this place was impressive. Just as huge, but the open design, sinking floor and curving walls made it feel...warm. As homey and warm as a ridiculously expensive mega-mansion could get.

The living room could fit three of his, but it still managed to look comfortable. An open, spacious gourmet kitchen in the back looked out into a room filled with wide, puffy couches and a theater-quality television equipped with every entertainment bell and whistle in existence.

Through the open archway Penny was hopping up and down in, Seamus could see books. *Walls* of books.

"It's here!" She cried happily, her face flushing from exertion. "The liberry!"

"Library," Bellamy corrected with a gentle smile.

"That's what I said. He gave it to her but it's here!"

"Who gave it to her?" Seamus asked, frowning. How many books were in that room?

"The Beast," Jake and Bellamy answered together.

Oh.

Oh.

Seamus joined her inside and wondered if maybe they *were* at Disneyland. A curved wall of books surrounding them, a small domed skylight made of stained glass above them, and a thirteen-year-old boy was already sitting at a desktop computer, his eyes nearly as bright with excitement as Penny's. "What are you doing, Jake?"

"This is the same computer they had at the campus, Dad. I told you about it, remember? It's got all the learning and research software already uploaded." He paused and clicked the mouse a few times. "Hey, Bell, this program says it can teach me how to speak and read French."

"It's a good second language option," Bellamy responded with a grin. "Very popular with college girls, I'm told."

Was his son *blushing*?

Seamus could feel those bright green eyes on him as he watched Penny run the width of the room, touching every book she could reach. "Daddy, they have more than you do here," she sighed happily. "They smell so nice. Can we have a room like this?"

Before Seamus could think of an answer, Dan poked his head in the open doorway. "The boys have found the pool. Should I let them in the room?"

"The what?" He spun on his heel and walked out into the living room without looking at Bellamy. "Wes?" he called, a trace of panic in his voice. "Sean? Where are you?" He followed the sounds of their excited shouts down a long hall and stopped dead.

There was an indoor swimming pool that looked a lot like the one at the hotel they'd stayed in. The glass doors were closed and obviously locked, which was a good thing, since Little Sean couldn't swim and he was desperately trying to find a way inside.

Seamus scooped him up in his arms. "That's enough, buddy."

"But—"

"No pool right now. And never without me, understand? Just like the lake."

His lower lip poked out, but he nodded.

Bellamy had set the dog down somewhere, because his arms were crossed tightly over his broad chest. "If you go further down the hall, there's a fully equipped exercise room—also locked for safety. And in the backyard, there's an outdoor kitchen and entertainment area, a clubhouse for the kids and a dog run."

Seamus was wound so tight he felt something was about to snap. "What's upstairs, Bellamy?"

"Seven bedrooms, three bathrooms and an office for telecommuting."

"I see." He set Sean down and looked at Wes. "Take your brother and go get Penny and Jake. I want you to wait with Dan in the car."

"But we just got here. We haven't seen the clubhouse." Wes looked anxious and Seamus took a deep breath and gentled his smile.

"I know, son. There's nothing to worry about, I just need to talk to Bellamy alone for a few minutes. Will you help me out?"

Wes nodded, obviously still confused and disappointed, and Seamus couldn't blame him. But there was nothing he could do about it. Bellamy had made sure of that.

"This house was your surprise." It wasn't a question.

"Yes. A damn good one, I thought." Bellamy sounded as belligerent and defensive as he looked.

"It's a great one," Seamus agreed in hushed angry tones. "It's perfect. A pool, a library from a children's story, Jake's dream computer. This is all absolutely perfect. It's the most beautiful fucking house I've *ever seen*."

His voice was rising as he spoke, echoing off the cathedral ceilings.

"Then why are you being so goddamn pissy, Seamus?"

Seamus knew he was overreacting, but he couldn't

seem to stop himself. "*Pissy*? Why am I *pissy*?" He started to walk away but turned back to face his lover. "We already have a house that I'm still paying the mortgage on. It has one shower, a hole in the porch roof and an old stove, but the kids were fine with it before today. Now nothing will be better than this."

Bellamy tried to reach for him but he backed away. "But they can *have* this," he said urgently. "I want them to. I want you to live here with—"

"I told you not to try and buy their affections. You agreed to that. They've only known you a few weeks and already they're sharing secrets with you and calling you Bell and relying on you to be there whenever they need you. Then you do something like this. Without asking me, without discussing this with me, you offer them everything they ever wanted on a whim…" He shook his head, dread and tension coiling in his stomach. *Like Murphy's. He always left a place better than when he found it.* "I knew this was a mistake."

He started walking away but Bellamy came after him, slamming him roughly against the wall. The reminder of their first fight made Seamus ache. "What the hell is your problem? I found a way for this to work for both of us. A home where neither of us would be a guest and we would have everything we needed to be together. You can't take a fucking step back and see how good this could be?" He swore under his breath. "Yes, it was a mistake not to talk to you, but I wanted to be with you the first time you saw it. I wanted everyone to be together. You told your parents about me. You told me you loved me and I thought we were… Hell, Seamus, I was trying to make you happy."

"We were happy before. I had things taken care of." He gestured between them. "*This* is the mistake, Bellamy. All of it. You belong in a place like this, but we don't. Tell your driver to take me and my children home. Our life might not be a fairy tale, but it's ours."

"No." Bellamy's voice rasped with pain. "What are you doing? You can't just leave like this. Not after this last month. Forget the fucking house. I'll sell it tomorrow, I don't care. It doesn't matter to me."

Seamus forced a laugh that came out sounding like a sob. "You see? It's all so easy for you. You come in and make one grand gesture after another. You make it all look so easy."

"It can be. With us, Seamus, it can be."

"It's not for me. It never is." He pulled away and made himself move toward the door. Bellamy was still calling his name when he made himself close it.

Through the door he heard a muffled shout and it made his body jerk as if he'd been shot through the heart. But he kept moving, walking to the car and making himself climb inside with his silent children and the whining dog.

When Dan came outside, he wasn't smiling anymore, but he was alone.

Like Seamus.

It wasn't just the house. The perfect dream house he'd tried to give them that was within walking distance of his sister and filled with everything Seamus and the children had ever wanted.

It was Bellamy. Everything he'd quietly hoped for alone in his bed. Everything he'd never let himself want because it was too much to ask for.

Seamus suddenly remembered the way he'd described his mother.

When Elle is focused on you, the world is full of color, anything is possible and you feel so loved you think you might burst.

That's how he felt with Bellamy. But it wasn't real. It couldn't be. Something like that couldn't last.

Coward!

Bellamy's muffled accusation ripped through him and cut him open. He was right. He was a coward. Seamus could tell himself he was protecting his children from heartbreak all he wanted, but he knew better. He was protecting himself.

Saint Seamus was a selfish bastard and a liar. He lied about Presley to protect himself. He kept his relationship with Bellamy from the kids, to protect himself.

But he hadn't lied to Bellamy. What they'd had was a mistake, but Bellamy had been the one to make it. He'd picked the wrong man. And Seamus wouldn't be able to put himself back together again if he stayed long enough for him to find that out.

He waited until three in the morning to go down to the living room. He moved quietly, making sure he didn't wake his children, and sat down on the couch. For a minute he stared at the pillow he'd brought down with him—the one that still smelled like Bellamy. Then he pressed it against his face to muffle his sobs.

Coward.

Chapter Fourteen

"But why, Jake?"

"Because he needs to sleep, Pen. Come on, let's get your bag."

"I don't want to go yet."

"Gram is waiting for us."

"No. I can stay next door with Carol. In case Daddy needs me."

"I always need my Lucky Penny." Seamus forced himself to open his eyes. "What's up, guys?"

"Daddy!" Penny jumped on him and hugged him, rubbing the stubble on his face as if she were petting the dog. "Are you sick? You can have my strawberries."

"Sorry," Jake said quietly. "She wouldn't leave until she talked to you."

He hugged his daughter tight and pushed himself to a sitting position, with her still clinging to his neck. "What is it, sweetheart?"

Her lower lip trembled. "I want to stay with you and Vini this weekend."

"I need to fix some things around the house, and you know you can't stay with Carol for a while."

"Because she has a new hip?"

"That's right. You'll have more fun if you go with the boys to see Angus. I bet he's learned a new trick already."

"He's not as smart as Vini," Penny said stubbornly. "Even if he can roll over."

"Penny, go upstairs and make sure you didn't forget anything." Jake pushed his dark hair out of his eyes when Seamus looked up at his words. "If you do, I bet I can talk Dad into letting Grandpa teach Vini how to roll over."

She was clearly torn, but the dog won the day and she kissed Seamus and hugged him one more time before running upstairs.

"Have you eaten anything since yesterday?"

God, did he look that pathetic to his son?

Yes.

Six days. He'd been like this for nearly a week. He still cooked dinner for the kids and made sure they got to school. He'd kept up with bar orders and deliveries from his phone and laptop. He was still breathing, but he felt like a hollowed-out shell. Like something was missing.

He rolled his stiff neck and groaned. He was too old to be sleeping on the couch every night, but he hadn't been able to relax in his bedroom. Too many memories.

Maybe it was time for a new mattress. One Bellamy hadn't slept on.

"Dad?"

"Yes, Jake, I've eaten," he lied. He looked into his son's somber eyes and felt a vise tighten around his heart. This was ridiculous. He had to snap out of it. "I'm sorry. It's been a rough week on you, I know, but when you get back on Sunday, things will be back to normal, I promise."

He just needed to forget.

Coward.

Jake came over and sat down on the edge of the couch, watching him with those eyes that saw everything. "It's okay, Dad. I understand."

"God, I hope you don't," he blurted, feeling his throat tighten.

"I remember when my mom died," Jake said in a calm voice that belied any memory of pain. "You sat in a chair beside the bed for weeks, slept there so I could see you if I woke up and got scared. So I'd know I wasn't alone." Jake leaned against him, offering his support. "I can sit with you now, if you want."

Seamus closed his eyes, focusing on holding his tears at bay. Jake had never talked about his mother. He'd been so young and so much had happened that Seamus thought he might have forgotten her, but he should have known better. Jake never forgot anything. "I love you, do you know that? You are, without a doubt, the best decision I ever made."

"I love you too, Dad."

He wasn't sure how long they stayed like that before the front door opened, startling them both.

"Good morning." Solomon strode in wearing jeans and a t-shirt, a papoose filled with a baby cradled against his chest. Stephen appeared close behind him with a dual stroller, pushing a set of twins that were wriggling like they were about to make a run for it.

"The jury's still out on that." Seamus smiled tiredly, wishing for coffee. "What's with the parade of tiny humans?"

His brother was studying him a little too closely. Yeah, he definitely wasn't looking good. "Younger is watching our newest Finn while Noah checks in at the firehouse, and the boys and I decided to keep him company. We're on a top secret mission, and we've come for your son."

Seamus snorted. "He's the only one I have left. Wes and Sean are already with Mom."

"Sorry, but he's crucial to the cause. Plus he's great with the twins and I need help. Are you ready for this, Jake?"

Seamus wanted to hug his brother for taking the worry out of Jake's eyes. Worry he'd put there. "I'm ready, but I'm not sure Penny is. I'll go get her."

When he left the room, Solomon sat down on the couch and wrinkled his nose. "I love you like a cousin, Seamus, but you really need a shower." He glanced at the baby. "Either that or baby Zachary is trying to tell me he doesn't like his first trip out."

Seamus stared down at Noah's new baby and shook his head. "Look at him. Barely a week old and he already has some red hair coming in. Jen should be happy about that."

"She is," Stephen said, kneeling to check on his boys.

Seamus smiled at their tight curls and matching outfits. "She says it makes up for the fact that there's yet another boy in the family." He glanced over his shoulder at Seamus. "How are you feeling?"

"I'm fine." *My heart is broken and it's my own damn fault.* "I'll be fine."

"Good," Solomon replied with an easy smile that transformed his face. "Because on our way over here we got a call from Thoreau. Young Mr. Wayne needs you to come in, ASAP. Some kind of brewer emergency, don't ask me what."

"Shit. What happened?"

Stephen smirked. "He told you not to ask him what."

"I'll call him. See if it's something I can fix over the phone."

"Now that I'm on leave, can I hit him?" Solomon asked Stephen as they both got to their feet. "Maybe a good pop in the head would snap him out of it."

"I'm thinking about it." Stephen stood, slipped his hands in his pockets and gave Seamus a look he was all too familiar with.

"Stephen I—"

"All I want you to do now is shut up, shower and shave. After that, you *are* going to go to the bar you haven't set foot in for a week to solve a problem only you can solve." He moved closer, compassion clear in his gaze. "I know you let me get away with weeks of this, and I know you're hurting, but you have four young children who rely on you and a bar with employees who need you. Fair or not, you aren't the guy that gets to wallow. You're the guy who fixes things. So go *fix something*."

It stung, but he was right. His mother had said something similar four days ago when she'd come to tell him that Father Drew and some women from her church were drawing up a visiting schedule for Parkridge. She'd agreed that she shouldn't be the one to visit Presley because it might agitate her, but that hadn't stopped her from finding another solution. "She carried my grandchildren, so I don't want to hear any arguments," she'd said. "You've done this alone for too long. You're not Atlas, honey. Share the load."

They'd discussed the children, and she said she understood why he was waiting to tell the twins about their mother. They were too young to understand, but when it was time, Camille had offered to come over to help him explain. Jake, however, was old enough to hear it from him. "Tell him, Seamus. He already knows something's wrong. Tell him about Presley…and your Bellamy."

So he had. Just the highlights about the latter. That he loved him, but it hadn't worked out. And that the reason it ended had nothing to do with the kids, and everything to do with Seamus being afraid to risk his heart.

Jake asked a few questions, but he didn't seem to have a problem with his father being gay as much as he did with learning about Presley. Seamus wasn't sure he'd ever seen Jake upset before. He tried to explain that Presley was sick, but Jake was too protective of Penny and Wes to be sympathetic. The next day Tanaka and Brady had come over and installed a security system, sheepishly informing them that Jake had given them a call. Now he was hovering around Penny, Wes and Seamus like a protective mother hen. It needed to stop, he knew, but the only way it would was if Seamus got his fucking act together and handled things so his son didn't feel the need to.

Yeah. It was time to let this go. "Tell Thor I'll be there in two hours."

"Exactly two," Solomon ordered as he stood and lightly bounced, smiling when the baby laughed. "Or we'll call the cops to drag your ass out of the house and make a scene. It's only been a week since I left so I still have some pull over there. Don't I, Zach?"

Seamus ran his hands through his ratty hair and shook his head at Solomon's transformation. The man actually looked relaxed. "What the hell have you done with my cousin?"

He gave him a pointed look. "I was about to ask you the same thing."

***

Thoreau Wayne was waiting for him out front with his brother Hugo. "Long time no see."

Seamus glanced down the road at the crowded sidewalks. "Is there a festival or something I don't know about?"

"End-of-summer thing," Hugo said as he shook his hand, his broad smile making his dimples pop. He was handsome, Seamus thought, suddenly remembering his suspicion about his cousin's feelings. "I came over to see if I could help Thoreau finish up so he could enjoy the party with the rest of the Waynes."

"I didn't get an email about an end-of-summer thing," Seamus muttered. As a business owner, he usually got a heads-up about art festivals and block parties. He sighed, unable to find the energy to be that upset about it. And he still hadn't had any damn coffee.

The front door opened before Thoreau could answer and Fiona was smiling at him, her pastel hair glowing in the sun. "I thought that was you. Get in here, old man. We need to hurry so we can make it to the—"

"End-of-summer party, yeah, I heard." Seamus studied them suspiciously as he stepped into the dimly lit but thankfully cooler bar. "I thought there was an emergency." People didn't usually look this happy about an emergency.

"This *is* an emergency, from what I hear." Hugo leaned against the front door and crossed his arms casually. "You know, the last time I was in here I was opening this door for strippers, do you remember? For your brother's bachelor party?"

"Of course I remember." Owen had been so damn happy and Stephen was on pins and needles, worried about leaving his pregnant wife at home. Of course, she was the one who sent the strippers. "That was a great night."

"That it was." Hugo tilted his head, watching Seamus. "And you said something about the bartender's curse, right? Knowing love when you see it? Good stuff."

Too bad he didn't know it when he had it. "Yeah. Well, I think Fiona's better at it than I ever was."

"So true," Fiona said with a laugh. She was standing behind the bar pushing an Irish coffee in his direction. It had extra whipped cream.

"Bless you," Seamus groaned, walking toward her. "Now if someone wants to tell me what's going on, that would be great."

"Pull up a stool, old man. I'll tell you anything you want to know."

He was too tired for this shit, Seamus thought, but he sat down and placed his elbows on the bar. "There's no brewing emergency is there?"

"Nope."

"That was a trick to get me here?"

She smiled and gave him a generous helping of foam. "Yep. Yeah, it definitely was."

"Why? You two have been handling everything just fine this week. You didn't need me to come in."

She looked at him as if he were missing a few brains cells. "Because you have people who love you, Seamus. You mean *so much* to them, that they decided to give you a uniquely tailored, specially designed for you

*Finn*tervention." She chuckled. "I love how you all do that, by the way. Just add your name to everything? It's adorable."

"No." *Hell no.* He spun off the stool and walked toward the Wayne brothers. Hugo shook his head and took a step forward.

"Sorry, we can't let you do that. Not yet."

He hoped Hugo was kidding.

Owen's voice had him closing his eyes and muttering a prayer for patience. "Watch out guys, he's got his *Hulk* face on again."

"I can take him." Hugo looked more thoughtful than intimidated.

"Owen?" Seamus spun around and saw his brothers, his sister, his cousins and their significant others, all spilling out from the back of the bar and quietly finding their seats. "*Another* family meeting? I don't need this, guys. I'm fine."

"Prove it." Fiona's lip ring glinted in the dimly lit bar. "Come back, sit down. There's someone in the back who went to a lot of trouble to put this together, so do it for him. What have you got to lose? More time on your couch feeling sorry for yourself?"

Seamus sighed and moved back to the stool, sending

a frown over his shoulder. "I wish I knew what privacy felt like."

"No, you don't." Fiona pushed his cup toward him and sat on a stool toward the back. "You wouldn't be the man you are if you didn't have your family."

"Yeah, I know." Seamus laughed, resigned, but it was muffled by the coffee he was already drinking. "Just keep these coming."

"Hey, Dad."

"Jake?"

When his son appeared beside Fiona, Seamus set down his cup so no one could see his hand trembling. "What are you doing here?"

And who put you up to this? I was just thinking I needed to hit somebody.

Jake had a stack of printed emails in front of him. "I was worried and I wanted to help, but I didn't know how. You're the one who always knows what to say. So I sent out an email and asked everyone to tell me the best advice you ever gave them. I got these back in response."

Seamus looked down at the sheaf of papers. "Son, you didn't have to—"

"Read them," Tasha said from her chair beside her

husband.

"Out loud, if you please." That came from Declan, Jennifer's professor.

With his son standing expectantly in front of him, Seamus didn't really have another choice. "Dirty pool," he muttered.

"What's that?" Thoreau called out. "A little louder for the people in the back."

"The first one's from Jeremy."

Jake,

The best advice your dad ever gave me happened one morning on my dock. Something pretty bad had just gone down and I was sure life as I knew it was over. Then every member of the family—over eighteen, so I'm not including you—showed up on my doorstep, made breakfast and told me in every way they knew how that I was a Finn.

I didn't think I deserved it, and it wasn't until I talked to your father that it started to sink in. He told me to stop moping like Van Gogh and then he talked about you kids. He said if you were in the same situation, he'd tell you—I'm quoting now—"Secrets rarely stay secret for long, so you might as well be honest from the start. And love is a blessing, no matter what form it takes."

He was right, but then he usually is.

Hope that helped,

Jeremy

"I sounded like I knew what I was talking about, didn't I?" Seamus said ruefully, his chest tight. But even back then, he'd been keeping Presley a secret from his family. He was never that good at taking his own advice.

Love is a blessing, no matter what form it takes. He'd been thinking about his children then, but he believed it now more than he ever had. Bellamy had been a blessing. He hadn't realized how much he was missing until the man followed him home.

"I'm sorry I gave you shit. I was worried." Owen said from somewhere behind him. "But I was wrong, Seamus. About all of it."

"It's okay, Owen. We're good."

"Read mine. We need to keep this love train moving." Tasha sounded impatient.

"Have somewhere to be? An end-of-summer thing, maybe?"

"How did you know?"

Seamus sighed and picked up her email.

Jake,

I've known your father most of my life and he's

helped me more times than I can remember. This would be a novel if I listed every word of wisdom I ever got from him—longer if I told you about all the times I regretted not listening—but I think it was when I was pregnant with the twins and leaving town that he gave me the best advice. It was after he yelled at me for breaking his brother's heart. You know how protective he can be.

Seamus cringed. If he'd known she was pregnant, he would have… No, the only thing he would have done differently was carry her over to his brother's house instead of walking away.

He told me that Stephen needed me and that I couldn't run from my life. And I'm so glad I didn't let my fear of not fitting into his world stand in the way of taking what I wanted, because it's the best thing that ever happened to me. That's because of your dad.

He gripped the paper, not trusting himself to speak as he looked over his shoulder at her. *Do not make me cry, evil woman.*

She sat up straighter and ran a discreet finger under her eyes. "I'm giving that advice back, Seamus. From what I understand, it's *exactly* what you need to hear." She rolled her eyes and started muttering. "A hot stick of dynamite like that offering you the world and you just run from it? Have I taught you nothing?"

Seamus set down the emails and dragged his hands down his face. "Jake, I appreciate it, I really do, but it's just making me feel like an idiot for not taking any of my own advice." He pushed his empty cup toward Fiona and accepted a fresh one. "None of it matters now, anyway. It's too late." *He's gone.*

"Are you a Finn?"

Seamus blinked as Brady's voice boomed through the mostly empty bar, sounding every bit the Marine that he was.

"Don't start." Seamus pointed at him, his voice rising. "I know what you're going to say, Brady Finn, and don't even start or I'll slip rum into every container of liquid I can find and you'll never see it coming."

Everyone laughed when Brady paled. Everyone except Jake.

"Dad."

When Seamus looked back at his son, Jake was smiling at him as if he knew the answers to the universe. "We're Finns, Dad. We go all in or not at all."

As soon as he'd seen him, Seamus knew. "This was your idea? Just yours?"

Jake nodded, his ears turning red. "Mostly. Fiona helped and...we were worried about you."

"I know you were and I'm so sorry, Jake. You shouldn't have to worry about things like this. This my job."

Jake's smile dimmed and he looked more grown up and irritated than Seamus had ever seen him. "It doesn't *always* have to be your job, Dad. Especially if you let us help too." He chewed on his lip. "Or if you had someone to take care of you while you were taking care of everyone else."

Fiona sniffled and Seamus caught a glimpse of her dabbing her eyes with a tissue. "Your son is an angel, old man. I love this job."

Seamus kept his eyes on Jake's. He was so damn proud. "You're right, Jake. Thank you for doing this for me. For taking care of me. It's more than any man deserves. I'm incredibly blessed to have such a wonderful family."

"It wasn't just me, Dad," Jake started.

Hugo Wayne interrupted him. "Is that him? *Sweet Jesus.*"

"I told you he was hot," Fiona sang from her perch.

Thoreau whistled. "They moved all the cars already. I

was wondering if they could set it up fast enough, but where there's a will, right?"

Seamus froze when he heard the music blasting in from the street and heard his family murmuring excitedly as they headed for the door.

Is that him?

It couldn't be.

He looked over at Fiona, afraid to turn around. She'd pulled Jake over to her and started dancing with him, all the while watching Seamus with a knowing expression that made his heart drop into his stomach.

"Guess what else your son did?" She winked at Jake, as if proud of him. "Beauty's back."

Bellamy.

"What exactly did you do, Jake? Is it as bad as it sounds behind me?" he asked his son softly.

"Probably worse." Jake was laughing at him. "He said you might freak out but I promised you wouldn't. That we'd get you here and talk to you first. It's so cool, Dad. Go and see."

Fiona shook her head. "*Lit*, Jake. Something like this? You say it's lit. Even a genius needs to keep up with his slang."

Seamus could feel his hands shaking when he pushed

himself off the bar stool and turned around.

His parking lot had been turned into a circus.

Not a circus. An end-of-summer thing.

What the hell was happening right now? He saw t-shirt vendors and food stalls and beer—fuck, *his* beer was everywhere. The bottles with the new logo he and Thoreau had worked on looked great, and people were lining up for it. How did they do this in a week?

Where is he?

He was scanning the crowd when his mother grabbed his arm.

"He's on stage," she said, her voice raised to carry over the blaring music. "I think I'm going to faint, Seamus. Don't tell your father. He's already jealous."

That distracted him enough to look down at her ruddy cheeks. Dad was jealous? "Mom? Are you okay?"

She looked at him the way Penny looked at the ponies. "*It's him*, Seamus. I didn't know your boyfriend knew *him*."

The stage had been set up on a giant flatbed trailer covered in speakers, and yes, a short, bearded man that looked a lot like the singer his mother idolized was at a piano surrounded by his band.

And then he saw Bellamy smiling down at him from

the center of the stage, and the rest of the insanity was forgotten.

You may be right

I may be crazy

Oh but it just may be a lunatic you're looking for

Seamus started laughing. He couldn't stop. Adrenaline, relief and joy were making him lightheaded. This was absolutely ridiculous. It was a cheesy, romantic over-the-top fucking fairy tale, and it had been plopped down right in front of his bar by his son, his family and Bellamy Demir.

And if it all disappeared right now, it wouldn't matter as long as Bellamy stayed.

He'd come back. *Again.* No matter how many times Seamus pushed him away, no matter how little sense it made, the man would not give up.

He forced his legs to move when Bellamy lowered himself off the stage, and finally they were face to face, the crowd dancing around them.

Bellamy was staring at him as if they were the only two people on the planet. He always looked at him like that. "I missed those eyes, gorgeous."

"I love you," Seamus said, moving closer to be heard before he lost his nerve. "I know I'm an idiot and I come with a lot of ba—"

The crowd cheered even louder as Bellamy grabbed Seamus, dipped him in his arms and kissed his fucking socks off.

Seamus wanted them all to go away. He wanted to be back in the basement covered in baby oil. He wanted to be...*anywhere* he could be alone with Bellamy, damn it.

When he lifted his lips, Seamus moaned, trying to pull himself together enough to speak coherently. "How did you get *him* to show up?"

"The entertainer? Those people I pay said your mother loves him." Bellamy pulled him close and buried his face in his neck. "So I doubled down."

"Doubled down?"

"You thought the tickets to Paris, the ponies and the doctor bills were too much. You thought the house was too much. I know you think this is too much too, but don't be upset. I needed to do something to get your attention."

Seamus slid a hand in Bellamy's hair. "The one thing you've always had is my attention."

He leaned into the touch. "This is who I am, Seamus Finn. Pushy. Rich. Impulsive. And you love me anyway. Also, I think this should be our wedding song. You *do* always call me crazy."

"That's because you are." Seamus dropped his hand and frowned at him. "Did you say wedding song?"

Bellamy changed the subject. "What do you think of it? The party? Thor thought this was a great time to see how your beer could go over with the masses. Did you know he has six siblings? Four boys and three girls and they're all named after authors because their dad is an English Lit professor. He's got a good head for business."

Seamus grabbed Bellamy by his shirt and growled. "Bell?"

He was refusing to look him in the eye. "Oh, and I rented those ponies again. Solomon took Noah's baby, Zachary, home and now he's on Penny duty, so you don't need to worry about her."

"Are you *trying* to pick a fight with me?"

"Usually," Bellamy said, his green eyes full of fire. "We both know I do that a lot. You're stubborn and classist, I'm rich and the puppy loves me best..."

Seamus raised an eyebrow. "I'm not classist."

"Good. Because once we're married, my money is your money and your kids are my kids. And I'm going to want *my* kids to live in our big house and come with us when we travel. And they need to learn French. That was Elle's one request for her grandchildren."

His blood was rushing in his ears and he felt lightheaded. "I'm not marrying you, Bellamy Demir."

"Is it the song?" Bellamy tried to joke but Seamus could see the vulnerability and hurt in his eyes.

"I'm not marrying you until you tell me why." Seamus needed to hear it. This was surreal and mad and very Bellamy. There were a million reasons why this couldn't be happening. Why it wouldn't work even if it was. But the only reason he was hesitating was because he didn't understand why the beautiful lunatic wanted *him*.

Bellamy took his hand and dragged him back through the parking lot and into the quiet bar. It was empty now, thank God.

He closed the door behind him and pressed Seamus against it. "I knew the first time I saw you."

"That was sex," Seamus said breathlessly. "You don't have to marry me to get that, Bellamy. You can have it right now."

Bellamy shushed him and nuzzled his cheek. "Of course it was sex. I'll never get enough of you, or knowing that I'm the only one who can make you go wild. But it was more." He kissed his neck, his chin and the corner of his mouth, as if he couldn't help himself. "I wasn't supposed to be in Ireland at all. I have an assistant who handles all our fundraisers, but I got a personal request to come to the hotel for a few days and go over plans face to face. I've known the owner for years, so I agreed. On my second night in town, I saw you."

Seamus slipped his hands under Bellamy's shirt, needing to touch him when he thought about how easily they could have missed each other. "I'm glad you were there."

Bellamy chuckled and the sound went straight to his dick. "So was I. You were at the front desk looking jet-lagged and frazzled and completely out of place. And you had no idea that the woman checking you in was flirting with you. Completely oblivious. I think you even took out a picture of your kids to show her along with your driver's license."

"No wonder you couldn't resist me," Seamus joked, moaning when Bellamy's hips rocked against his.

"Exactly. Something in me knew, even then, that I couldn't let you out of my sight. I followed you to Murphy's bar, found out everything I could about you and, when I saw you with Gillian, I finally worked out a way to get your attention. She had a good business plan, but that wasn't why I was there. That was never why. It was all about you. I knew you were mine, Seamus Finn. Even then, I knew. And I was willing to do whatever I had to do to help you see it. See me."

"Oh God, Bell." Seamus felt himself sliding down the door, but Bellamy was there, holding him up in his strong embrace.

"I've always been impatient. Looking for something new. Something exciting. As soon as I kissed you, I knew I could stop looking. You are it for me. You, Jake, Little Sean and the twins. Now all I want to do is take care of your family with you and cherish and protect them as if they were my own." He took a shuddering breath and pressed closer. "I told you I didn't want you to take care of me. But I need you to let me do all of this because I'm in love with you, and being without you is unacceptable."

Seamus didn't know how to respond, so he kissed him. He'd never heard anything that romantic in his entire lonely life. It was still so hard to believe—Bellamy loved him—but he couldn't walk away. Jake had told him to go all in, and his son *was* the genius in the family.

He lifted his lips. “I’m sorry I pushed you away.”

“I was moving too fast. I do that.”

“And I move too slow. We’ll fight like that again.”

Bellamy nodded, waggling his eyebrows. “And then we’ll make up and I’ll make you scream my name until you forget.”

That sounded too good to resist. But he had to lay down a few more ground rules. “You can’t go around renting ponies and bringing singers to my mother whenever we have a fight.”

“Only for proposals and birthdays.” His lips were twitching. “Is that a yes?”

“I did just get some really good emails about following my heart.”

Bellamy’s eyes were brilliant with need. “And where is your heart, Seamus?”

He ran his hands over Bellamy’s scruffy jaw, a part of him still unable to accept the fact this was really happening. “I think I’m looking at it.”

He moaned when he felt Bellamy’s thick erection pressing against his hip. “Can we lock the door, gorgeous?”

Seamus reached for the top button of his jeans. “I do

own the place."

"Shameless," Bellamy murmured when his fingers closed around his cock.

Only for you.

Chapter Fifteen

4 months later…

"I knew I'd find you in here."

Seamus smiled, floating on his back in the heated pool, his eyes still closed. "I should be at the bar. It *is* New Year's Eve."

Bellamy snorted. "Thor and Fiona have things well in hand. If the new server is overwhelmed, Fi can just snap her fingers and Wyatt will appear."

He was right. Wyatt had been following the colorful bartender around like a whipped puppy lately. It worried him at first. He'd been sure Thoreau was dating her, and it would have put Seamus in an awkward position if his new business partner was stuck in a love triangle with his cousin. Luckily, he seemed more entertained than threatened.

Finn's pub was still Seamus' pride and joy, but he'd decided to team up with Thoreau when it came to expanding the brewery capacity to handle distribution and local marketing of Finn's beer. He was a natural, and he'd become a good friend over the last few months, really stepping up since the wedding to give Seamus and Bellamy a chance to settle into their dream house and start building new memories together as a family.

He was married.

Bellamy had only been willing to wait long enough for his parents to arrive, and *Seamus* had only been willing to have a civil ceremony with just the family on the guest list. It had ended up being the perfect day for everyone except Penny, who was now harassing Uncle Necky to have a big ceremony so she could be a real flower girl.

His husband had made it up to her by taking them to Disneyland for the honeymoon and getting them all the kind of VIP access reserved for, well, people like Bellamy Demir. Penny had been in princess heaven, and all was forgiven.

It was hard to believe anyone could be as happy as

Bellamy had made him. Or as angry. Or as continuously aroused.

He could no longer say his life was boring.

Seamus heard the splash a few minutes before big hands were tugging him against Bellamy's naked body. "Mmm. I was feeling guilty about the kids still being with Mom and Dad until you did that. We'll have to find a way to thank them."

"It's already been done," Bellamy muttered before sensually biting his shoulder, making him groan.

"What do you mean?"

"They enjoyed their last cruise so much I decided to give them another to St. Barts. They'll love it."

Seamus frowned. "Was this another Christmas present I didn't know about? You already spoiled everyone so much that Tanaka and Declan are planning for next year. Christmas isn't a competitive sport, Bellamy."

"Says you." He sounded smug. "But the cruise was for taking care of their grandkids all day. Especially now that Penny won't stop singing the lullaby Elle taught her. You know what they say, what you do to ring in the New Year is what you'll do all year long. I didn't want them to think they'd be babysitting and dealing with

Vini chasing Angus around the house for the next twelve months."

Seamus licked his lips. "I should be mad at you, but you're spoiling my parents, so I'd feel like a dick if I told you that you shouldn't have."

Bellamy wrapped his fingers around him and started to stroke him roughly. "Exactly. Don't waste your breath. Just let me take you."

"Take me where?"

A growl rumbled in his chest when Seamus rubbed against him. "Out of this pool, for one. I want to make sure you know what you'll be doing all year."

Bellamy got him out of the pool and dried him off swiftly. "I have a surprise for you." Before Seamus could ask what it was, he was being dragged down the hallway.

Another surprise? Bellamy couldn't stop showering him with gifts and elaborate gestures since he'd accepted his proposal. He'd brought Gillian and Connor—now engaged to each other—over for the wedding. He'd bought the old house, done some repair work and added a bathroom before letting the newly arrived Irish cousins move themselves in.

They were going to be a handful.

He'd taken Seamus on weekend trips to New York to meet his friends and employees, though they'd spent most of their time in the bedroom of his penthouse apartment. Not that Seamus was complaining.

Every time he tried to protest, Bellamy swore it was Seamus who had given him the real gifts. A family. A home that was filled with chaos, laughter, music and love. His love.

The only things that mattered.

Bellamy was still an arrogant bad boy, but he was also a sappy son of a bitch. Seamus couldn't get enough of him.

"Stop, Bell."

Bellamy scowled over his shoulder. "Can't stop. I told you, I have a surprise. We need to get dressed."

"That is *not* what I was expecting you to say." Seamus crowded Bellamy against the hallway wall, dropped their towels and wrapped one leg around his hip.

Bellamy groaned. "Don't tempt me."

"Too late," Seamus whispered before taking his earlobe between his teeth. "I want you right now, Bell. Right here."

"Bathroom," Bellamy snarled.

The guest bathroom was only a few steps away and he knew why Bellamy wanted to get there. "I love it when you compromise."

Bellamy shoved him roughly into the bathroom, closing the door and yanking open the cabinets to find the small bottle he kept there for this exact situation.

"Hands on the sink, gorgeous."

Seamus shivered and obeyed, loving the chemistry between them. Knowing it wasn't going anywhere. That Bellamy wasn't going anywhere. Not without him.

"Look, Seamus."

He looked up at Bellamy's reflection over his shoulder. His dark skin was flushed and his features were sharp and tight with need. His eyes were like green fire and they burned wherever they touched him. "Please, Bell. This is what I want to be doing all year."

He felt the cool liquid between his cheeks and two blunt fingers pressing impatiently inside. Stroking as Bellamy bit down on his shoulder. "All year isn't enough."

When his lover's thick cock stretched him, his moan echoed loudly in the tiled room. "Yes. God, *yes*."

Bellamy cupped his forehead and pulled his head back against his shoulder. He wrapped another arm around his middle to hold him while he thrust deep. *Fuck, so deep.* Seamus could see them together in the mirror. See Bellamy sucking the skin of his neck. See the mirror and cabinets shake when he started losing control and taking him harder.

Harder, Bell. Don't stop.

"Is this what you needed?" he growled. "You wanted to make sure my cock would be buried in this ass all year?"

"*Yes*. Fuck, Bell, faster."

"Every day," he groaned, hips like pistons pounding against him. "Every night, every *year* until I die."

Seamus dropped his hand to his own erection, his fist pumping in time to each powerful thrust. "Love you so much. So good, Bell. God, I'm close."

"Yes," he moaned, his cock expanding inside him before Seamus felt the warm flood of his release. He came with him, chanting Bellamy's name as his body shook with the force of his climax.

This was where he'd spend the rest of his life.

He hoped it was long enough.

They leaned against the door, kissing and mumbling incoherently to each other as they recovered. Seamus smiled at the way Bellamy wrapped himself around him, rubbing his face against his neck as if marking him. As if no one else existed in the world.

The banging on the door made Seamus jerk and shout in Bellamy's arms.

"Seamus? Sorry, I was sure we were making enough noise for the neighbors to hear us." The voice paused. "Say something, son, or your mother will think I've given you a heart attack."

"*Dad?*"

"Oh good." His father sounded relieved. "I was looking for your husband. The caterer arrived and she wanted to talk to him about setting up. Everyone's here so…"

Seamus leaned back and stared at Bellamy. "Should I ask what my surprise is now?"

Bellamy's shoulders were shaking in silent laughter. "I must have lost track of the time."

Seamus closed his eyes and leaned his forehead against the door. "Dad? We need someone to go up to our bedroom and get us something to wear. We were… *Taking a shower*."

Shawn Finn was silent for a long, awkward moment. Then Seamus heard it. The chuckle on the other side of the door that turned into a guffaw so loud and uncontained, Seamus couldn't help but smile.

"Will do, Seamus. Hold tight." He must have started walking away because his voice was fainter when Seamus heard him say. "Honey, you have to hear this."

"This is your fault," Bellamy said quietly, amusement in his beautiful eyes. "If you hadn't distracted me, we'd be dressed by now."

"Oh no." Seamus pulled out of his embrace and crossed his arms. "This is *your* fault. If you'd told me the entire Finn clan, including our kids *and* a caterer, was coming over, I wouldn't have been so tempted to distract you."

Liar.

Bellamy shrugged carelessly. "I knew it was what we'd be doing all year anyway, so I thought we'd make it a party."

"What? Hiding in the bathroom?"

His smile was beautiful. "Enjoying our family."

Damn it. "I love my surprise."

And you.

"Wait until they leave. You'll love the second one even more."

Seamus sighed. "Just tell me now."

"Oil and leather pants might be involved."

He couldn't stop his huff of laughter. Or the fresh wave of arousal. "A rematch for New Year's? Great. Now I'll spend the whole party thinking about you covered in oil."

Bellamy's gaze heated again. "I can send them all home right now. I'm sure your parents would keep the kids overnight."

"You're crazy if you think they'll leave before the caterer does."

"You may be right." Bellamy kissed him again, distracting him. "How long do you think it will take him to get our clothes?"

Seamus leaned into him, unable to resist his touch. "It's a big house. It could take hours."

"Maybe we should shower again."

Bellamy did something with his fingers that had Seamus panting. "Good plan. God, I love you."

"I love you too, gorgeous. Now bend over."

***

Kenneth Tanaka…

He'd finally told Seamus and Bellamy what he'd done. Ken didn't like lying to them, even by omission, but the situation had been too fragile at first. He hadn't wanted his tampering to affect the outcome, so he'd avoided them for weeks.

Maybe the hotel owner in Galway was an old friend and maybe Ken had mentioned Bellamy Demir's need for a quiet vacation. They both knew he needed something. Running with the bulls, wrestling, sky diving… If he wasn't working, he was risking his neck in search of something he couldn't seem to find. And it was getting worse as he got older.

Ken knew that wasn't his nature. Bellamy was more romantic than adrenaline junkie, he just needed the right outlet. The right guy. He was waiting, and it was something Ken recognized because he'd been waiting too. Until Brady.

He'd made Seamus reservations in the same hotel at the same time and taken a step back. He wasn't even sure if Brady's cousin was gay or not. It had just been a feeling. And when he found out about Gillian, he almost felt guilty for interfering. Almost.

In reality, all he'd done was move a few pieces on the board. They could have missed each other in the giant hotel. They could have hated each other on sight.

But they hadn't. Bellamy had proven him right,

sweeping Seamus and his children off their feet and bulldozing his way into the family with his big, generous personality.

What did Seamus call him? A cocky bastard? Yeah, that was definitely Bellamy. He was also a damn good friend.

"Move over, Cupid."

Brady came in and leaned down to kiss his neck, making him shiver. "What are you working on?"

"The Finn Project," he murmured. "Only a few more to go."

Brady chuckled. "Actually, we have three new arrivals. At this rate you'll never make an honest man out of me."

He'd forgotten about them. *Fuck.*

Ken closed his laptop and let Brady drag him to his feet for a passionate kiss. "Maybe we don't have to wait until the project is finished."

"I like the sound of that."

Ken didn't tell him that Solomon already knew what he wanted and was doing his matchmaking job for him during his leave of absence. He didn't tell him that things were already in the works for Noah and Wyatt.

He didn't tell him what he'd found out about James.

He might need help for that one. And that help was probably going to have to come from Trick Dunham and a few of his shadier contacts.

Until then, he'd count this as a win.

THANKS FOR READING!

I truly hope you enjoyed this book. If so, please leave a review and tell your friends. Word of mouth and online reviews are immensely helpful to authors and greatly appreciated.

To keep up with all the latest news about my books, release info, exclusive excerpts and more, check out my website RGAlexander.com, Friend me on Facebook, or follow me on Twitter.

If you love my ***Finn Factor*** series and want to hang out with like-minded others, as well as get access to exclusive discussions and enter the frequent ***contests*** and ***free book giveaways*** each month contests, join THE FINN CLUB on Facebook:)

Friend me on **Facebook**
https://www.facebook.com/groups/911246345597953/
for contests, and smutty fun.

Check out *Curious*, Book 1 of the Finn Factor Series

*"Everyone go buy the f***ing thing. Curious. Go now."* tweet by author of Love Lessons,
Heidi Cullinan

"When I got to the end of this book, I wanted to start over... RG Alexander is one hell of an author!"
USA Today bestselling **Bianca Sommerland**,
author of Iron Cross, the Dartmouth Cobras

Are you Curious?

Jeremy Porter is. Though the bisexual comic book artist has known Owen Finn for most of his life—long enough to know that he is terminally straight—he can't help but imagine what things would be like if he weren't.

Owen is far from vanilla—as a dominant in the local fetish community, he sees as much action as Jeremy does. Lately even more.

Since Jeremy isn't into collars and Owen isn't into men, it seems like his fantasies will remain just that forever…until one night when Owen gets curious.

Warning: **READ THIS!** Contains explicit m/m nookie. A lot of it. Very detailed. Two men getting kinky, talking dirty and doing the horizontal mambo. Are you reading this? Do you see them on the cover? Guy parts will touch. You have been warned.

Available Now!
www.RGAlexander.com

The Finn Factor Series
(for the reader who enjoys variety)
Book 1: *Curious* (m/m)
Book 2: *Scandalous* (m/f)
Book 3: *Dangerous* (m/m)
Book 4: *Ravenous* (m/f/m)
Book 5: Finn Again

Big Bad John
Bigger in Texas series, Book One

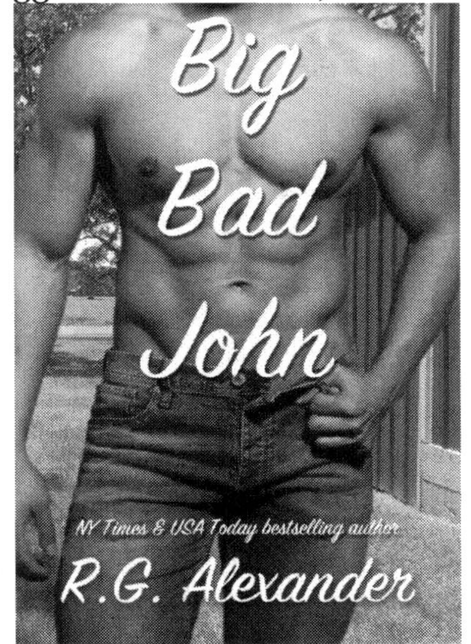

Available Now!
www.RGAlexander.com

Kinda broad at the shoulder and narrow at the hip…

Trudy Adams never planned on going home again. Not to that sleepy little Texas town where everyone knew her business and thought she was trouble. She ran away to California years ago, and now, after what has felt like a lifetime of struggling, her lucky break might finally be around the corner.

And then she got that email.

John Brown has been waiting patiently for Trudy to return, but his patience has run out. He's had years to think about all the things he wants to do to her, and he's willing to use her concern for her brother, her desire to help her best friend get her story, and every kinky fantasy Trudy has to show her who she belongs to.

The explosive chemistry between them is unmistakable. But will history and geography be obstacles they can't overcome? When Trouble makes a two-week deal with Big Bad…anything can happen.

Warning: **READ THIS!** BDSM, explicit sex, voyeurism, accidental voyeurism, voyeurism OF voyeurism with a sprinkle of m/m, exhibitionism, ropes, cuffs, gratuitous spanking, skinny dipping, irresponsible use of pervertables…and a big, dirty man who will melt your heart.

BILLIONAIRE BACHELORS SERIES

Available Now!
www.RGAlexander.com

Glass slipper shopping can be a dangerous pastime…

The CEO's Fantasy-Book 1

Dean Warren is the billionaire CEO of Warren Industries. He's spent the last five years proving his worth and repairing his family's reputation. But the rules he's had to live by are starting to chafe, especially when it comes to one particular employee. He doesn't believe in coincidence, but when Sara Charles shows up suddenly unemployed and asking him to agree to a month of indulging their most forbidden fantasies--there's no way he can refuse.

When reality is better than his wildest dreams, will the CEO break all of his own rules to keep her?

The Cowboy's Kink-Book 2

Tracy Reyes is a man who enjoys having control. Over his family's billion dollar land and cattle empire, over the women he tops at the club, and over his life. When teacher Alicia Bell drops into his lap with a problem that needs solving and a body that begs to be bound, he can't resist the opportunity to give her the education in kink she needs. But can he walk away from his passionate pupil when it's time to meet his future bride?

The Playboy's Ménage-Book 3

Henry Vincent and Peter Faraday have been friends forever. The royal rocker and polymath playboy have more than a few things in common. They're both billionaires, they both love a challenge...and they've both carried a long-lasting torch for the woman that got away. Finding Holly again brings back feelings and memories neither one of them wanted to face. But they'll have to if they want to share her. Keeping her from running again and making her admit how she feels about them will take teamwork. Hours of teamwork...and handcuffs.

The Bachelors

We know every debutante's mama wants a piece of their action, but if you could choose without repercussions, which of the Billionaire Bachelors would be your fantasy? The true hardcore cowboy who has enough land and employees to start his own country, but no dancing partner for his special kind of two-step? The musician with a royal pedigree, a wild streak and a vast fortune at his disposal, who's never been seen with the same woman twice? His best jet-setting buddy who can claim no less than five estates, four degrees and three charges of lewd public behavior on his record? Or the sweet-talking, picture-perfect tycoon-cum-philanthropist who used to be the baddest of the bunch but put those days behind him when he took over as CEO of his family's company? (Or did he?)

Pick your fantasy lover--rocker, rancher, rebel or reformed rogue. Glass slipper shopping is a dangerous sport to be sure, especially with prey as slippery as these particular animals, but I'll still wish all my readers happy hunting.

From Ms. Anonymous

Available Now!

www.RGAlexander.com

OTHER BOOKS FROM R.G. ALEXANDER

Fireborne Series
Burn With Me
Make Me Burn
Burn Me Down-*coming soon*

Bigger in Texas Series
Big Bad John
Mr. Big Stuff-
Big Trouble-*coming soon*

The Finn Factor Series
Curious
Scandalous
Dangerous
Ravenous
Finn Again
Shameless

Billionaire Bachelors Series
The CEO's Fantasy
The Cowboy's Kink
The Playboy's Ménage

Children Of The Goddess Series
Regina In The Sun
Lux In Shadow
Twilight Guardian
Midnight Falls

Wicked Series
Wicked Sexy
Wicked Bad
Wicked Release

Shifting Reality Series
My Shifter Showmance

My Demon Saint
My Vampire Idol

Temptation Unveiled Series
Lifting The Veil
Piercing The Veil
Behind The Veil

Superhero Series
Who Wants To Date A Superhero?
Who Needs Another Superhero?

Kinky Oz Series
Not In Kansas
Surrender Dorothy

Mènage and More
Truly Scrumptious
Three For Me?
Four For Christmas
Dirty Delilah
Marley in Chains

Anthologies
Three Sinful Wishes
Wasteland - Priestess
Who Loves A Superhero?

Bone Daddy Series
Possess Me
Tempt Me
To The Bone

Elemental Steam Series Written As Rachel Grace
Geared For Pleasure

ABOUT R.G. ALEXANDER

R.G. Alexander (aka Rachel Grace) is a *New York Times* and *USA Today* Bestselling author who has written over 45 erotic paranormal, contemporary, urban fantasy, sci-fi/fantasy and LGBTQ romance books for multiple e-publishers and Berkley Heat.

She has lived all over the United States, studied archaeology and mythology, been a nurse, a vocalist, and for the last decade a writer who dreams of vampires, airship battles and happy endings for all.

RG feels lucky every day that she gets to share her stories with her readers, and she loves talking to them on Twitter and FB. She is happily married to a man known affectionately as The Cookie—her best friend, research assistant, and the love of her life. Together they battle to tame the wild Rouxgaroux that has taken over their home.

To Contact R. G. Alexander:

www.RGAlexander.com

Facebook:

http://www.facebook.com/RachelGrace.RGAlexander

Twitter: https://twitter.com/RG_Alexander

Made in the USA
Columbia, SC
09 July 2020

13552563R00209